LAST PAPERS
(Fiction & Nonfiction)

LAST PAPERS
(FICTION & NONFICTION)

BY

STEVEN G. FARRELL

www.celtic-badger.com

www.bookstandpublishing.com

Published by
Bookstand Publishing
Morgan Hill, CA 95037

And

Celtic Badger Publishers
Greenville, South Carolina

4251_2

ISBN 978-1-63498-080-7

Printed in the United States of America

CONTENTS

PAPER 1

BOWERY RIPPER ON THE LOOSE

CHAPTER 1

The summer heat was so intense on the first day of September that not one of the Irish Clowns paid much attention to the morning newspapers. Headlines screamed out all over the neighborhood that a young woman had been murdered the night before there on the Bowery. Nothing much actually bestirred the Irish Clowns unless it was another street gang crowding in on their territory. The gang's turf was based on a block or two in each direction from their headquarters at Hughie's Bohemian Café situated on 3rd Street and Canal. Their second biggest motivator was Rat Rice, the head cop on the Bowery, who enjoyed picking on them no matter what sort of crime had been committed in his bailiwick. Third on the list of their constant headaches were their very own parents with their constant bellyaching about jobs, marriage and leaving home.

Admittedly, the Clowns' turf had shrunk more than a few yards on all four sides since their golden heyday when they were known as Gordon Swartz's and the Irish Clowns. It was funny how it took a tough Jewish kid to use his fists to hammer the local Mickeys into a cohesive fighting force to be reckoned with on the East Side. Rat Rice, Chief Inspector of the Ninth Precinct, liked to put it out to the newspapers that Gordon and his Irish lads had become the toughest thing near the Five Points since the days of the Dead Rabbits, the Bowery Boys, the Five Pointers and the Monk Eastman mob. Be that as it may, the Irish Clowns had long since dropped into the second division once Gordon went legit and moved to the southernmost edge of the Bronx to open up a hot dog joint across the street from the New York Yankees baseball stadium.

Marion McMaster, aka "Bugs", became the chieftain of the Irish Clowns once Gordon effectively retired from the position. Bugs had always been the second best brawler in the crew but his brain power was decidedly

1

third rate. Short and stocky, he had personality and charisma but not too much ambition.

Moving up to second-in-command was Jordan Warden, a cynical tough guy, who could talk a meaner game than he actually could play. His main mission in life was to mooch free ice cream from Hughie Kressin and to second guess Bugs McMaster every move. Jordan didn't have the reputation as being criminally inclined but he was famous for his love of the sight of blood. In notorious rumbles of the past, he would become a mightier warrior once one of the opposite was cut and squirting blood. Bugs was constantly teasing Jordan for his blood lust.

Whitey Kelly, real first name unknown, was the only member of the gang who had a steady paying job. He actually had a pretty good reputation going in the upholstery business and he was slated to replace his father, Creepy, at the head of the Kelly family shop. Whitey wasn't as weird and threatening as his old man, but he was a lad full of quirks. He could also scream like a banshee and he was as brave as a wolf hound in combat.

Murphy was a tough fighter only when Bugs was successful in setting fire to his lazy tail. His old man owned a funeral parlor, so he had no real need to earn much more than the pocket money that his father and mud doled out to him. He was heavyset and above average in height and had a bad County Cork temper when provoked. Murphy's ranking fell somewhere in the middling of the pack.

Gyp and Benny were minor members of the gang. Their last names were probably unknown by most people in the Bowery as well as to the other members of the gang. Their sole purposes in life were to at the bottom level of the Irish Clowns and to run the most mundane of errands for Bugs. Like most boys from the Bowery, they had at least had enough savvy to put up their dukes and fight by side with their comrades in arms when the occasion called for it.

Mario and Bosco Ferro, the only two Italians ever sworn on as members of the all Irish gang, were handsome and rangy young men with pleasing smiles and good right hooks. However, with their new jobs with the *Park Row Review* newspaper, they were not really considered full and real members of the gang anymore. Their main function was to serve as go-betweens between Chief Inspector Rice and the boys. The Ferro brothers still popped into Hughie's on occasion to pay their respects.

It was hard to place Clarence Darrow Shaw, one 'Shem,' on the pecking order because he couldn't fight his way out of a wet paper page and he was the village idiot as well. Tall, somewhat slender and a moron, Shem somehow had worked his way into the good graces of Gordon years before

2

and his right man status had been continued as a matter of tradition when Bugs McMaster assumed command. Like the others, he lived beneath the roof of his parents and was a bum. However, he had earned some degree of respect by working odd jobs at the Fulton Fish Market.

Last, but not least, was Hughie Kressin, the pudgy and crankily sweet owner of Hughie's Bohemian Café. Hughie, who spoke with an old-time off-the-boat Yiddish accent, claimed to have been born in Prague over somewhere in the former lands of the Hapsburg, but he had long since become a flag-waving American citizen. The boys spent just enough cash in his joint to prevent Hughie from tossing them out on their collective ears. Besides, as far as Irish Mickeys went, they weren't bad kids and they served as an unofficial law enforcers on his premises. The bane of Hughie's existence was his wife, Mary. "Momma", was also a terror of the neighborhood and was unloved because of her shrewish behavior and sharp tongue.

Bugs McMaster and the Irish Clowns formed a decaying Irish street gang in the crumbling heart of the Bowery, the most decayed part of the city. There were still plenty of thriving shops, restaurants and churches in the neighborhood, especially close to the enclaves where some lower middle-class and working class residents still lived, but the outer edges were rapidly giving ground to the encroachment of the skid row area. A new element, brown-skinned Spanish speakers, were pouring in off of the boat from San Juan and chasing away the Micks. The good old days were just about to be over on the Bowery.

CHAPTER 2

"Get a job, louse!" shouted Mr. Shaw immediately before shoving a forkful of scrambled eggs and bangers into his mouth.

"Father, I won't have you hollering like a lunatic beneath me roof so early in the morning at me son, Clarence," jumped in Mrs. Shaw, splashing more coffee into the old man's mug.

"Thanks for defending me, ma," said Shem, tossing a huge second helpings on to his plate as his father simmered.

The storm blew over very quickly as it usually did in the Shaw household. The family shared deep affection for all of their bickering over the breakfast, lunch and supper table inside of their modest household. After

3

the head of the household had had a long and steady job at Tammany Hall and some of children had progressed out of adolescence into the mature world of eight hour work days and weekly salaries. Shem was just a benign galoot and it was difficult for anybody to hold a grudge against him for very long. Even the old man couldn't stay mad at the boy; for every Irish family had a Shem to deal with and it was a cross to be bored.

"Maybe you can see if the Ferro brother can get you a job down at their newspaper, son?" suggested the mother.

"You have to be able to read and write, ma," snorted one of the younger brothers.

"That'll be just about enough of that, young fellow," said Shem.

When the family were finished discussing Shem's career possibilities, somebody mentioned the noise made by all of the police squad cars and fire trucks in the neighborhood. The very sky of the neighborhood had been lit-up in the wee hours of the morning. The intense August heat had made sleep difficult enough as it was in the first place. The old man had even escaped to the fire escape with his pillow and blanket to catch a slight breeze.

"Probably another knife fight beneath the elevated tracks," noted the father.

"Ah, the neighborhood is worse than Dublin north of the Anna Liffey River," put in the mother.

"Maybe we should move to Brooklyn," said the smallest girl which provoked a hearty round of laughter.

Shem could never leave the house without receiving a kiss from a mother and a fistful of change from his father. The family had a set routine that they enacted every morning before everybody went their own separate ways. "Here's a few extra cents for a newspaper so you can check the *Help Wanted* section," said the eldest brother, adding, "I want to read about whatever caused the racket."

The closest newsstand to Hughie's Bohemian Café was the one run by Squirt Sheridan, one of the meanest gang bangers in the Bowery. Many felt he could give even Bugs a run for his money when it came to an old fashion donnybrook with fists. However, Squirt had an evil reputation as a handler of a pearl handle switchblade. Shem was afraid of Squirt but he was on assignment to fetch a newspaper.

"What do you want, punk?"

"How dare you raise your voice to a paying customer!" shouted back Shem, rattling his coins in the palm of his hand. "I have half a mind to report you to the Bowery's Chamber of Commerce."

"You have a half mind all right."

"Never mind the running commentary and make with the latest edition of the *Park Row Review*. I want to read my friend Mario's latest article."

Shem was steps away from his final destination to Hughie's when he got wind of the terrible news on the front page. The headline screamed out: *A Young Woman Has Her Throat Ripped Out on the Bowery*. It was always a crying shame to read about the growing crime rate in their neck of the woods, but what caught his eye was the name of the victim.

"Chief, somebody croaked Mary Ann Nikolai!" roared out Shem, bolting into Hughie's.

It was too early in the days for root beer floats, chocolate malts or hot fudge Sundays, so the place was filled with the aromas of eggs, bacon, buttered toast, hash and coffee. The gang was nested in the very back of the place in their usual chairs with Bugs McMaster presiding.

"Take it down a few notches!" roared Momma Kressin, shaking up the block.

Hughie was washing dishes, plates and cups in the kitchen sink behind the fountain. He was very fond of Shem and he had known him for years. A shouting Shem on a hot summer morning was something he could do without. He shot a silent glare at his wife for her rudeness towards the boy. His ears pointed upwards when he heard the name of Mary Ann Nikolai; for hasn't she been a steady customer of his for years and still a sweet girl until she had taken a turn for the bad.

"Shem, you're disturbing our morning concentration," said Bugs, forever searching for words he had no idea what they really meant.

"What this about Mary Ann Nikolai?" asked Jordan.

"She's gone and got herself croaked!" shouted Shem, throwing the newspaper down on the table in front of Bugs to prove his testimony.

"Say, didn't we go to St. Thomas Aquinas Grammar School with her?" asked Gyp.

The memories of Mary Ann came fast and furious and they all decided it was a shame that she had been murdered. What was the neighborhood coming to?

"Who would do such a thing to such a sweet and innocent lamb?" asked Hughie.

"How would you know if she was so sweet and innocent?" asked Momma, putting her hands on her hips.

"It's merely a figure of speech, momma," said Hughie, turning red.

"She wasn't all that sweet and innocent these days and I saw her numerous times with my very baby blues under the elevated tracks plying her trade," said Jordan, warranting dirty looks all around.

"Hard times can turn a saint into a sinner," threw in Shem, repeating something he had heard his mother say about somebody in their very own family. Shem didn't like talking about such matters.

"She still was only a dirty tramp and got what was coming to her," snapped Jordan.

Bugs was about ready to clobber Jordan with a well-deserved right cross when Murphy beat him to the punch by cracking Jordan in the right shoulder with his fist. Gyp got into the act by attacking Jordan's right shoulder. Benny was going to add insult to injury by pouring a glass of ice water over the loud mouth's greased back hair-do. Hughie came to the rescue by threatening to throw them out onto the street for being too rowdy.

"If you want to rough house like Cochise and the Cherokees out west then go outside. It would be even better if you Bowery Mohicans moved out west," fumed Hughie.

"Cochise was an Apache and the Cherokees were down south," corrected Jordan.

"It's time to vacate these premises," said Bugs before Hughie could blow a gasket. "Besides, let's take a gander at the murder site. It's only a few blocks over to Houston Street."

"We might see some blood," chirped Jordan.

"I see all the blood I want at the Friday night fights," said Shem.

Bugs and his boys reluctantly braved the heat of the day in order to troop their way to the spot where Mary Ann Nikolai had been killed. The boys slowed their pace when they were passing the Kelly's upholstery business. They peered into the shop window to get a look at Whitey, who had a tool of his trade as he started work on an old chair. He waved to them before hunching over to attack his work.

"He's none too friendly," said Gyp as the boys moved along.

"You would be none too friendly if you had to toil eight hours in this heat," said Bugs.

"Working with Creepy would make me none too friendly," put in Shem.

The fellows gassed about Creepy Kelly all the way to Houston. They noticed their friends the twins working the scene before they noticed the blood stains splattered all over the cement. Shem jumped back and refused to come closer. The other boys seemed to get a kick out of the gravel smear until Bugs reminded them that it properly belonged inside of the lovely female body of their old classmate Mary Ann. Mario was scribbling inside of his notebook while Bosco was snapping away pictures.

"Any suspects yet?" asked Bugs, acting official.

"Chief Inspector Rice is fairly certain some wino did the knifing, but I'm not so certain about that myself."

"Usually Rat Rice is certain the Irish Clowns are somehow involved in every caper on the Bowery," said Murphy.

"That's a lie," protested Shem. "We'd never cut a girl even if she wasn't a good one."

Gyp used his foot to smear the fresh blood. The others gave him the business for being a messy pig.

"You don't sound so convinced yourself, Mario," said Bugs.

"Bugs, Bosco and I were among the first on the scene when the taxi cab driver phoned in the call just shortly after it got light out. We saw the body and it wasn't pretty.

"I almost lost my lunch," said Bosco, pushing Shem aside.

"The attacker had to be a real nut job because he craved her up, but good," said Mario.

"It was like he was trying to drill through her body to reach China," said Bosco.

"Where's Rat Rice?" asked Benny.

"Rounding up the usual suspects, no doubt," observed Jordan.

"He'll be looking for us sooner or later," cracked Gyp.

"We have nothing to hide," said Shem.

"It wouldn't hurt for you guys to play ball with Rice and help him out with this one," said Mario. "It might help you out further down the road."

"What would you suggest?" asked Bugs.

"Scout around the neighborhood and see if you can unearth any evidence for the cops."

Bugs McMaster and the Irish Clowns were lost in their own thoughts when they once again crossed the Kelly's storefront. They were jarred back to the mean streets of their existence by all of the screaming and shouting coming from inside of the upholstery business. From the window they could see Whitey chasing Creepy around furniture waiting to be attended to with a blood-stained chisel in his hand. The scene was like something out of an old silent Keystone Cops film. Creepy, a blood stained weapon of his own inside of his hand, suddenly spun around and attacked a retreating Whitey.

"They're going to fracture one another!" shouted Bugs, opening up the door.

"You ever pull another stunt like that and I'll tear your kidney out with me bare hands!" shouted Creepy.

"If I ever get out of here I'm going right down to the precinct and reporting you to the police!' shouted back Whitey.

"Hold everything!" shouted Bugs.

The bold leader of the Irish Clowns stepped into the family feud. It was a mistake, for Creepy slashed off his tie with one deft flick of the wrist. Everybody watched as the tie landed on top of Shem's head.

"No, thanks, Mr. Kelly," joked Shem. "It doesn't match my eyes."

The other Irish Clowns had to restrain Creepy Kelly by wresting him down to the ground, where he continued the fight. Whitey, out of breath and his face red, began to peel them off one by one. After all, Creepy was still his father. It took several minutes before Bugs was able to restore some semblance of law and order. Before the court went in session, he called for the weapons to be handed to him as exhibits A and B. He felt the sharp edges in spite on the blood coated on them.

"Are you two trying to turn this into a morgue?" asked Bugs.

"Mind your own business!" roared Creepy. "I'll take of my lad in my own way!"

"Like some kind of a nut," badgered Bugs.

"Who asked you to butt in, Bugs?' asked Whitey, who was almost as loud and irate as his old man. Creepy was of average height and of dark features. He sported a grisly salt and pepper moustache. Whitey was short but compact and he had very blond hair. The two did not resemble one another in the least.

"The way you two were carrying on I thought you were kinsmen of Squirt Sheridan our best known knife fighter in the Bowery," said Jordan.

"You put me in mind of the Hatfield and the McCoy hillbillies who live in Kentucky," laughed Bugs.

"West Virginia, you mean," corrected Jordan.

"You reminded me of the dangerous wino who killed Mary Ann Nikolai," said Shem.

At the mentioning of the girl's name, Whitey began to ring his hands over and over. As if in a chain reaction, Creepy began to do the same motions with his hands. The impression a keen observer would have made was that the father and son were trying to clean the blood off of their hands: old blood as well as new. They both stopped when they realized that they were being observed.

"Somebody is cuckoo here and it isn't me," said Shem.

"It isn't you for a change, you mean," said Bugs.

"Get out of me establishment before I call Kennedy the beat cop to have you all arrested for trespassing!" threatened Creepy.

"Better do as he says, fellows," warned Whitey. "He isn't kidding."

The boys had been put off by the sight of the crazy father and son and they were put off their food and drink for the day. Shem suggested they all go to Wall Street and apply for jobs as messenger boys. Somebody else mentioned that some of the newspapers were seeking copyboys.

CHAPTER 3

Mario Ferro, rising ace reporter for the *Park Row Daily,* rapped on the door of Mary Kelleher. He had waited until after sunset because he didn't want prying eyes to observe his visit. The Bowery was as nosey and as small as any small town in Wisconsin or South Carolina, and people had tongues that wagged like the tails of eager puppies. Besides, people would only think the worse if they knew that a healthy young man was paying a night call to a woman with a steamy past. He glanced across the street at the point beneath the track where Mary Ann had been found. It still troubled him more that Mary Kelleher had predicted it.

"Mario, darling," cried out Mary in that gleeful Irish immigrant way of her as she climbed into Mario's arms and smothered him with kisses.

"That's a swell greeting to come home to, Mary," gushed Mary, always flustered by the sweet kisses of the naughty girl he had grown to love so deeply.

"I have tea brewing and sausage grilling."

Mary hurried to the kitchen to attend to the meal while Mario took a place on the expensive sofa. The costly furniture was always a reminder that Mary Kelleher lived a head or two above most of the residents on the Lower East Side. Well, that part of her past was over, and she had moved onwards with her human career; although Mario, as a Catholic, wasn't quite certain how respectable a tarot card reader and fortune teller was in his worldview.

"See anything in your crystal ball today?" he asked as she set out utensils on the dining room table.

"I see many things that I don't always understand, Mario," Mary answered carefully. "I know Father Higgins doesn't approve of my calling, but it is a gift the good Lord above gave to me at birth."

"I see it more like a curse," stated Mario, regretting the tune of self-righteousness that had crept into his voice. "You predicted Mary Ann Nikolai's murder."

"It was dreadful and I hate thinking about it. I saw the ambulance take away her remains, May God have mercy upon her soul. I didn't predict it, either. I saw a vision. I did not see her face clearly in the vision. I could not have forewarned her as much as I would have liked to have done so. The gift takes its own course."

"What a course it took."

Mario wasn't sure what to say as they ate quietly. He glanced at her beautiful face and he just knew he loved her no matter what her past was or if she was doing evil with her gift. He also had enough savvy to realize that he must accept her as Mary Kelleher or not accept her at all. She was too Irish and too individualistic to ever just be like his mother or anyone's mother. She smiled back him when she caught him looking at her with such intensity and he smiled back sheepishly.

"A penny for your thoughts," she said.

"You can read my thoughts already, my roisin duhb."

She frowned and stared down into her tea as if she were searching for answers.

"There shall be four more victims before the monster goes away"

"He won't be caught?"

"He'll wander away…and start again. He does have some love in his heart; he's not all evil."

"What does love have to do with it?"

"There are a few people he loves here in the Bowery and he watches over them and he protects them."

"Does he protect you, Mary Kelleher?"

"He does just that."

"I want you to be my wife so I can get you the hell out of this hell."

She smiled but shook her head.

"I love you with all of my heart, Mr. Ferro, but your destiny leads you to another love while my destiny leads me to a lonely spinsterhood."

"I love only you, Mary, and I want you to bear my children."

Mary Kelleher, who wasn't one for tears, began to weep. Mario rushed over to the other side of the table to comfort her. He was surprised and pleased that it didn't take much goading to get the young pretty to speak her mind.

"My blood is tainted by a strain of madness and evil that I can control through my sincere prayers and faith as well as my gift. However, the touch of madness that is a seed that can be passed onwards for many generations. I don't want our great grandson, who carries the Italian name of Ferro, but is infected with a germ and a curse that can trace itself back to Ireland."

"I'm too American to believe in such superstitious tittle tattle."

"I speak tragic and true words," declared Mary Kelleher, turning Mario passive with her colleen kisses. "Tonight we shall all as we roll in sport in one another's arms."

CHAPTER 4

Bugs McMaster, for all of his Irish blarney and American baloney, also had a soft spot for a young lovely who lived on the Bowery. The current flame of his heart was one Maria Colombo and her folks ran a tiny pizzeria on Canal and Fourth. The family served up Italian food with a Tuscany touch, which made them unique in a city filled with Italians from Naples and Sicilians from Syracuse. The Colombo family also sported blond hair, fair skin and blue eyes that made people think that they were of German, Swedish or even Irish stock, instead of Italian. Maria, who had been born over in the old country and was fluent in her native tongue, spoke with a New York accent that one could cut with a knife. However, to a street thug who was smitten with the love bug she was everything that was European and refined.

The entire Colombo family was taken with Bugs McMaster and considered him a good catch even though he was Irish and rough around the edges. Papa Colombo always ushered him to quietest table in the place and immediately delivered freshly baked bread and the best red wine. Momma always put her three hundred pound frame and large heart into serving up her best lasagna, sausage and spaghetti. The boy had the fists of an Irishman but the taste buds of an Italian.

Papa and Momma also made sure that Maria had a few minutes to sit with her beau so they could plan for the future. Worse came to worse, they could transform the Mick into a Wop and make him a true chef.

"We heard the awful news about Mary Ann Nikolai."

"Don't put me off my feed, Maria."

"Will the killer strike again, Bugs?" she asked, lowering her voice.

"They always strike again, Maria."

"Where and when?"

"Here, there, everywhere."

"Can't the police stop him?"

"Don't hold your breath, lover."

"Can you stop him, Mr. McMaster?"

"The Irish Clowns will stop him before the cops."

"It could open up the doors for you, Bugs."

"Open the doors for what?"

"You could develop a detective agency with the other boys and solve crimes."

"Would you like me to be a private dick?"

"I'd be happy with any honest line of work you did as look as it was steady and it provided a living for you, me and our Bowery bambinos."

Bugs McMaster was full of delicious Italian cuisines and thoughts of Maria as he headed homewards to his warm bed beneath his mother's roof. The Depression had ebbed and Roosevelt's campaign had people sing 'Happy Days Are Here Again'. Perhaps it was time for this Bowery Boy to follow the other Bowery Boys to settle down with a job and a wife and all the rest of it. He didn't want to become a Studs Lonigan, who was author James T. Farrell's Irish street kid, who never grew up and died a bum.

CHAPTER 5

Things were starting to go weird shortly after the murder of Mary Ann Nikolai, and they were about to get progressively weirder as the final days of summer began to click off and the heat refused to simmer down. There were numerous reports of unsolved murders over on Bleecker Street in Greenwich Village. A wild urban legend was rapidly working its way down from the northernmost part of the Bronx to the southernmost region of Brooklyn that average New Yorkers were vanishing into the thin air. The Irish, Jewish and Italian organized syndicates even went so far as to issue official memorandums that their hands were clean in the epidemic. It was a season of blab about kidnappings and graves being dug up. The mayor was quick to deny in the newspapers and on the radio that anything was out of the ordinary while he ordered the hiring of more beat patrol cops and put the pressure on the Police Commissioner.

Bugs McMaster, in his usual cool and what he thought analytical way, liked to spend much of the empty hours of his days mulling over what was going on his turf. Like many others, he wondered if it was a Communist or Nazi plot to create turmoil in the biggest and most important city in the land. He had enough of the superstitious nature of his humble soil-toiling peasant ancestors to wonder if there was something supernatural afoot. The Irish were a keen race for vampires, ghosts and ghouls.

Bugs enjoyed it when his elderly mother retired for the night so he could have the parlor to himself. He liked to rest up on the couch with his shoes on and gaze out at the New York City skyline, going over things in his head; his thoughts uninterrupted by talk or swing music on the radio. However, on one hot and humid night, the couch only made him hotter, so he moved over to the window to see if any breeze was stirring on the moon beams. He pulled out the screen window so he could stick his out into all of the pollution of the night air. After failing in his mission, Bugs sank back into his late father's overstuffed reading chair.

Bugs' revelry was penetrated by the sound of something tapping. At first he sought to drown out the sound, but soon the methodical rhythm of the tapping became so loud that he was forced to look outside of the window and down at the sidewalk below. The gang leader, who was long venerated for his valor, literally jumped out of his skin when his eyes meet those of Creepy Kelly three stories below and peering upwards. Creepy Kelly, decked out in a top hat and long dark cape leftover from the reign of Queen Victoria of England, lifted up his cane and pointed it at Bugs. The old man made two or three stabbing gestures at the boy before he chuckled and went on his way.

"What was that all about?" Bugs asked the street lamp that shone just outside of the window.

Bugs watched Creepy Kelly descend down the street; his cane still tapping out his progress. He was almost out of sight and Bugs was sliding back into the parlor when Whitey Kelly went lurking by. He stopped in almost the exact same location that his father had occupied, but he didn't look upwards to get a load of Bugs in the window.

"For Pete's sake," Bugs mumbled to himself. "If this doesn't take cake I don't know what does. Whitey is tailing Creepy."

Bugs McMaster didn't sleep a wink the rest of the night as his brain was furiously trying to make some logical deductions about Creepy and Whitey. He could have used Sherlock Homes and Peter Abelard that night to help him formulate his major premise, his minor premise and his general conclusion.

CHAPTER 6

The voodoo was still hanging thickly in the Bowery air only a few nights later when the entire neighborhood was treated to a knife fight between Squirt Sheridan and Whitey Kelly right next to Squirt's newsstand just outside of the entrance of the 3rd street elevated station. A crowd quickly gathered as Squirt and Whitey circled one another, waiting for openings to take stabs and swipes. Cuts began to appear on their faces, hands and arms. Generally the Irish have never been known as knife fighters, leaving that to their Italian brethrens, preferring skin or something to throw or bash with like bricks or rocks. However, Squirt and Whitey had always been the gauchos of the district, both having a few notches on their knife handles. It was always reckoned they were almost dead even with Squirt have a slight edge from more experience.

"Cut his heart out, Whitey!" one of the Irish Clowns shouted out encouragement.

"He's bleeding like a stuck Irish pig," shouted Jordan in a shrill voice.

Most of the crowd cheered on Whitey while a few of the decayed 3rd Street Celtics gang rooted on their champion. Blood squirted all over the crowd as Squirt punctured side flesh. Whitey, however, was quick on his feet, landing a return blow on Squirt shoulder, showering the daily newspapers with their vendor's blood.

"Where's Kennedy?"

"He's probably......" somebody responded with an off-color remark.

More blue comments followed as an elderly woman scurried off to find the neighborhood flat foot. Later on, it was claimed that Officer Kennedy, a mouth full of egg cream, was standing inside of an all-night candy store, where he was enjoying the spectacle as much as the next Bowery resident. An Irish Clown and a 3rd Street Celtic doing one another in was no skin off of his nose.

"Make way, peasants!" shouted out an angry old man's voice as an angry old man pushed his way through the crowd. The old gaffer swung a solidly built night stick to clear a way to the brawl. Before anybody could grab his arm, Creepy Kelly cracked his cane across the bullet-shaped head of Squirt Sheridan, bringing the knife fighter to his knees. Whitey was also caught off guard by his old man's interference.

"The villain was attacking one of me lads!" roared the old man.

Steven G. Farrell

"Foul!"

"Two against one isn't fair!"

"Fight is over."

Bugs McMaster and Shem Shaw, home from the boxing matches at Madison Square Garden, jumped into the center of things to play referees again.

"Break it up, break it up, folks!" roared out Kennedy, who had decided to finally make his appearance and to earn his pay packet.

The man in blue began to blow on his whistle once he got a quick look at all of the blood spilt and at the look of the condition of the two boys. The crowd, including Creepy Kelly and the Irish Clowns, quickly faded into the night as more cops began to appear. Soon a paddy wagon came tearing around the corner to haul off the bloodied Whitey Kelly and Squirt Sheridan.

The night was only half-way finished, for only about two hours after the knife fight another act of violence broke out in the Bowery. This time the bloodshed occurred in the Chinese Chop Suey place right next to Hughie's Bohemian Café known by the locals as *Chopsticks*. The middle-age Chinese man from Hong Kong and his wrinkled wife were known as *Mister and Missus* Chopsticks out of respect more than working-class bigotry.

Oddly enough, Mr. Chopstick poked out Mrs. Chopstick eyes with a chopstick before he chopped off her right hand with a butcher knife that was very skilled indeed at chopping. Mrs. Chopstick was going into deep shock by the time the ambulance arrived to cart her off to the emergency room. Everybody was sad the next day when the newspapers proclaimed that the dainty Asian lady had died just minutes before she was transferred to the operating table. The Chop Suey joint would be forever closed as Mr. Chopstick was no doubt headed to the gas chambers on Riker's Island.

"Maybe they had a quarrel over the menu," somebody quipped to start-off a long series of tasteless rounds of Confucius Says jokes.

However, more than a few gossipers in the know began to speculate that perhaps Mr. Chopsticks, driven mad by his oriental lust for young white flesh, had used his butcher knife to cut open Mary Ann Nikolai when she turned down his request and money. People were so engrossed in the Chopstick mystery that very few of the locals paid attention to the reappearance of Squirt Sheridan at his newsstand by noontime. He was all black and blue, bandages appearing all over his body. Fortunately, Squirt had a spare worn-out shirt to replace that had been torn asunder by Whitey's knife.

Shortly after six o'clock, Whitey Kelly joined the boys inside of Hughie's. He didn't have much of an appetite, but Hughie was able to force a free 7-Up into his hand.

"What was the fight all about?' Bugs demanded to know.

"Squirt made a rude remark about my father and I got wind of it and decided to nip his rudeness in the bud," said Whitey.

"What kind of rude remark?"

"Something about my father being the daddy of several illegitimate children in the Bowery, who were abandoned on doorsteps."

"Say, Bugs, wasn't Sailor abandoned on your mother's doorsteps."

"Be quiet, Shem."

"He threw it in my face that father had been in cahoots with all sorts of low-life ladies dating back to the last century."

"Squirt is quite the regional historian," cracked Bugs, adding, "Does Squirt even know who his father is?"

"Maybe it is Creepy," Shem said innocently enough.

"Squirt Sheridan is no brother of mine," stated Whitey.

Whitey refused to say any more about his epic encounter with Squirt Sheridan and the conversation quickly turned back to the Chopsticks. Whitey began to twist, turn and shake his hand as though he was shaking off the dripping blood. Bugs McMaster was watching Whitey's every move; others were too.

CHAPTER 7

After paying the twenty-five cent for his shave and a haircut, plus another five cents for a tip, Jordan took one final look in the room wide mirror, admired his appearance and adjusted his tie, before stepping on to the pavement. He skipped over a puddle of water made by the street cleaner as he started to head over towards Hughie's Bohemian Cafe to meet the fellows. He usually timed his arrival before Bugs McMaster arrived, because it gave him a few minutes to be the reigning monarch until the true emperor arrived. He had more brains than Bugs but the pugnacious Mickey could still take his measure when it came to the old toe to toe.

"One day Bugs will move on and I'll move up," Jordan said out loud as he crossed at a corner while the light was still red. He laughed out loud as he dodged cars and trucks. He was used to being cursed out for disobeying the traffic signals.

"First there was Schwartz; now there was a McMaster and, some day it would be Jordan at the head of the helm of the Irish Clown."

Fancy that: a nice Jewish boy in charge of a crew of Irish thugs. After all, Schwartz had been Jewish, and he had founded the gang years ago. He could beat all of the Mickeys at their own game. It just went to show that a Jewish guy could be as tough...or even tougher.... than either the Irish or the Italians. Just look at all the Jewish gangster who had made headlines over the years like Meyer Lansky, Bugsy Siegel, Arnold Rothstein, Dutch Schultz, Abe Reles and Bug Workman. A Jewish lad on the make could get ahead using their mitts as well as their bean. He was part of a New York City tradition.

Jordan started to think back to the slaughter of Mary Ann Nichols. The other Clowns had known her from grammar school, but it had been a Catholic school run by the nuns so he hadn't really known her. Besides, he had spent most of his lower elementary school grades over further south on the Lower East Side near Little Italy. Moving to the Bowery had been a shock to his system. However, once he learned how to stick up for his rights and to fight back the Irish kids had accepted him as one of their own. Getting back to Mary Ann, he didn't have much sympathy because of what she was and how she earned her living. The neighborhood was a purer and cleaner place without her or her kind.

"So people think ole Chopsticks was Mary Ann's murdered," Jordan said with a chuckle. "It won't be long before they're all in for a big, big surprise; it's at least my prediction that the merry-go-round of mayhem has only just begun its spin here on the Bowery."

Jordan, who looked both ways first, ducked into an alley on Elizabeth Street. It was filled with trash cans and rubbish of all sorts, but it held a special place in his heart; for the Irish Clowns had once beat the River Street Raiders in that very same alley, with Jordan felling three of the opposition by himself. Of course, Bugs McMaster had chomped down four of them, but he had been leading the way and thus more opportunities.

"This is a nice spot for a murder," said Jordan, observing that there was no exit for escape once you were inside of the alley unless you went through one of the back doors into a building. "No escape from death!"

Jordan whipped out an invisible switchblade and began to take invisible stabs at the invisible woman in front of him, her back up against the wall. He stopped back and imagined the blood escaping his victim. Then he felt slightly ashamed of himself as he wiped clean his harmless weapon and put it back into his pocket.

"Get out of here, punk!"

Jordan was startled by the sound of a gruff voice behind him. He spun around and saw nothing behind him.

"Who's there?"

"Up here, jerk!"

Standing on the fire escape three stories up was a middle-aged man with a cigar stuffed inside of his mouth and his burly, hairy arms revealed poking out of a sweat-stained undershirt. The man dared Jordan to smart-off back to him. Discretion was the better part of valor as far as Jordan was concerned. He dashed out of the alley and didn't allow a smile to appear across his mug until he was safely inside of Hughie's and surrounded by the Irish Clowns.

CHAPTER 8

The smile was wiped off of his Jordan's face when the police hauled him down to precinct headquarters the next morning. The boy had just stuck his nose into the morning edition that was proclaiming the slaying of a second streetwalker in the Bowery. His heart had skipped a beat or two when he realized that the girl had been found in the alley off of Elizabeth Street where he had play acted his own scene of violence. Was it a mere coincidence that the madman had selected that alley to strike again? Or had the murderer been watching him and then carrying out the reality?

Rat Rice had plenty of his own questions to ask. And he was none to gentle with his wording. As soon as he had returned to the office he found the mayor waiting on the other line demanding resolution to the two murders. Worst than that was he found a letter in his office mail entitled "DEAR RAT." It was a missive direct from the bloody hands of the Ripper himself, taunting him.

19

"So you're in trouble again, Jordan," said Rat Rice in that Louisiana drawl of his that made people laugh out loud behind his back.

"I have an alibi for that night, Chief Inspector," said Jordan, knowing when to be respectful.

"Make with the alibi," another copper said.

Rat Rice nodded his head in agreement with the request. In spite of his southern accent, Rat Rice was a graduate of Texas A&M University and a long-time fixture at the precinct. He was by no means a fool and he was as tough as any dockside brawler.

"The night that lady was killed I stayed in all night to play cards with my dad and two brothers."

"The Warden family is okay, Chief."

"The old man has run a tailor shop for years on 4th," somebody else noted.

"So where has this boy gone wrong?" asked Rice.

"We played spades until midnight and then we all turned in," said Jordan. He was beginning to panic.

"Maybe you snuck out on the fire escape when everybody else was asleep."

"I share a room with my younger brother and he's a light sleeper. He would have woken up if I had opened up the window to take my leave. Besides, it was raining at that point, and I hate getting soaked to the skin. You can call home and verify all of what I'm saying. I think you're trying to make me the patsy for all of this junk."

"Check it out," Rice said to one uniform as he ordered another one to fetch pen and paper.

"Now as we wait for the feedback that could decide your fate, we're going to examine your penmanship and see what kind of job the P.S did for your cursive skills," said Rice.

"Write cleanly, punk," another cop said.

The sweat pouring down his pour, the Irish Clown accepted the pen into his right hand; his left hand was dripping sweat all over the clean sheet of paper put in front of him. Rat Rice reached into his suit coat and pulled out the letter he had received only a few hours ago. It was the thing that had made him determine to crack the case wide open.

"Print what I read to you," commanded Rice, adding, "and do it the way you would if you were hand printing a note to a friends."

"You can write, can't you, punk?"

"He's Jewish, not Irish, so he can write."

Rat Rice began to read:

Dear Rat,

I keep on hearing the police caught me but they won't fix me yet. I have laughed when they look so clever and talk about being on the right track. That joke about Chop Sticks gave me real fits...."

Jordan, who had always been proud of his educational abilities, limited as they may have been, took great care to follow Rice's dictation. He wanted his writing to impress as well as to clear his name in the eyes of the cop.

".... Good luck. Yours truly, Jack the Ripper. Don't mind me resorting to my old trade name.....

Jordan also jumped out of his skin when he heard the name of *Jack the Ripper*; for every American school child knew of the dastardly deeds of London's 19th century arch criminal. Other eyes inside of the warm room rose over the mentioning of the name. It just couldn't be! After many years of silence, it appeared Jack the Ripper had moved stateside to continue his bloody career. It just didn't add up. It was true Jack the Ripper had never been captured by the bobbies but he surely would be dead after all of these years. It was over sixty years in the foggy past.

Chief Inspector Rice lifted up Jordan's offerings to his eyes to carefully read the results. He then held up the original letter so he could compare the handwriting side by side. The two letters made their way around the room. There was no match between the two, but they all suspected that Jordan was clever enough to disguise his true handwriting in one or the other. The Bowery Boy was obviously no fool.

"Don't leave town, boy," the Inspector said slowly.

CHAPTER 9

M ario Ferro, who had an access to Inspector Rice that was denied to all the other reporters on the New York dailies, was the first to get a look at the *Dear Rat* letter before it was sent to the crime laboratory to be dusted for prints. By the time Chief Inspector Rice made his revelation of the letter know to the rest of New York's media world, Mario and Bosco Ferro were rushing back to their office to get their scoop ready for a special edition. Mario, who was a news hound to the tip of his toes, came up with the headline of *The Bowery Ripper On the Loose*. From that moment onwards, the serial killer loose in the Bowery would be known as *The Bowery Ripper*. Mario had found the story that would cement his name in the annals of investigative reporting.

The *Dear Rat* letter actually compelled Mario to take a detour to the New York Public Library where he did some research on the career of the original Jack the Ripper. He read that five murders were part of the Ripper's canon but several more could have been on the roll call list. He found out some other interesting facts that he would only share later on. Jack the Ripper career had only last about three months before he simply fell off the globe.

"But that all took place many, many years ago," said Mario, repeating what the police had said only a few hours before when they were drilling Jordan.

It just had to be a copycat killer; somebody who had read a book about the Ripper and who was now reduplicating the crimes in order to make a name for themselves.

CHAPTER 10

I nspector Thomas Farrow, a long-time member of Scotland Yard, always looked forward to his spot of tea and a biscuit or two late in the afternoon when he was beginning to feel tired back in the Records Department. Short, fat and easily winded, Tommy had long ago been promoted up and off of the streets of London's East End. He had never been one to use his fist and to swing a night stick; instead, Tommy Farrow was a bloke who used his bean to unfold cases. Other officers of the law discovered the clues while Tommy collected them, added them all up, made a deductive reasoning about it, and then presented in the court room at the Old Bailey.

Tommy put a generous amount of sugar and cream into his tea before stirring it all together with a vigor lacking in the rest of his life. He munched on the sugary biscuit, savoring its sweetness. Tea time also gave him a chance to think deeper on the case of the recent serial killings over in white Chapel.

"I'd be considered barmy if I came right out and said it that it was the work of Saucy Jack himself," the Inspector said to himself. "Jack the Ripper alive and well in 1938. That's a cock and bull story.'

Not even the more sensational British newspapers had compared the recent slaying in White Chapel to the slayings committed by Jack the Ripper back in 1888.

"Why that was how many years ago? Perish the thought, old boy."

Actually his attention had been drawn to one suspect who had stood out against all the rest in the current state of affairs with the murder of White Chapel's prostitutes: Morrison McMaster, aka 'Sailor McMaster.' Tommy recalled to mind the thick New York accent of the Yank McMaster, who was so clearly low breed and uneducated. A telegram from New York indicated that the boy was a foundling and had been reared by an adopted family. The inspector had even sat in on an interview with McMaster, concluding that the thuggish young American had the killer instinct even if hadn't killed the street girls. Tommy could see murder and mayhem in the young tough's eyes. Unfortunately, there hadn't been any evidence to hold the foreigner, so he was released; and then he disappeared.

"Presto, the man clears out! Sailor McMaster was gone! No doubt he hopped a ship to America or Australia where, if he is a murderer, he'll carry on his career until he slips up and falls into the hands of the authorities."

The door to Records and a female secretary poked her head and called, "Tommy, the Superintendent wants to see you after you've finished your repast."

Tommy gobbled up his second biscuit, wiped off his lips with a napkin, and straightened up for his visit with the top man on the totem pole.

"You're to go home immediately and to pack a grip for a short jaunt to America," said the Super, without any ceremony or build-up.

"America, sir?" asked Tommy, unruffled.

"It's this Ripper business rearing its ugly head again," said the Super.

An assistant to the big man went on to explain to Inspector Thomas Farrow that the New York Police had contacted Scotland Yard through Interpol to assist them with a duet of Jack the Ripper copycat cases in some place called the Bowery.

"Yes, I have read a little about it in the papers."

"Silly Yanks want an expert on the 1888 Jack the Ripper case to assist them with this modern murder spree. You fit the bill more than anybody else on the force, Farrow."

"I have never been to the colonies before, sir."

"I believe it's damnably cold over there this time of season," said the Super. "Get the best winter coat you can find and put it on your expense account."

"May I venture forth with some of my own speculations upon the case?"

"What is it, man?"

"Do you remember the American we hauled in a few weeks ago in regards to the current murders on the East End?"

"Released because of insufficient evidence, what about it, man?"

"He was called Sailor McMaster and, if I recall correctly, was a New Yorker. He's vanished from this port. When he left these shores the murders stopped. He mustn't be ruled out as a suspect. Also, if you recall, the murders fell on the anniversary of the Ripper's murders."

The Superintendent paused for a moment, "I see where you're going with your line of thinking, Farrow."

"What is your official directive?"

"Carry on."

"The newspapers will howl for our blood if and when I put forth my theory that Sailor McMaster is the grandson of Jack the Ripper. If we announce that bad genes from the original Jack the Ripper have passed on nobody shall buy it."

"I'm not sure if I buy it myself, Farrow. You found this out by digging through every single official document in London since 1880."

"Mary Kelly, the last victim of the Ripper, had delivered a child into the world only a few months before her death and the child...one James Kelly... was placed in an orphanage in Liverpool. James was put out to apprentice with an upholstery business, but he fled his master when he was about fifteen. The authorities surmised that the lad washed up on American shores."

"It's just so much history to me, Farrow. What about the Ripper's son?"

"Back in 1888, an officer who work the East end stepped forward with the testimony of a worn-out prostitute or two that the father of the boy was one James Kelly."

"James Kelly and Mary Kelly, you say? What sort of game we're they playing. It's quite unnatural: brother and sister…even for the Irish."

"Kelly was a common enough name in London and Dublin in those days, and nobody ever mentioned that they were siblings."

"Who was this James Kelly and when he was at home?'

"James Kelly was also an upholsterer and he had been placed in Broadmoor for the stabbing murder of his legal wife. He ripped her throat out."

"Out with it all, man."

"James Kelly escaped from prison just before the outbreak of the murders in white Chapel, but he had shipped out of England by the time the police had started to make inquiries about him. James Kelly was a Jack the Ripper suspect in 1888. James Kelly is my own personal favorite."

"And you think this James Kelly is still a-foot?"

"In 1923, he showed up at the gates of Broadmoor and turned himself in. He died an old man in 1927. At least that's what the death certificate reports."

"James Kelly senior, James Kelly junior and Sailor McMaster all figure in it. Well, you sort it out, Farrow."

"By the by, sir, this is the fiftieth anniversary of the Ripper's criminal spree. He could be alive today, certainly, but it'd be very, very old."

"Farrow, I don't put my faith in your line of reasoning, but you're the expert. Close the door on the way out."

CHAPTER 11

" **I** got to get on safe ground before the Ripper hits the streets," Shem fretted out loud as he made a dash for it as soon as the doors of the elevated train opened.

Clarence Darrow Shaw, aka 'Shem,' member of the Bowery's Irish Clown social club and an infamous loafer of the Lower East Side of Manhattan, disembarked the 3rd Avenue Elevated Train at Canal Street. He had spent another fruitless day seeking an executive position on Wall Street, now it was time to get back to his real occupation, goofing off with the other Bowery's Irish Clowns. The job-hunting façade was just a scam to keep his old man at bay in the Shaw family's tenement apartment. He would do anything to keep his parents from yelling at him. It usually worked. After coughing-up the fare to and from the city Shem had just enough of the money he had bummed off his Ma for a coffee and piece of pie at "Hughie's Bohemian Café", the official hang-out for Bugs and the other Clowns. Hughie Kressin, the ancient Yiddish-spewing innkeeper of the Bohemian Café, was an easy touch in spite of all of his ranting at the Irish corner boys who cluttered his place. Shem knew he wouldn't feel secure until he was with the gang. The Ripper wouldn't dare step into the holy grounds of the café. Hughie was particular about the quality of the people who stepped into his establishment.

"Gee, Bugs will understand why I can't get my career off of the ground," Shem said out loud as he descended the stairways of the station. His moronically bugged eyed looks and mumblings always drew stares. He just knew his folks would start harping on him about going back to his old gig at the Fulton Fish Market. "They're both nothing but Irish harpies."

Shem drew a bead on Hughie's just down the block but his vision was blocked when his Dodgers baseball cap fell over his eyes upon his collision with Squirt Sheridan, the tough newsboy who worked the corner and who was a sworn enemy of the Bowery Irish Clowns. Squirt was known for carrying a switchblade knife.

"Watch it, punk," growled Clancy. "I hope the Ripper cuts your throat before Christmas unless I slice it before Thanksgiving."

"Excuse me for breathing, young fellow," shot back Shem. "Never mind Christmas; let me live past Halloween."

"Get a job, wastrel!"

"Lay a finger on me and I'll tell the chief," retorted Shem, adding, "knife fighter."

Squirt knew he could have mopped up the sidewalk with Shem or any of the other losers in the gang but he didn't fancy tangling with Bugs McMaster, who was still accounted as one of the best East Side sluggers since the days of Monk Eastman, Razor Reilly and Eat Em Up McManus. Shem Shaw was the best insurance policy in the entire rapidly decaying neighborhood. Sheridan thought to himself that soon the Bowery would have nobody left in it but winos, bums and the Irish Clowns.

Shem scurried pat Kennedy the beat cop.

"Are you still running with the Tinkers from the County Kerry?" hooted the flat foot.

"Oh, go back to the Ninth Precinct," shot back Shem.

Standing just outside of Hughie's Bohemian Café was Sarah Shaw, a second cousin of Shem and a third rate hooker on the Bowery. She had once been a very charming and pretty slip of a lass, but now she was beginning to look a bit shopworn. Most of the family, as well as the old families on the Bowery, were ashamed of Sarah's carrying on. Shem remembered better times and felt pity for a good girl who had gone to the bad. It wasn't like she was getting rich at it or enjoyed the life.

"Sarah, you better move on before Hughie blows his top or Bugs comes along," said Shem, peering into the diner to see who was around. Hughie was making a banana spilt for two fat dames while Bennie, Gyp, Murphy and Jordan were taking up valuable space at a table in the far back of the shop in between the rarely used jukebox and the too often used restroom. Whitey was probably just closing up the holster shop he operated along with his tough old gaffer Creepy Kelly. The Ferro brothers were still down at their office at the newspaper where they were making a name for themselves as a reporter and photographer with the inside scoop and glossy and gross photographs on the two serial killings that had taken place in the old burg. And the chief, Bugs, was probably finishing up his supper at home where his Ma always put on a good feed since she inherited loot from her bachelor brothers who were all firemen, police detectives and undertakers before they kicked their buckets. Shem was wondering why the Ripper had cut the throat of two lowly street walkers in the Bowery instead of hunting up in the Bronx or down in Brooklyn. One would think the Ripper would find fresher and prettier girls somewhere on Coney Island. Shem could almost imagine the smell of the popcorn, the taste of a hot dog, and the sounds of people screaming on the Ferris wheel. Too bad it was October and the fair days were over.

"If you let me hold your spare change, Cousin Clarence, I could go home and escape Bugs' wrath for another night. You're still wrestling mackerel at the Fulton Street Fish Market, aren't you?"

"Everybody by the name of Shaw has the Fulton Street Fish Market on the brain. Besides, I'm flat broke and have been out of work since I lit-up my box of firecrackers beneath Mr. Silverstein's chair during his afternoon nap."

"That wasn't smart thing to do to your boss, Clarence."

"It was the fourth of July, Cathy," snapped Shem. "Where's your sense of patriotism, lady?"

Sarah suddenly froze in position. Her ears perked up as she tried to hear something over the noises of night time New York City. She peered long and carefully across the street. She studied the spaces in between the pawnshop, the Chinese restaurant and Battleship Marge's Boardinghouse. Her gaze stayed the longest on the alleyway further down the street and away from the elevated station. Her silence and stiffness scared Shem who was easily frightened.

"Somebody is watching us right now."

"Stop it right now, Cathy!"

"Do you suppose it's him?"

"I hope you don't mean who I think you mean," responded Shem, biting on his fingernails.

"I bet it's the Ripper, Shem, out to get us both." "We going to be number three and four."

"I wish the chief was here," whined Shem, starting to cry like a half-wit.

"Boo!' shouted Cathy, grabbing him by the neck.

Shem's terrified scream brought Kennedy huffing and puffing down the street and Hughie bolting towards the front door of his dive. By the time the two adults could rescue the boy Sarah was laughing and skipping across the street. Soon she ducked out of sight into the alley that had once held so much fear for her. The copper socked Shem on the arm for issuing a false alarm and Hughie was going to bar him from the Bohemian Café for the night until Shem pulled out a handful of loose coins to prove he was a paying customer for a change. Momma Mary, Hughie's hefty spouse, glared on at the moocher.

"Hughie, go prepare me a nice bowl of chicken soup and a cup of hot tea while I wait out here for Bugs to show."

"I'll chicken soup you," snorted Hughie, cracking Shem with his cleaning towel. "Millions of Jews sipping chicken soup in this city and I get the Irish kid who likes mine."

"You mean he likes my chicken soup, Poppa," countered Momma.

"Bless your heart, Momma."

CHAPTER 12

S hem Shaw was alone for only a few minutes when he heard a blood curdling scream issue from the alley across the street. He immediately recognized Cathy's voice. He raced across the street to the entrance but he didn't venture any further because he assumed that this was probably more of his cousin's larks. He was peering into the gloom of the dusk when Bugs came up to him and cracked him on the top of the head with his battered hat that was yet another inheritance from a deceased uncle.

"Shem, are you watching Alice's rabbit disappear down the magic hole again?"

"I heard Sarah screaming down there."

Bugs frowned at the mentioning of the name of an old flame of his.

"The only screaming that one does is when she's on her back and earning pennies off of the waterfront riff raff who patronize her."

"Chief, that isn't nice to say about a girl down on her luck."

"She's down on something," said the chief, shaking his head sadly as he tugged Shem over to the café. It was time to check-up on the troops. The two had just made their way back to the table that now served as their clubhouse since their numbers had decreased over the years and the younger Mets had chased them away from the old underground clubhouse. The greetings and insults were still in progress when Whitey Kelly strolled in looking pensive as ever. He was forever whipping his hands because he felt he could never get them clean after working in his old man's all day. The clowns started in on the newcomer when their taunts refocused upon the Ferro brothers, Mario and Bosco, who rushed in from the street. Mario, the reporter, flapped his notebook in the boys faces while Bosco, the photographer, called out for a pose.

"If it isn't our very own print boys and the Bowery's number one newshound and his brother the snapper," shouted Bugs, making no sense to anybody but himself. Mario ignored the uproar as he ordered a cherry cola from a Hughie, who was wondering if the soda was to be paid for in currency or placed on the boys' ever-expanding tab.

In between gulps Marion clued the others in on the latest scoop about the Ripper.

"The coppers are anticipating two attacks tonight."

"As if one wasn't enough," put in Shem. "And now I'm worried about Sarah."

"Go on, Mario, you interest me for a change of climate."

"It seems that Scotland Yard of London contacted the Bowery's very own Chief Inspector Rat Rice when they got wind of two Ripper murders here on the Lower East Side of New York City."

"Why would the Scottish in anyone's yard be interested in the Bowery?" asked Shem

"Shem, you're an idiot," snapped Bugs, smacking Shem with his hat again before turning his attention back to Ferro. "Mario, what's ole Rice doing about all of these Ripper murders?"

"Scotland Yard, the London police, sent over here to our fair city one Inspector Tommy Farrow to assist Rice and the lads at the Ninth with the Ripper spree because they think our Bowery madman is copying their man in every detail."

"What? The Scottish invented another Ripper?

"For once Shem has asked an intelligent question," said Jordan.

Hughie set a fresh cherry coke down in front of Mario as he proceeded to blow his stack. "Haven't you hooligans ever heard of Jack the Ripper? He was the original Ripper. The neighborhood's nut case in this neighborhood is a copycat. Jack the Ripper was in all of the newspaper back when I was a fresh off of the boat from Prague in 1908 or so."

"Try 1888 on for size," corrected Mario as Hughie fumed.

"Is this Prague in the Queens?" asked Shem.

"Did this Jack the Ripper lurk in the immense London fog and kill girls with a knife?" asked Bugs.

Light bulbs went on all over the café as everybody began to put two and two together.

"My old man told me all about Jack the Ripper," rumbled Whitey. "You know the old guy lived in White Chapel, London around that time."

"I thought you were Irish?" asked Hughie. "You're all Irish or Italian and not a good Jew among you."

"Hush, Poppa," Momma scolded as she brewed more coffee.

"A lot of Irish lived in London back in those days," grouched back Whitey, "so what about it?"

"Surely Mario, Rat Rice doesn't think it's the same Ripper after all of these years."

"The heel isn't saying, but I'm saying so in my next article entitled *The Ripper on the Bowery*. Sounds catchy, doesn't it?"

"You could say it's ripping."

"Anyways," continued Mario. "I was at headquarters today when the Chief Inspector introduced the limey bobby from England and the first thing the foreigner said was that in 1888, on September 30th, the Ripper struck twice, in two different spots, and put the end to two girls."

"You don't say," said Bugs, rubbing his jaw. "The first attack was in late August and the second one was in early September so I guess the Ripper would be ready to strike again."

Mario consulted his notebook and confirmed Bugs observation. "August 31st and September 8th, which were the exact dates that Jack the Ripper done his dirty deeds in London. If he goes ahead according to schedule September 30th is circled on the calendar."

"This way it doesn't require any guesswork on the part of chief Inspector Rice."

"Chief, Squirt Sheridan is pretty handy when it comes to sticking people with a knife," blurted out Shem.

"Shem has a point there, Bugs," said Jordan as some the other nodded their heads.

Bugs took a long pause before he finally responded by saying, "Squirt Sheridan has earned himself some serious consideration as a suspect but he's more of a galoot than a night stalker."

"And here's the kickers, boys," announced Mario, waving everybody closer in for a whisper of a cover-up as he drew the attention back to himself. "The two girls our Ripper killed were named Mary Ann and Annie just like...."

"Jack the Ripper!" the gang sang in harmony.

"So it stands to rationalization that the police know the name of his two promising victims tonight," said Bugs.

"Smart boy," said Hughie, clapping Bugs on the shoulder.

"And if the police know that all they have to do is put guards on all of the girls in the Bowery by those names."

"Elizabeth and Catherine," said Mario, answering Bugs' unspoken question.

"The Bowery must have dozens and dozens of girls with the first names of Catherine and Elizabeth," said Hughie. "Where do the police even start?"

"Cathy's real name is Catherine," Shem said to Hughie.

"Don't bother your Poppa Hughie right now, Shem."

"Cathy!" roared Bugs, leaping to his feet and racing to the door. "Cathy was in the alley."

Unfortunately, Bugs was too slow on the draw and Cathy's bloody remains had already been found by Kennedy. By the time the Irish Clowns reached the far end of the alley a crowd had gathered. Shem, against his will, was pulled forward to identify the body of his deceased cousin. The crowd was angry and they began demanding that Kennedy take action immediately. The man in blue immediately blew his whistle for more assistance.

Bugs, Shem and the Clowns were all shaking their heads with disbelief as Kennedy began to force the rest of the onlookers to clear the way for re-enforcement. Nobody seemed to pay much attention when Bosco began to snap a picture. The exploding light bulb made everybody jump back.

"Say, what's the idea?" asked Kennedy, pushing his hat backwards on his head.

"Let's show more respect for my cousin, young fellow."

"Evidence," answered Bosco, popping in another bulb into his camera.

"A scoop, you mean," said Bugs.

"We need to burn some images to warn the public that a madman is at large," Mario said in a rhetorical manner.

Bugs would have had more cross words for the newspaper brothers but the alley was soon full of all sorts of city employees. Sirens filled the autumn night air as uniforms crowded into the dark alleyway. Kennedy elbowed a few of the boys aside to usher in Chief Inspector Rat Rice. A roly poly fellow with a Charlie Chaplin followed close behind him. The two bent over the dead girl's body and examined the mess that had once been her throat and stomach.

"The bloke's gone and made a mess," said the chubby man in a thick Cockney accent as he pointed out the gore splattered all over the brick sides of building and all around the alley. "We're all standing in the blood and guts of this poor and unfortunate soul."

CHAPTER 13

The foreigner's last sentence did the job of clearing out the alley that Kennedy hadn't been able to accomplish. The last thing Bugs and the Bowery Irish Clowns heard was Rice shouting out orders in his bossy tone of voice of his. Nobody was in a mood for a banana spilt when the gangs retook their old chairs inside of the Bohemian Café. Bugs looked around to see that several of the key members of his crew were missing in action.

"Hughie, you can fade as I take a head count," said Bugs. "Go listen to the radio and have Momma Mary rustle up some grub."

"On your tab, I suppose."

"Yellow bellies," laughed Jordan. "They took off running at the site of blood."

"Not everybody gets a thrill by the sight of the ketchup like you, Jordan," snorted Bugs.

"Shem had to rush home to tell his family about....you know," said Gyp.

"Whitey said he had to check on his old man, Creepy Kelly," said Bennie. "You know that Creepy can get up to no good if somebody doesn't keep a close eye on him."

Bugs rested his chin on his fists and began to ponder the situation. The Ripper was intruding on his territory even if his turf was confined to a few grubby blocks in the lowly Bowery. What's more the Ripper was now attacking people who the Irish Clowns knew.

"Say, fellows, didn't Mario say the Ripper was suppose to attack two girls tonight?'

"What about it?" asked Benny.

"He was penciled in to kill a Catherine....and he did; now he's suppose to kill an Elizabeth."

"More police have arrived," noted Jordan. "Rice has called in the reserves."

The boys paused as more sirens could be heard in the distance. The tiny diner seemed to be engulfed in the loud screams of squad cars and fire trucks. The noise was deafening. Bugs started to holler above the racket. "It is up to us to start patrolling the Bowery to see if we can catch the Ripper. We won't have any females left if we leave it in the hands of Inspector Rice, Kennedy and the moustache from Scotland Yard."

"Bugs!" shouted Hughie, bursting out of the back room and racing over to grab Bugs by the arm. "The Ripper has struck again! I just heard a news flash over the radio! The Ripper struck again!"

Benny and Jordan caught a hold of Hughie and forced him to take a seat. Gyp tossed a glass of lukewarm water into the little man's face in order to settle him down and to get some sense out of him.

"Hughie, if you decompose yourself long enough to speak plain English to us, we're all ears."

"The Ripper struck again just down Canal Street here only a minute away. It occurred near the East River."

Hughie's words rang true as the Bowery was alive with excitement, panic and rage that night. The police and civilians alike padded their way from one site to the other. The Irish Clowns had just arrived at the second murder site when Inspector Rice looked at them and said, "Just the boys we wanted to see."

"Why us?" asked Jordan.

Kennedy pointed to a chalked graffiti that stood out against the backdrop of blood dripping off of the back of a tattoo parlor.

"The Clowns are the men that will not be blamed for nothing," Bugs read out loud.

"Shakespeare it's not," cracked Jordan. Nobody laughed at his remark.

"But the message is a positive identification," Rice announced grandly. "Boys, you're all under arrest!"

CHAPTER 14

"So you the Irish Clowns are in trouble again," Rat Rice said with a wicked smile once he had the gang safely down in headquarters.

"You know full well that murder is not in our line," said Bugs, refusing to let the Chief Inspector get under his skin.

Rat Rice and the Irish Clowns had a history that dated back many years now, and both sides knew the other inside out. In recent years, Rice had relaxed his grip on the Irish Clowns due to his professional relationship with Mario Ferro, who was a good egg once he got a regular job and drifted away from the clutches of Bugs and the gang.

"Somebody is slicing up bellies in this old parish of ours," stated Rice.

"So that gives you the right to put the Bowery under Rat Rice's bayonet law," snapped back Bugs.

"Why would I want to hurt my cousin, Cathy?" Shem asked with an innocent pout.

"The boy-o has a point there, Chief Inspector," said Kennedy, who had a soft spot for the Bowery Boys.

"You've already racked me over the coals before," protested Jordan. "You found out I was clean. Why not give the fellows here a chance to prove themselves by giving them the same test you gave me?"

"We aren't in school," Shem protested himself.

"Good idea, Chief Inspector."

"May I interject something at this junction," butted in the normally sedate Tommy Farrow.

"Hey, fellows, this guy here speaks the real king's English," jeered Bugs, pointing to Tommy.

The cut of Bugs' jive and facial appearance had reminded Inspector Thomas Farrow of a similar interrogation back home in London. There could be no mistake about the resemblance between this McMaster and another McMaster.

"Go right ahead, Inspector Farrow."

"Do any of you lads here by any chance know one Morrison McMaster?"

The Irish Clowns looked at the runty little limey with awe and a new found respect.

"Hey, Bugs, isn't that Sailor's real name," said Shem, receiving frosty looks from his mates.

"Shut up, Shem!"

"Bugs, if you do happen to see your cousin, Sailor, let him know his old pal Chief Inspector Rice would like a casual chat with him. Tell him I know he was a foundling. Your mother took him in."

"What's this all about?" Bugs demanded to know. "What do you care about his pedigree?"

"Sailor sails the seven seas," put in Shem. "And Ma McMaster found him on her doorsteps. Maybe found Mugs that way, too."

"He sent us a post card from Australia last year," Bugs slowly admitted, turning his attention back to Shem. "Leave my heritage out thi, mug!"

"Nothing from England?" asked Inspector Farrow.

"We never knew he was in England," answered Bugs.

"That'll be all, boys," Rice announced Rat Rice, pointing to the door of his office with his forefinger.

CHAPTER 15

The arrest of the Bowery's Irish Clowns must have been some sort of ruse by Inspector Rat Rice in order to prove that he and his department were on top of the Ripper Case; for they were almost immediately released. A telephone call to Hughie at the Bohemian Cafe provided them with an airtight alibi. Bugs wondered if Rat had them arrested merely as some sort of twisted joke. Whatever Rat Rice's motivations, Bugs was worried that a lynch mob would be awaiting their return back to their headquarters at Third and Canal. However, their long-time mascot Hughie must have quelled the mob, because all was quiet when the boys marched in to reclaim their table at the back.

"Inspector Rice was just grandstanding for the reporters," exclaimed Hughie, dishing up free ice cream to smooth over any hard feelings the gang might have for the Inspector. He had done it more than once or twice over the years.

"And for that we're going to show up Rat Rice by putting our mitts on this so-called Ripper of the Bowery and pulling down his ironed trousers in full view of the radio and newspaper public," said Bugs. "And his remarks about Sailor were uncalled for. So what if he was an orphan? We gave him a home, didn't we? Is still my cousin, isn't he?"

"The Irish Clowns to the rescue!" said Jordan, rallying the others to the cause.

"The Irish Clowns should get paying jobs instead of butting their noses into police business. If the Ripper doesn't cut them off, Rat Rice will break them off," fretted Hughie.

However, once Bugs McMaster had made-up his mind nothing in Heaven or on Earth could dissuade him from the task at hand. The whole affair was had turned personal. Besides, the malt shop kingpin reckoned that he and his crew knew the nooks and crannies better than all of the cops in Manhattan put together. It stood to reason that as neighborhood loafers that they could sneak into every shadow of the Bowery. Bugs came up with the division of labor, sending Jordan and Bennie northwards towards to the outer edges of the Bowery at Fourteenth Street while Gyp, Murphy and Whitey covered the waterfront along the East River. Mario and Bosco were the most useful at their place of employment where they could get tabs on Chief Inspector Rice and Inspector Farrow as well as filter to the gang about any new bulletins about the Ripper. Bugs and Shem would handle the business district beneath the elevated tracks, going from shop to shop to ask question. Bugs decided it as was only a mere formality to stop at the Kelly's

Upholstery Shop to question Creepy Kelly, Whitey's forever cranky and threatening father.

"I don't want White Chapel's hooligan mates under me roof!" shouted Creepy, waving some sharp work instrument beneath Bugs' nose. The old gaffer's accent was hard to place; for it was not an Irish brogue or a Cockney dialect but rather a broth of two stirred together.

"Who's this White Chapel when he's at home?" asked Shem, ditching behind Bugs' back.

"I think the old gent is referring to our mutual pal, Whitey," explained Bugs.

"It's a good a name as any other and sure wasn't the lad born over in White Chape,l where I had me shop back in London?' challenged Creepy. He suddenly shrunk away from the boys as though he had let the cat out of the bag.

"So Whitey is English and not Bowery Irish?" asked Bugs.

"That's none of your business, you corner boy, you."

Bugs didn't reveal his hand to the other boys when they regrouped at Hughie's Bohemian Café just before dusk. He spent much of the time studying Whitey's face and body language as the others recounted their long day of detective work. Bugs had long since realized that the old Jack the Ripper murders had occurred in the crumbling White Chapel section of London's East End before they had suddenly rematerialized in the crumbling Bowery section of New York's East Side. The boss of the Irish Clowns knew he didn't need to be any Sherlock Holmes to deduce that Jack the Ripper was Creepy Kelly. Bugs McMaster was nothing if he wasn't loyal to his fellow gang members and he wasn't about to help Inspector Rat Rice and Precinct 9 to do their job in locating the murderer. Stopping the Ripper from striking again on the Bowery was altogether a different ball game. Some of the fellows had spied upon Squirt Sheridan at his corner newsstand but it had just been racing forms and girlie magazines all day long.

"Fellows, the best thing we can do is just sit tight until the November 3rd when this Ripper character is poised to strike again," announced Bugs, finalizing his decision.

"Shouldn't we warn the neighborhood that the Ripper could strike again on the 3rd of next month?" asked Jordan.

The public telephone began to ring and it refused to stop until Hughie picked it up.

"Can we trust the Ripper to keep to the old schedule?" Gyp asked sensibly.

Hughie shouted over the boys: "Bugs, it's Mario, and it said the last victim of Jack the Ripper was a dame by the name of Mary Kelly."

"Whitey, isn't Kelly your last name?" Shem asked innocently.

"So what about it, mug," growled Whitey, clenching his fists. "There are plenty of people with the last name of Kelly in the Bowery. Besides, we don't own a Mary."

Shem turned away from the wrath of Whitey to address: "And Hugo, Momma's first name is Mary."

Hughie rubbed his chin in reflection.

"You're forgetting that Momma Mary isn't a night walker…if you catch my drift."

"More like a nightmare," Hughie mumbled under his breath but still thankful that his wife was in the kitchen flipping hamburgers for the boys. She had always been known for her fiery temper back in the old country. She was also one jealous old nag. Maybe Momma was Jill the Ripper. Nah, she couldn't be. Well, one could never tell.

The Bowery's Irish Clowns spent the entire month of October going from door to door to warn people about the upcoming event of the Ripper's November appearance. Anybody named Mary was strongly cautioned to stay behind locked doors on in during the opening days of the eleventh month. Catching wind of the Irish Clowns civic deeds Rat Rice decided to get into the act by hammering up flyers all over the joint re-stating the same advice. The Chief Inspector promised the public that he would beef-up the number of beat cops in the area and went on to promise that on the 3rd he would be pounding the pavement along with Inspector Tommy Farrow, the Jack the Ripper expert sent over by Scotland Yard. The implication was that Farrow had something up his sleeve. The Mayor of New York City had even posted a $10,000 reward for the ripper. As the neighborhood proceeded to set up its defenses, Bugs McMaster was doing some snooping around on his own. He thought it was best to keep his own counsel about his discoveries. The only one he felt comfortable in confiding with was Mario Ferro, who had access to the real inside dope from all sorts of sources.

CHAPTER 16

"Sweet Mother of Mercy!" exclaimed Bugs McMaster the very second he got a load of his cousin sitting in Bugs' late father's overstuffed arm chair.

Sailor McMaster, who had the same mannerisms but none of the dark looks of Bugs, put his newspaper down and smiled over at his cousin. Bugs momentarily frowned when he observed that Sailor was wearing his best night gown as well as his night slippers. The mug was trying to egg him on. The two laughed before they shook hands. The McMaster clan was not huge on hugging. When the greetings died down, Mrs. McMaster, mother and aunt, an ancient and worldly-wise old Irish lady, summoned the two to the supper table, where she served Irish stew, homemade bread and hot tea. She ordered the boys to bow their heads as she said the Lord's Prayer over their meal.

All sorts of small talk and family news was exchanged before Bugs slowly turned things around to Sailor's whereabouts.

"Bugs and Auntie, I have been in every port in the world by this point: from New Zealand to Peru."

"What about London, England?"

"There, too," Sailor answered slowly as he gave Bugs the once over.

The boys avoided a clash until Mrs. McMaster was out in the kitchen preparing the dessert.

"We're having strawberry shortening cake with whipped cream," she called.

"So you've been to England?"

"So what's the big deal?"

"What's the big idea getting sore at me over an inquiry?"

"England is a stop on most sea voyages and the captains of every ship like to give their crew leave there because the natives speak some sort of English."

"Alright, alright, don't get sore," said Bugs, looking at Sailor but searching for some resemblance to Creepy. Same dark features but Sailor was short and sturdy like Whitey. Whitey and Sailor didn't look a bit like one another. What if Creepy was his real father, too! Perish the thought!

Mrs. McMaster came bustling into the room carrying the boys' desserts first. She scolded the boys about quarreling as she went back to fetch her own. It was just like the lads to set to feuding after not seeing one another for years on end. It was the like the olden days when Bugs and Sailor would fistfight up and down Canal Street before joining forces to take on all comers. They were a throwback to all the fighting Irish back in the old country, where clan fought clan until they united to fight the English.

The cousins had to make nice until Bugs' mother decided it was time to go to bed, where she would say her rosary beads before turning in the radio to catch some of the latest tunes. The boys huddled close together in the parlor, not wanting to be overheard. No sense in alarming the auld one.

"Four girls have been killed lately down here in the Bowery."

"I know, Bugs; they get the newspapers down in Hell's Kitchen."

"What does the lower west side have to do with the price of tea in China?"

"I was holed up there for several weeks, spending my doe for the merriment on the water front," Sailor answered with a wink. "What auntie doesn't know won't hurt him. A merchant seaman gets lonely after all those weeks on a floating tub."

"Spare me the details."

"So I heard about the murders. And, yes, I recognized all of the names."

"The coppers hauled down to headquarters because somebody had tried to frame the Irish Clowns."

Bugs went on to give Sailor a report about what had taken place in Rat Rice's office. He then slowly went over, word for word, about what the tubby little Englishman had said. Sailor's face flushed red as he turned away.

"Got anything to add?" asked Bugs.

"I'd never set-up you or the Irish Clowns no matter how desperate I became in a jam. You should know that by now."

"Why is the Englishman chasing you?"

"There were several girls cut-up over in London when I was there, and I was called in for a line-up session. Before you get in an uproar, I'm going to proclaim my innocence to the rooftops. I think they wanted to pin it on an American Yankee with no cash on them for their defense."

"You arrived back and the murders start-up over on this side."

"It isn't me, Bugs," roared Sailor.

Bugs put his finger to his lips; they both waited, but the elderly woman remained in bed.

"Any alibis for your stay in Hell's Kitchen."

"Only the bad kind, Bugs."

"Is somebody setting you up as the patsy?"

"Could be that, but I doubt it. Nobody in the Bowery knows I'm back except for you and Auntie."

"I have my beady eyes on a suspect here on our home turf, but the English will have to solve their own mystery," said Bugs.

"I'll do anything to clear my name."

CHAPTER 17

A light rain was whipping off of the East River the late October morning as Chief Inspector Rat Rice of New York's finest and Inspector Thomas Farrow of Scotland walked over the gangplank and stepped on to the Chinese junk boat. The crew, who were all Chinese, all huddled close together, exchanging frightened looks. Finding a dead white man on board their vessel was no way to start their morning. A uniformed police officer led the two high-ranking officials to the crumpled body at the other end of the floating vessel. It was hard to avoid the blood smeared across the deck. The body had been heaved on to the deck and then dragged out of sight.

"One of the McMasters," announced Rat Rice, giving the corpse a hard look.

The dead man, his eyes still opened, had had his belly slashed to ribbons.

"It's Sailor, sir," said Farrow.

"It isn't Bugs," answered Rice.

"The Chinese found the victim here when they boarded this morning. He was slumped over dead at about six this morning. They have dropped anchor and had abandon ship just before midnight," an officer read from his notebook.

"That gives us a six hour window," said Rice.

"Did somebody get the Ripper, or did the Ripper get somebody?" asked Tommy, deeply disappointed.

Somebody was watching the crime scene from a nearby grog shop. He got up off of his stool and decided to use the back door to avoid any prying eyes. It was only a matter before the constables came in to ask questions of the early morning riff raff. Creepy Kelly was furious when he saw Squirt Sheridan plunge his knife into Sailor McMaster's heart. He was enough of an Irishman to know that revenge was warranted in this case. Squirt Sheridan would have to pay back in blood for what he had done to Sailor McMaster.

"See you later, Kelly," said the bartender.

"Don't be using me name so freely if you please," snapped back Creepy Kelly, giving the bartender a look that chilled to the bone.

Creepy Kelly headed back to his shop. His intention was to open up the place and start working before his son was out of bed. At least White Chapel didn't have to worry about Squirt Sheridan anymore, because his old man had the goods on the newsboy. He had seen the knife fight in the wee hours of the between Squirt Sheridan and Sailor McMaster. It had been over accusations of who was the Bowery Ripper. They both could have lived up to the name by the way they slashed their knives in the darkness, each drawing blood until the scales of the battle tipped in Squirt's favor. However, not one of them had the sand of the original Ripper.

Squirt Sheridan's triumph whoops had turned to yelps of fear when it dawned upon him that he had now committed cold blooded murder. He looked in all directions in panic before he regained his head just long enough to draw the body over to a tied up boat. Creepy watched with interest as Squirt disposed of the body. Clever lad was trying to blame it all on the Asian fishermen.

Squirt had just returned to his newsstand beneath the Third Street Elevated when he heard a voice thunder out from the darkness of the alley.

"I saw what you did, Squirt Sheridan!"

"Who's there?"

Creepy Kelly became visible by stepping under the glow of a streetlight so Squirt Sheridan could see who was addressing him.

"Stay clear of the Kelly men or the Kelly men will do you in one way or the other."

Creepy Kelly issued his warning as he ditched back into the shadows. Squirt decided not to go after him in pursuit. He saw the old man turn off at the end of the alley.

Later that very day, the Park Row newspaper released a copy of another missive from the Bowery Ripper that was entitled *From Hell's Kitchen*. The note was addressed to Inspector Thomas Farrow of Scotland Yard and closed with *Catch me when you can Inspector Farrow*. The police had received the note the day before Sailor McMaster was murdered.

CHAPTER 18

Morrison McMaster's funeral mass was well attended at St. Thomas Aquinas Church. It was rather unsettling that it took place on Halloween, a day the Irish had always given over to the celebration of ghosts, spirits and watches, dating back to the golden days of the Celts. Mrs. McMaster, dressed in widow black, sat in the front row, sobbing her eyes out. Bugs McMaster, his arms around his mother, stared directly ahead at old Father Higgins; his thoughts drifting back to the morning after Sailor's return. Sailor had stated he had a lead on something. What was it?

A few rows back sat Shem Shaw with the entire Shaw family. His eyes were red from crying, but then his thoughts drifted to happier times. He remembered making his first Communion in this very church with Bugs, Sailor, Whitey, Benny, and Gyp. It was a long time ago. Who would murder Sailor, Cathy and the others?

Whitey Kelly sat in the very last row with his father. Whitey's nose twitched as his father always had a foul odor lingering over him. Was it old age that made him stink so much, or was it the aroma left-over from the bad deeds he had committed over the years? Whitey didn't really know his father, and he had never cared to learn anything from him about the past. It had to be hideous and disgusting could see Murphy, Gyp and Benny with there with their family. He longed to be next to them.

Coming in after the Mass had started was the entire Wiercinski family: father and four sons. Jordan gave Whitey a nod before taking a seat without kneeing. The Wiercinskis were Jewish but they came to pay their respect as the gang would have gone to the synagogue to do likewise if the situation was reversed. The Kressins were also in tow.

Halfway to the altar, and on the St. Mary side of the church, sat the massive Ferro Italian family. Momma Ferro cried out loud as the priest gave the homily. Mario, like Bugs, was lost in thought. He was no dummy and he knew the slaying of Sailor McMaster was somehow tied in with the Bowery Ripper case. In fact, with shivers running up and down his spine, Mario knew that the ripper on the Bowery defiled the entire religious rituals with his unholy presence. It was evil beyond mere evil.

Chief Inspector Rat Rice and Inspector Farrow, both devout Catholics, blessed themselves with the sign of the cross, readying themselves for the offerings before the Holy Communion ritual. The men tried to drive out thoughts of violence to concentrate on the ringing of the bell and the lifting of the Host. Rat, Tommy, Mario and Bugs all felt the presence of the Ripper nearby.

Squirt Sheridan, his eyes bloodshot and his face wrinkled from lack of sleep, would have liked to have receive but his soul was dirty. He hadn't made his confession since he had killed Sailor McMaster. The church had to forgive him if he were heartily sorry….and he was all of that. The Church would forgive even if the state didn't forgive. It was at that moment that a plan popped into his head.

Squirt Sheridan tugged on the rain coat of Chief Inspector Rice before he could get in his black draped squad car to make the trek to the nearby Catholic cemetery.

"I know who the Ripper is?"

"Do you know who killed sailor McMaster as well?" asked Tommy Farrow.

"I killed Sailor McMaster….the Ripper….for the reward money."

Rice and Farrow exchanged looks. Then Farrow locked eyes with an old man who was giving him the once over. Farrow had a precision sharp memory and he immediately recognized the old fellow. No, but it couldn't be. That bloke had to be dead by now. It was James Kelly alive in the flesh.

"Let's bury him first."

The two policemen and the newsboy skipped the luncheon so they could hurry back to the Precinct, where Squirt Sheridan made a statement.

"When do I get my doe?"

"You'll get the reward money when all of the pieces are put in the puzzle."

"What do I do until then?"

"You'll go about your business."

CHAPTER 19

I t was a perfect Halloween night as the fogs got denser and denser as the evening progressed and the streets had cleared. There had been very few tricksters dressed in scary outfits that night as people locked themselves inside because of their collective fear of the Bowery Ripper. No need to take any chances for a few pieces of candy. Instead, Father Higgins and the nuns at St. Thomas Aquinas had decided to hold a party in the school basements for all of the neighborhood Catholic children. The Jewish kids were invited out of diplomacy.

"The Ripper was never one for young blood: Catholic or Jewish or Protestant."

Creepy Kelly decided to give the children a cheap thrill by peering long enough at a basement window for some of them to notice him. However, as soon as the cry the Ripper, the Ripper, went up, he decided to hightail it before somebody decided to investigate. If some old nun apprehended him he could just claim he had been looking for Whitey and the Irish Clowns.

The old man crossed over to Canal Street and stood in front of Hughie's Bohemian Café, a place he had utterly no use for. When Hughie Kressin stepped outside and locked the door behind him, Kelly decided to move on.

"Good evening, Mr. Kelly," Hughie said politely.

"And the same to you, Mr. Kressin," said Creepy.

"It appears we're both dressed to the nines as the young always say," chirped Hughie, holding up his cane and tapping the top of his hat.

"Quite so, sir," said Creepy, cutting the conversation short.

"So what am I, chopped liver?" Hughie mumbled to himself as the old man silently turned the corner.

Hughie was happy that the coast was clear and he didn't have to share the pavement with that old grouch, Creepy Kelly. No wonder Bugs and the Irish Clowns avoided that one like a plague. Hughie had also felt sorry for Whitey Kelly for having such a father. No wonder the boy was always so high strung and edgy.

"Good evening, Officer Kennedy."

"What do you hear, and what do you say, Hughie?"

"I'm just taking a stroll to unwind."

"Don't tarry too long, Hughie; for the Ripper could be on the prowl."

"I have it on good authority that he isn't do to make another Bowery call for a few days."

Kennedy went his way while Hughie went his way. Kennedy was a good man and had an indulgence attitude towards Hughie and his midnight visits to the ladies beneath the Third Street Elevated Tracks. Hughie reluctantly greeted squirt Sheridan, who was still open for the late night traffic. Squirt, who owed the Bohemian Café a considerable sum on his bill, was friendlier to the old European than he was to ninety-nine percentage of the residents of the Bowery.

"So the old lion is roaring again tonight?"

"Mind your own business, Mr. Sheridan," Hughie said cheerfully.

"I hope I'm that frisky when I'm one hundred years old," teased Squirt.

The two men would have bantered for a while longer but they both felt hot eyes pouring upon their activities from the nearby alley. The men exchanged glances before they both began to laugh nervously.

"It's probably Creepy Kelly," whispered Hughie.

"Old man Kelly is watching us all and knows all of our deep and darkest and dirtiest secrets," said Squirt, only half joking.

"Maybe he's spying on the Bowery Ripper as well," intoned Hughie.

"Curiosity killed the cat," said Squirt.

"Amen to that, brother."

Hughie continued on to his destination. However, he couldn't shake off the sensation that he was being followed. He wondered if it were his imagination when he something tapping on the pavement. He spun around to see nothing. The taping began once he started to walk again.

"Who needs this type of echo affect when the Bowery Ripper is still on the loose?" asked Hughie as he circled around and started to head home. He could have sworn that he heard somebody laughing his head off. It was the sound of a mad man laughing.

CHAPTER 20

November 1st, All Hallows Day according to Ma McMaster's calendar, must have been the strangest day in the long and strange history of the Bowery; for it was the day that Jordan Warden took it upon himself to invest a new dance that was quickly christened the "Ripper's Rumba." The dance was ghoulish, especially considering that poor Sailor McMaster had only been interned the day before, but the poor, especially those who were Irish, Italian and Jewish, have always had a morbid sense of humor that probably dated back to the Middle Ages and the constant presence of the Grim Reaper and violence hanging over the village air. However, it could have been that the madness in the autumn air unleashed by the presence and the violence of the Bowery boys. Jordan failed to greet his pals in the Irish Clowns where he went to the jukebox and slipped a nickel into its slot. He carefully made his selection. The song had to have a heavy Latin beat with perhaps some with some Cuban calypso in it. Jordan wanted something that would stir-up the fire inside of his soul.

"Check this out, fellows."

As soon as the music started to blare, Jordan started his dance with his swingiest swing move that nobody in any New York dancehall could match. It was a recording that had made the hit parade during that summer of 1938. Some younger couples jumped up and began to do some sort of teenage jitterbug that Jordan completely ignored.

"Look at that cat cut-up the rug!" hooted Gyp, starting to dance with a chair.

"Cut that out, you hooligan!" called over Momma Kressin.

"Momma, let them have some fun," said Hughie.

However, Hughie blew a fuse when one of the would-be hipsters knocked over a root beer float and the floor got slippery.

The ruckus had just begun.

"Heat us up, dad!" roared out a pretty young thing.

"Get me, fellows! I'm the Bowery Ripper cutting up his victims!"

Jordan began to stab away with an invisible knife. He pretended to duck from invisible blood. He then used his hands to choke his invisible victim to the ground. He then did a ballet before he flipped and started all over again. The other dancers mimicked his moves.

"Poppa, this is getting ugly."

"Ugly, what's ugly about honoring the dead with a waltz," shouted Hughie, grabbing a teenager for his own fancy footwork.

"Stop it, Ripper!" said Murphy, running up to Jordan and landing a punch or a fake punch on the chin that sent him spinning against the wall. The effect added to his dance as he started stabbing away again on the rebound.

"Get the Ripper," gushed Gyp, lifting Jordan up into the air, where he caught a hold of the rafter and pulled himself free.

Gyp began to dance with Murphy as Benny pulled Shem to his feet and began dancing with him. Everybody was dancing in the joint except for Bugs McMaster, who had more important things on his mind than dancing.

Momma used a broom to chase the kids out onto Canal Street, where they continued their shouting and dancing.

"Hey, everybody, Jordan just originated a new swing dance!"

"Let's all do the Ripper Rumba!"

Officer Kennedy was soon on the scene but he had enough of the primitive Irish culchie inside of him to kick up his heels and add his own County Kerry jig to the mulligan stew of a dance that was steaming up and down Canal Street.

Shem Shaw rushed back into the Bohemian Café to fetch his buddy Bugs.

"Come and join the party, chief."

"I'll war dance another night, Shem."

"What's wrong?"

"Surrealism belongs next to Seine River in Paris, France, and not along the East River in the Bowery, US of A."

"Way and up the Seine River....far, far away!" sang Shem.

"What will the Catholic father day all about this?" Momma asked herself as she began to close up the place before the crowd came back for more.

CHAPTER 21

Inspector Thomas Farrow was the most at home when he was buried in old files and ancient police reports. He sipped away at a big mug of what the Yanks were passing off as coffee. Somewhere in the files of Sailor McMaster and the rest of the Irish Clowns he felt rested the answer to the Bowery Ripper mystery.

A large shadow appeared at the window of the door of the cubby hole that Tommy had set-up as his make-shift office away from Scotland Yard. He had felt all along that Sailor was the Ripper, and Squirt Sheridan had signed a sworn statement to the same. So what was hounding him? Something was dreadfully amiss here. Then he recalled mind that old man at the funeral.

There was a light rap at the door.

"You may enter," called out Tommy.

"Well, Tommy, you'll be on your way home in a day or two as we put the final touches on all of the reports and testimony. I'm sure you'll be glad to get back to your old lady and your home," Chief Inspector Rat Rice said in a cheerful southern accent.

"I'm not married and I live in dreary tiny bed sit in Soho. I'm quite happy with my arrangements over here, sir."

"There is nothing to keep you here now that Squirt Sheridan has spilled the beans on Sailor McMaster."

"November fourth is coming very rapidly and I'd be much obliged if you extended my stay until it has passed on by. Then, and only then, will be one hundred percent certain that the Bowery Ripper is no more."

"I don't understand what you're getting at, Farrow?"

Tommy Farrow picked up the valise he had brought over to America with him that was filled to the brim with documents, photographs and police drawings. The tubby little man put his hand into the mess and pulled out a photograph of a man. Without a word he put the photograph into the Chief Inspector's hands.

"I had taken the liberty of borrowing from Scotland Yard's filing system some old photographs of possible suspects in the 1888 Jack the Ripper case."

"What are you getting at, Tommy?"

"The photograph you hold in your hand is of one James Kelly."

"Was he the man?"

"Several members of Scotland Yard thought Kelly was Saucy Jack; others thought it was this man."

Farrow handed rice a picture of a man with a bizarrely long mustache.

"Looks like a dandy," commented rice, still unsure of the direction Farrow was taking him in.

"Francis Tumblety was a dainty, an American and a quack doctor who was selling patented medicine in London at the time of the Ripper murder."

"Was he a good suspect?"

"He was a ripping suspect," Tommy said with heat that was unusual from him. "In my earlier days on the force I met the bloke who followed Tumblety across the Atlantic Ocean once Tumblety fled England. It was reported that he died in St. Louis sometime around 1903."

"Scotland Yard let him slip out of their fingers?" Rice said in a pompous and self-righteous.

"He had been picked on a morals charge, but discharged pending more evidence."

"What was he doing that was so immoral?"

"He had a taste for young male prostitutes."

"And whatever became of your man, Kelly?"

"He fled too."

"Don't tell me he came to New York as well."

"Aye, he did. Years later he turned himself in to the mental institute he had escaped from in 88. It was reported that he had died in 1923."

"So that crosses them both off of the list, doesn't it?"

"Not quite."

"Spell it out slowly for me, Tommy."

"I saw James Kelly at Sailor McMaster's funeral."

For the first and last time in his long career on the New York police force, Rat Rice fainted dead away. When he came to Tommy Farrow was completely in charge of the situation. Rat Rice could only listen and nod his head in agreement.

"The Ripper is following a script and in a few days he'll be on the scent of fresh blood. He wants somebody by the name of Mary."

"There are plenty of girls walking the streets by the name of Mary."

"The last recorded victim of Jack the Ripper was one Mary Kelly, and she wasn't murdered on the streets, she was murdered indoors. It was never clearly established if she was a Maggie May or not."

"It makes our task all the harder."

"In my research today I did happen to chance upon two possibilities: one Mary Bridget McMaster, aunt of Sailor McMaster."

"Who is the other piece of bait?"

"One Marion McMaster, aka 'Bugs McMaster'."

"You have hatched a plan."

"Aye, I have done just that, sir," answered Tommy. "We'll need your newspaper mate to assist us."

"Mario Ferro is a good man and won't let us down."

"He was an Irish Clown at one time?"

"He's gone straight," Rat said defensively.

"I trust that Mr. Ferro still has the trust of Mr. McMaster."

"I read you loud and clear now, Inspector."

CHAPTER 22

On November 2nd Bugs McMaster was seated inside of Hughie's Bohemian Café waiting for his tribe to gather for their war paint and instructions when Hughie ushered him over to the public telephone where Mario was waiting at the other end of the line.

"Any information about Creepy Kelly?" asked Bugs.

"I hope you're all ears, Bugs; for there was a Jack the Ripper suspect by name of James Kelly, a convicted maniac."

"You don't say? Creepy could be James. It can't be. He'd be over a hundred."

"One James Kelly was sentenced to a life in a lunatic house by the name of Broadmoor for the murder of his wife shortly before the Ripper's murdering spree. He escaped by using some tricks that would have made John Dillinger proud of him. He also went underground for years until he showed up one day at the main gate of Broadmoor requesting readmission. The British fuzz began a search for him back in 1888, but they wrote him off when they figured out he had fled to the United States; and by 1923, the year he resurfaced, they no longer considered him a prime suspect."

"It adds up."

"There's even more, Bugs," interrupted Mario, adding, "according to Inspector Farrow of Scotland Yard, there was always a long standing theory among British crime experts that Jack Ripper had brought his hobby over here. A few prostitutes were found sliced and diced here on the Bowery years before we born. He was never captured and it was believed by the authorities that he took off when the police began to close in on him."

"It must have been before Inspector Rat Rice's time."

"Scotland Yard and the London Metropolitan Police have long theorized that the Ripper then continued his murdering all over the country and these attacks being spread-out over many decades."

"Isn't Creepy Kelly a bit past all of that now?" asked Bugs, thinking of Whitey.

"Maybe he has an able-bodied assistant," whispered Mario, thinking of Whitey.

"What else is on your mind, Mario?"

"According to the files James Kelly died in 1927."

"If Creepy Kelly is indeed James Kelly maybe he pulled a second Harry Houdini escape act."

By the time Bugs got off the party line the gang was starting to gather. Hughie and Momma were in the kitchen getting hot coffee, soup and sandwiches ready for the boys. Hughie had promised to keep the Bohemian Café open all night long so the boys would have a headquarters and a place to warm up. The Irish Clowns planning session pulled to a grinding halt when Squirt Sheridan strutted in and put in an order for hot pastrami on rye and coffee to go.

"Put it on my bill, Momma Mary," grunted Sheridan, seeming the worst for drink.

"I will but this is the last time. You're up to seventeen dollars and twelve cents and that's getting too high up there for Poppa and me," she said. She didn't want to quarrel with a mean drunk.

Squirt Sheridan glared at the gang but held his tongue as he disappeared into the gathering mist of the late autumn night. He left behind the fumes of cheap whiskey.

"Squirt Sheridan has become a true skid row rummy," proclaimed Jordan, waving away the sour air.

"He must be burning the candle at both ends," noted Gyp.

"Let's keep an eye on the flames of those candles," said Bugs.

"Where's Shem?"

"Where is Shem?

CHAPTER 23

Ma McMaster had been careful to bolt the door the second her son Bugs had took his leave. She pleaded with him to stay in with her during the long night of the Ripper's last call upon the poor souls of the Bowery. However, that son of hers had a mind of his own and his mind was set on spending the night with his gang, the Irish Clowns, looking for the demon before he could strike again. Sure, it was a noble deed her Marion and the lads were after doing for the neighborhood. Even Father Higgins had praised the lads from the pulpit that very day. The good parish priest had even compared Marion to St. Patrick, patron saint of Ireland, who cleared the Emerald Isle of all snakes, demons and druids.

Ma turned on the radio to see if she could find some cheerful jazz to take her thoughts off of her fears and all of her miseries. She snapped the wireless off when all she could dial in where more news bulletins about the Bowery Ripper and his upcoming attack. Some of them appeared to be filled with glee over the scent of blood. No girl, no matter how sinful, deserved such a fate. It just had to be an Englishman sent over by the royal family to do in more innocent people.

Out of nervous tension the old snapped the radio back on, spinning the knobs around until she got the right wave for some perky orchestra music being progressed lived from Radio City. The music made her relax just to doze off for a few minutes. Something made the elderly women wake-up and jump out of her rocking chair. For a just a flash of a moment she saw somebody standing on the fire escape, looking in at her. She made a dash for the window, but by the time she arrived at the sill the person was gone. She pulled down the shade to protect her privacy. Could have just been a pesky tenement kid larking around, or maybe one of the Clowns calling on her lad.

The old woman was now filled with an intense feeling of unease and fear. Her backside had barely touched back down on the wood of the chair when another rustle of noise made her retake her feet. This time she hurried over to the front door to have a listen. There was nothing doing out in the deserted hallway. Her imagination was just working overtime. Wait! There it goes again. Somebody was most definitely lurking just outside her apartment doorway.

"I have the solution to this problem right here in the hallways drawers!" Ma McMaster declared loud enough for the stalker to hear her through the door.

Ma opened up and a drawer with a great bang, shuffled inside with more noise, before pulling out her late husband's service revolver.

"It's already loaded!" she shouted, leaning up against the door and clicking back the trigger in hopes that the sound would travel.

She made a great show of unlocking the door.

"I'll teach you to bother Ma McMaster's when her dandruff is up!"

Mrs. McMaster pointed the gun into the hallway so she could prove she was armed to the teeth and ready to blaze. She cautiously stuck her head out to peer to her right towards the stairwell that led to the ground floor. A hand grabbed her by the wrist and twisted it until she dropped the weapon to the floor with a thump. She was gently turned towards the invader.

"You don't want that thing to go off, do you, Mrs. McMaster?"

"Shem Shaw, it's only you."

"I came to collect Bugs," he said, reaching down to pick-up the 38 and handing it back to her.

"Was it yourself who was looking in the window before?"

"I only just arrived at this very moment," said Shem, protesting his innocence.

"Is there any problem here, Mrs. McMaster?"

Shem and Ma turned to face the person who had asked the question. They were both shocked to see Creepy Kelly standing there in his work clothes. Before anybody could speak two uniformed police men arrived on the landing.

"What is this, the county fair?" asked one of the coppers.

"Any trouble here, Mrs. McMaster?" asked the other one.

Mrs. McMaster had just barely enough time to hide the pistol behind her back.

"Nothing doing up here, officers."

"Let's clear the hallway then."

The two men in blue gave Shem Shaw baleful looks as he start skipping down the three flights to the sidewalk.

"Do you live here, sir?" one of the officers asked the old man.

"Don't be shoving me now, man," shot back Creepy. "I just came by to thank Mrs. McMaster here for always being so kind to my boy."

"Sure, it was no trouble at all, Mr. Kelly," said Ma.

Creepy Kelly bowed his head at the old lady as he made his way downwards to the night outside.

CHAPTER 24

The Irish foggy dew had thickened into an old-fashion London pea soup fog as the midnight hour approached and past. Shem was happy to be close to Bugs but he would have been happier to be closer to his bed at home. The weatherman on the radio had forecast that the drizzle would intensify in the wee hours of the morning and that that the rain would eventually turn to sleet before it became solid snow. The sidewalks of the Bowery appeared to be uncommonly cluttered with all sorts of people considering the Ripper was about to strike again. Shem wondered how many were onlookers hoping for a bloody show. Then again, any person passing by could be Jack the Ripper on the prowl. He thought of his dead cousin and hoped that he and Bugs would save the day. He dearly would love to get in a clout or two for Cathy's sake.

"There should be a curfew tonight of all nights," said Shem.

He was debating whether or not to tell the chief about his encounter with Creepy Kelly and the police when he had gone over to pick him up.

"There hasn't been a curfew on in the Bowery since the draft riots during the Civil War," said Bugs.

"The Ripper is a one man civil war."

Bugs poked Shem in the ribs for quiet.

"Do my eyes deceive me?' asked Bugs, pointing at a figure that loomed a few blocks ahead of them.

The two young men picked up their paces to close the gap between them and the hunched over figure that loomed in front of them. It appeared to be an elderly man. It was also quite obvious he was wearing some sort of top hat that had been out of fashion since the "Gay Nineties". In his right had the man held a walking stick that he nervously clicked on the cement sidewalk as if he were propelling himself forward; on his left he was carrying a black leather bag.

"Is he going to the opera?" asked Shem.

"He looks like a doctor making a house call back in the olden days."

The words were no sooner out of the chief's mouth when the man suddenly whirled around his tracked, lifted up his cane, and charged the two boys at full speed. Creepy Kelly was only inches away from crashing in some skulls when suddenly men leapt out of the shadows and wrestled the man down to the ground. It was Rice, Farrow and a squadron of plains clothes officers.

"Chief Inspector Rice!"

"So you're still meddling in police business, McMasters," said Rice, turning away to instruct his men to cuff the struggling menace to society. "We've been tailing you all night and we knew you would serve as useful bait to lure Jack the Ripper out into the streets. After all, isn't your name Marion?"

"Marion!" hooted Shem.

"It's my maiden name," said Bugs, stumbling over his words.

"We were hoping Marion was close enough to the name of Mary."

"My premise was correct," Inspector Farrow crowed like a rooster.

The chief was in no mood to thank the police for rescuing them. Instead, he was interested in the black bag that had fallen to the ground during the shuffle. All eyes were turned on Bugs as he snapped open the latch and turned the bag upside down. A sandwich and a thermostat of coffee tumbled to the ground.

"Smells like pastrami," noted Shem.

"It's me late night snack, you Yankee ruffians," shouted Creepy. "And why am I in cuffs when I was defending myself against these footpads who intended to rob me of my meal?"

Rat Rice didn't have the time to sort out the mess because Gyp came running down the street and roaring his head off that somebody had snuck up behind him and pulled his cap over his eyes and had slammed him up against a wall. In between gulps, Gyp explained that by the time he was able to see again, Whitey and the attacker had vanished into the night. He speculated that Whitey was giving chase to the Ripper at that very moment. Gyp was barely finished with his narrative when Murphy tore around the corner shouting bloody murder.

"Bugs, somebody stuffed a trash can over my head and by the time I had gotten the tin off of my noggin the attacker was gone and Jordan had disappeared into thin air.

Chapter 25

Events were tumbling in from all points and things were going to get even more obtuse.

"Bugs, help!"

"It sounds like Hughie."

Soon the chubby little café owner had discovered the small gathering.

"Jordan is hurt and I just saw Whitey racing towards the East River. The Ripper attacked Jordan and he's dying on the footsteps of my café and Whitey is in hot pursuit of the Ripper. Come away quickly!"

In front of Hughie's Bohemian Café the boys found Jordan who was up on his feet and holding a hanky to a bloody cheek. However, he was far from death's doorsteps. Nobody bothered to take a close look at his wound. Meanwhile the police followed Whitey's footsteps in the thin covering of the fresh snow.

"Get Jordan inside and out of the cold!" ordered Bugs.

Hughie and the gang were greeted with the sight of blood and gore splattered all over the shop. In spite of all of the slashes across the face and the derange destruction of the body, it was still possible to identify the still warm remains of Momma Kressin.

"I was only gone for a few minutes," said Hughie before he fainted into Murphy's arms.

"I didn't hear a thing," announced Jordan.

"I think Whitey Kelly is the Ripper on the Bowery and not Creepy Kelly," decreed Bugs.

The police did follow the footprints up to the very edge of the docks where the abruptly evidence stopped. Rice and Farrow surmised that whoever had made the run had concluded by leaping into the East River. The two men were rapidly coming to the decision that it was a fake suicide. The word "fake" was dropped from the official report a few days later when some rough and tough dock worked pulled a body out of the drink with their hooks and it was immediately identified as being the bloated remains of White Chapel "Whitey" Kelly. It would be ruled that the boy was pushed into the river from behind. Oddly enough, it was never recorded if there was another step of prints. The murder was attributed to Jack the Ripper. The Inspector was still supervising the investigation of the mysterious footprints when he hailed by Murphy and informed of the slaughter of Momma Kressin inside of the Bohemian Café.

By the time Rice and Farrow arrived to the latest crime scene the Ferro brothers were already there snapping pictures and conducting interviews. The police wanted confessions, not interviews. The next few hours were filled with shouting, crying and accusations. It wasn't until a snowy dawn was breaking out from over the Atlantic seaboard that Shem asked the least dumb of all of his questions.

"Where's Creepy Kelly?"

In all of the excitement that old man had managed to drift away into the swirling snow without notice.

"He won't get far with the bracelets on his wrists," said Rice, hoping for the best.

"Creepy Kelly must have killed his own son in the shuffle at the waterfront," declared Farrow, seeking approval.

"I think you have it all wrong there, Sherlock," butted in Bugs, a smug grin smeared across his pug-nosed face. "It's true that Creepy Kelly was the original Jack the Ripper but it's also true that Whitey was his apprentice and he was Ripper on the Bowery."

"So it's true what they always say: father like son," wisecracked Jordan.

"So where's Creepy?'

"Maybe he jumped into the river with his son," suggested Bugs.

Chapter 26

However, the body of Creepy Kelly was never recovered from the icy river. Years later, a rumor was whispered along the streets of the Bowery that Farrow had wired Rice that James Kelly had reappeared at the gates of Broadmoor Lunatic Prison for a second time. There was also tattle that the old documents were never replaced by new ones. James Kelly had officially returned to the institution in 1923 and that he had been buried on the prison's grounds in 1927. The English per usual were trying save rather than solve the mystery. It was believed by most that all of this gossip had been spread by the Ferro brothers who had gotten the tip-off from various reliable sources.

Chief Inspector Rice never pointed any fingers at Creepy or Whitey, but their reputations were tarnished in the newspapers. The police had found the perfect fall guy the next day when Officer Kennedy discovered a drunk and groggy Squirt Sheridan slumped inside of his battered wooden newsstand; his clothes being smeared all over with fresh blood stains. The thick-headed Mick became the hero of the day when he searched the hood's pockets and discovered a recently used switchblade.

"I've been framed!" screamed Sheridan as Kennedy booted him into an awaiting paddy wagon.

"Tell it to the judge, Jack the Ripper."

Bugs McMaster for once was heard coming to the defense of his old arch-enemy: "for once in his life the Squirt is telling the truth."

"Come again, chief," requested Shem.

"Last night we heard with our own ears Squirt ordering a pastrami sandwich and coffee to go and we also found the same such items inside of Creep's black back. It's a bit fishy to me."

"You mean Creepy stole Squirt's stuff and framed him."

"Somebody by the name of Kelly set-up Squirt for a fall."

"Aren't you going to tell the police, chief?'

"I will if I have to in order to save his neck from the noose."

Bugs Moran never had the opportunity to present his testimony the police and Squirt Sheridan never had a chance to sing like a canary on the witness stand. He was found a few days later swinging from the rafters of his cell. It probably saved him a trip to the hangman's gallows at Sing-Sing as Bugs McMaster pastrami sandwich theory probably would have been rip to shreds by the district attorney. Bugs didn't lose any sleep over the suicide ruling that was allowed to stand. Many residents of the Bowery thought it was good riddance to an evil man and it saved the taxpayers money on a trial and an execution.

"It was a bloody good yarn while it lasted," Jordan was always fond of saying after the Bowery returned back to its grimy and gritty ways. "Somebody should take it to Hollywood and make a movie out of it."

"You must be the grim reaper," Bugs once said to Jordan.

"Maybe Jordan here was the real Ripper on the Bowery and he did it just for the heck of it," blurted out Shem.

Jordan responded with a sickening laugh. He made no denial to the charge.

"Maybe Jordan did it to provide material for a screenplay that he intends to write for a Hollywood B movie," chipped in Gyp.

"Say, that isn't a bad idea," Jordan said coming to his own defense. "I heard California is still sunny this time of season and there are plenty of pretty girls."

"And victims," said Shem.

Some of the fellows laughed at Shem's remarks but they weren't laughing when January rolled around and they received a gloating postcard

Steven G. Farrell

from Jordan out on the Pacific coast that closed with the cryptic message of "the Clowns are men that will not be blamed for nothing."

Jordan made a handful of motion pictures before he eventually died of a drug overdose. Nobody could really verify if he was in a police line-up during the Black Dahlia case.

"Oh, I think Momma would have loved to see Joan Crawford playing her up on the silver screen," gushed Hughie.

"Hughie, you're just as bad as Jordan," fumed Bugs.

"I miss Momma's chicken soup," put in Shem before tempers could flare.

Poppa seemed very peaceful and happy once Momma was out of the picture. He had become the scandal of the neighborhood when he started dating a very young Irish colleen from Sixth Street. Nobody had the heart to tell Hughie that it was an established fact that his new sweetheart had been a paid sweetheart beneath the tracks of the elevated tracks. More than a few suspected that the little old Yiddish-speaking man from Europe was no dummy; some even were even whispering that Hughie Kressin was really the Ripper on the Bowery who had manufactured the murders with the ultimate aim of getting rid of his pesky wife.

It was right around St. Patrick's Day when the residents of the Bowery were putting up their shamrocks, cooking their corn beef and cabbage and dying their beer green when Chief Inspector Rat Rice made an unannounced visit to the Bohemian Café. Lukewarm greetings were exchanged before the Chief Inspector got right to the heart of the matter.

"As far as the mayor and city hall is concerned Squirt Sheridan was the Ripper on the Bowery and his last two victims were your pals Creepy and Whitey Kelly. It's too bad about the second body not being dragged up with the nets. Poor Creepy was probably food for the sharks and the crabs somewhere at the bottom of the Atlantic," said Rice.

"Sounds reasonable to me," said Bugs.

"You fellows wouldn't be holding out on me?" asked the Inspector.

"We're no wiser than Precinct 9," responded Bugs.

"So case closed!"

"So case closed," Bugs said slowly.

When the Giants were just about to open up the new baseball season at the Polo Grounds against the Brooklyn Dodgers, Mario put a serious question to Bugs behind the closed doors of Hughie's backroom.

"So you'll go to your grave believing Creepy Kelly was the Jack the Ripper of White Chapel, London and Whitey Kelly was the Ripper on the Bowery here in New York City?"

"I'm 100% positive."

"And I'm 100% positive that Creepy Kelly was the Ripper both times."

"And I'm 100% positive that I miss Momma's chicken soup but I don't miss Momma one bit," said Shem; his eyes bulging in his village idiot-like.

CHAPTER 27

Only Mary Kelleher and Creepy Kelly knew the complete story and neither of them would have revealed their secrets to you or I. Creepy did always regret that he had to finally do away with his own grandson, Whitey, by shoving him from behind into the icy river where could not interfere in the family's business as well as the family's destiny. It was regrettable, but Creepy Kelly was a man of many regrets. It was most regrettable that Sailor had to do away with his own father, Clarence, in order to make sure that he didn't spill the beans on the family secret. Scotland Yard had put the scare into Clarence and Sailor had to toss him into the Thames River and flee England in order to preserve the silence that hung over Jack the Ripper. James "Creepy' Kelly confessed his sins numerous times in the confessional to numerous doubting priests. Even his keepers at the bedlam hospital back in England realized that the ranting and ravings of a deranged old man was the truth. He had been the one and only Jack the Ripper.

Mary Kelleher went completely undetected on the morning of the murder of Momma as a Chinese junk smuggled her out of the New York harbor and unloaded her in Philadelphia. In a few short days she arrived at Cohn, County Cork, Ireland, where she would resettle with the vow that Momma would be her last victim. However, she could vouch for her brothers and sisters she had left behind in the Bowery. Sooner or later the slaughter would begin all over again. She truly had been the daughter of Jack the Ripper…but not more!!

Steven G. Farrell

PAPER 2

THE CRIMSON DRUID OF WISCONSIN

T he huge man in the bloody red hood and the matching red outfit first made his appearance in the modest but growing port city of Kenosha, Wisconsin in December of 1884. His violent reign of terror lasted slightly less than a year when he concluded with his final piece of slaughter in October of 1885. By the Christmas season of Eighty-five the Crimson Druid of Wisconsin was front page news throughout the nation that just had survived the bloodshed of the Civil War. From the capitol of Washington DC to the Barbary Coast of San Francisco the serial killer from Kenosha was on everyone's lips. Even newly-elected President Grant issued a proclamation that he would order federal troops into the southeast corner of the state to flush-out the notorious bad man unless Governor William E. Smith took drastic measures to halt the Crimson Druid's career. The governor, for his part, threw up his hands, sending a nasty telegram to Mayor Z. G. Simmons of Kenosha and demanding resolution. Mayor Simmons quickly passed the buck on to Gleason, chief of police. The chief, an immigrant from Cork City, Ireland and a veteran of the War Between the States, doubled the police force and put in place an unpopular (and lightly enforced) curfew that began at nightfall. The Kenoshans hollered for stronger measures. Gleason played his ace in the hold and wired New York. His urgent message summoned the infamous Major Stuart O'Farrell to our paralyzed, as well as polarized, village that nestled up snug on the southern and easternmost border and the northern easternmost point of Illinois.

Chief Gleason, who was a second cousin of mine, requested that I be the one to meet O'Farrell at the Northwestern Railroad Station when the famous detective arrived from the Empire State. He also had me telegraph the official details of the police report to the great sleuth at his hotel suite at the New Yorker in downtown Manhattan. It would give the Irishman reading material on his long journey to the Midwest. I followed the chief's orders to the smallest detail. As my twin chestnut horses trotted northwards on Sheridan Road towards the depot, I had a strong feeling that a

65

professional snoop like the Major already possessed all of the released facts concerning our puzzling case in Wisconsin. The memories of the five bloodied corpses and the screams of the two unfortunate survivors of the attacks rang-out inside of my ears. I tightened my scarf against the bitter February winds gusting off of Lake Michigan that lied less than a half mile away to my right.

My name is Steven Gerard Farrell and I am known mostly as 'Farrell' by my friends and colleagues. My relatives and intimate friends call me 'Gerard.' In spite of the similarity in our names, I was not a known relative of Major O'Farrell. I, like most newspapermen and news readers, was keenly aware of the man's reputation as the man's reputation as the solver of crimes and the dispenser of justice. He was also truly a man of mystery.

The man, who was a self-proclaimed Irishman via England, had started building his reputation many years before when he tracked down the murderers of Charles Dickens' German scholar friend Professor Wisenbaker. He had been employed over the years by the Pope of Rome, Bismarck of Prussia and the Emperor of Japan. Mostly his fame was built upon the cobblestone roads of London, England. More than a few critics suggested that Conan Doyle's Sherlock Holmes had more than a passing resemblance to the bulky Celt. The daring Irishman must have wanted to disassociate himself from the pen of the equally made-up Dr. Watson by fleeing to the new world and setting up headquarters in New York City, hub of the criminal classes of the United States. He kicked off his American career with an investigation that landed John 'Ole Smoke' Morrissey, heavyweight prizefighting champion turned State Senator, in prison. He quickly moved on to break the hold of the Hudson Dusters Irish street gang on the waterfronts of the lower West Side. He proceeded to build up his star status by recovering heavyweight John L. Sullivan's stolen bankroll and by rescuing Lillie Langtry, the British actress, from her kidnappers. It was also whispered that the Major had located Jesses James, America's number one bank robber and stage coach stick-up man, in St. Joseph, Missouri only days before western bad man was shot in the back of the hold by Charley Ford A very few even whispered that it had been O'Farrell himself who had pulled the trigger of doom. It was food for thought.

Many Kenoshans believe that I am the very best reporter on the *Kenosha Port Daily* (KPD) and that nothing ever misses my analytical mind and my sharp eyesight. Now I shall try to my best of my abilities to impress you, my readers, with my reporting skills, as well as my memory for details. Please be patient as I briefly set-up the situation for you, so you'll be prepared for Major Stuart O'Farrell's regal entrance into my humble Midwestern city.

It was only a few days before Christmas when the Druid of Wisconsin struck wrecking the holiday spirit for our tightly-knit if ethnically diverse community perched along the western shores of the greatest of the Great Lakes. Why anybody would feel the touches of Venus on a cold winter's night is well beyond the logic of a middle-aged bachelor such as I. Jill Lovett and Clyde Kennedy had found a snug place right behind Simmons' Baseball Stadium, home of the Kenosha Celtic-Badgers in the Northwestern Baseball League, and hard by the railroad tracks on the Chicago-Milwaukee line. Perhaps they were hoping to catch the rays of the passing oil lamps from the speeding train to assist in their undressing. As fate would have it the two never left the buckboard. I imagine the two lovebirds locked in an embrace and a kiss when a man stepped out of the brush and approached the driver's seat of the wagon. The police speculated afterwards that it had been the young girl who had viewed the man first, for she had leapt off of the wagon in a panic. A bullet in the back of her skull dropped her a mere five yards away from the passenger seat. She was discovered face downwards in the snow. The boy had probably never been aware of the Grim Reaper sneaking up on them from behind. One bullet to the head had also polished him off. Neither of the corpses had been tampered any further with according to the autopsy report.

The murders had been reported within a half hour of the event when Jared Jennings rushed into the police station. The fool was roaring his head off that he had heard the sound of gunfire ringing outside the door of his house on Sheridan Road right across the street from the ball yard. Constable Swartz, a beat cop, verified everything when he barged in to file his report that there were indeed two bloody bodies lying next to the train tracks. I chanced to be in the station when the commotion started. I was among the first to have a look. I didn't know either of the young lovers, but I still felt an outrage surge through my body and soul over the carnage. Footprints in the snow lead southwards towards the Irish Prairie, but petered out at a busy crossroad heading close to the county line with Zion, Illinois. As the tracks tailed off, Chief Gleason approached on horseback out of the darkness. He was the Irish Prairie's most important resident. It was certainly on the crime scene in a flash.

"I sensed something was amiss," the chief responded when he was asked what had brought him out into the cold. The grounds were thoroughly examined as we all agreed that the shooter had had a decent eye. Two shots: two targets hit! Police questioning and my own bloodhound nose sniffing produced very little as far as clues went. More than one witness reported seeing a stubby little man running southward on Sheridan Road. An old woman, one Selma Saudinger, was perhaps the best lead as she swore-out a statement that the man was dressed in a red hood and swaddled in a massive red cloak. Her testimony, however, was universally discounted as the ravings of a bitter and ancient busybody. Luckily, two or three other night voyagers stepped forward and verified her overall description. One man referred to the night walker as a 'monk.' Kenosha is a predominantly Catholic city, so no outbreak of irrational anti-Catholicism reared its ugly head…yet. Dick Andresen, a writer from the rival *Shoreline Post News* seemed to delight in pointing out the Irish connection to me. I, for one, blamed a 'Fib' (flipping Illinois boaster) as the culprit.

The attack was starting to fade from the mind of the public when the 'monk' struck again. The second attempt occurred on the Fourth of July. The vast majority of the city's inhabitants were down at Southport Beach watching the fireworks after spending the day celebrating the holiday and the victory of the Union over the Confederacy by watching the annual parade on 22nd Avenue and 60th Street. Pamela Rizzo and Anthony Mello, another pair of lusty youngsters, had found a comfortable spot beneath an apple tree in Columbus Park on the north side of the city limits and in the heart of the city's Little Italy district.

The two were once again waylaid before they could disembark from their wagon. They were also ambushed from a man approach from behind. The murderer was strolling away at his leisure when he chanced to glance behind to see Anthony trying to crawl away to safety. The 'monk' calmly reloaded his pistol and retraced his footsteps to finish off the carnage. There had only been one witness: Louie Mockus, the town drunk. Louie, who was on a summertime bender, was rudely yanked out of his whisky-induced slumber by the sound of gunfire. Chief Gleason usually put no stock in Louie's drunken tirades, but when the rummy gushed on about seeing a "fat goblin in a fancy red hood and gown" performing the dirty trick, he was believed. The saints be praised: Anthony was rushed to the hospital in time to stem the bleeding and save his life. He verified Louie's account of the big bloke in an outfit. He went one further by adding the detail that the attacker had a pair of spectacles on beneath his mask.

On the same day of the second attack, a mysterious letter found its way on to Chief Gleason's desk in the police station.

Dear Chief Sceamson,

I want to report a double a double murder out at Columbus Park last night. I'm the one who did it. I also am the one who did in the couple at Simmons Field last December.

Goodbye!

The neat writing had a large reddish hand print upon it. Either the hand had been smeared in blood first or the writer had used some sort of artistic invention to reproduce the appearances of the real McCoy. Many surmised that the 'monk' must have been somebody familiar to the police squad to have access to the chief's office.

Poor Pamela was already dead and growing cold when the authorities arrived on the scene. A mad dash to the emergency room on the gallop had barely saved the life of Anthony. The boy, who had the reputation of being an apple thief and a no-account, didn't have much to say to me as he wallowed in pain, fear and misery. He would only say that the attacker was of stocky built and had a cubby and round face jutting out from beneath his red face mask. The boy also mumbled out before the morphine took hold that Pamela was constantly talking about a guy named 'Dick" who was bothering her about a date in recent weeks. The police duly picked up and questioned every teenage boy going by the names of Richard, Rich, Rick, Dick and Dicky, all to no avail. I suggested a few 'Dicks' of my own but the chief wasn't amused by my vulgarity.

Anthony was not anywhere near recovered when he crept out of the hospital one midnight. His friends reported that he had mentioned that he was heading for the Mississippi River and a riverboat ride southward to New Orleans and a new life. The little children of Kenosha firmly believed that the 'mad monk' had abducted the boy while he was asleep in his bed. A ghoulish children's song emerged about the body parts of Anthony being scattered all over the city was a morbid reminder that Kenosha was under siege by a lunatic.

The third attack took place in the very core of the city in beautiful Lincoln Park. The onslaught became the bloody signature of the series of murders. The 'mad monk' had tied up two young lovers who had been enjoying a picnic near the park's boat house. Once they were knotted up, he had proceeded to stab them over and over again with what police suspected was a rifle bayonet left over from the 61-65 war. The invasion became notable for three things: first, it occurred right before sunset in the late autumn which made it a daylight attack; second, the stalker had engaged the young couple in a rather lengthy conversation before he had the girl, Catherine Owens, hogtie the boy, Mick Lonigan, with a long piece of rope provided by the man himself. Once the boy was tied up, the man ordered the girl to the ground where he proceeded to bind her up tightly; lastly, although the girl died as she was being transported to St. Catherine's, the boy had survive the attack and was able to provide a detailed account of their encounter with the attacker.

The man had been dressed in a long red gown that had a strange hand-like emblem on the chest. Mick described the get-up as looking like the nightshirt the KKK wore down in Dixie to frighten off carpetbaggers. It was too bad that the lad couldn't provide a sketch of the man's face to the police artist, for he had worn a red hood over his head and a Halloween costume red mask had covered the upper portion of his face. However, Mick added fact that the man wore smoked glasses beneath his mask. How queer it all was!

Young Lonigan provided bits and pieces of the conversation that flowed between the three of them.

"I'm a former rebel and I spent the war as a prison camp down by Lake Michigan. I have never returned to Greenville, South Carolina because the Yankees laid waste to my homestead. Now I'm going yonder out to South Dakota to prospect for gold and I need your loot to serve as my grub stake."

"He has kin in the Dakotas," Miss Owens had said hopefully. "Maybe he can help you."

Mick recollected how he had shot his girlfriend an icy look before holding up his coin purse.

"My poke isn't much."

At that point the keen witted realized this 'mad monk' was immense like a member of the Swiss Guard while the 'mad monk' observed fleeing down Sheridan Road after the December murders had been described as 'short and squat.' This was a different man altogether.

The gun-wheeling man motioned for the boy to toss his pouch of coins on the spread-out picnic blanket on the lawn. It was still lying there with a few crumpled dollar bills and a few coins when the police arrived on the scene. Mick went on to note that the man had no southern drawl although he claimed to have been a 'Johnny Reb.' He also related how the man walked slowly away as though he hadn't a care in the world. He exited the park from Lincoln Drive that fed into 18th Avenue. Mick managed to unravel himself from the rope and to stagger a less than a hundred yards until he reached the shore of the lagoon. His blood dripped freely as he pulled himself onto the bridge that spanned across the body of water. Luckily, two fishermen were still riding the waves in a boat and he was able to flag them down.

I was able to interview the boy the day after the surgeons sewed him back together. The poor fellow was lost in a haze due to all of the pain reducing drugs that had been main-lined into his blood system. I felt very sorry for the fellow's condition.

"He was a big man like you, Mr. Farrell."

Mick and I both hailed from the Lincoln Park neighborhood where most of the residents were either of Irish or Welsh origin. Mick was a fellow Irishman although he belonged to another Catholic parish than my people.

Chief Gleason gave me a fishy look, so I rapidly explained that I had spent that entire Saturday at a Knights of Columbus event over in the basement of St. Thomas Aquinas Church over on 63rd Street and 25th Avenue. When the gathering finally broke-up some of the diehard drinkers reassembled at Donovan's Tavern on the corner of 65th Street and 18th Avenue. I lived in the middle of the block south of the tavern. I suppose every man in Kenosha was now a suspect. It also troubled me that the 'night walker' had now intruded upon my domain.

Things got crazier when a resident on my block snitched to the police that they had peered over their fence to see their next door neighbor cleaning blood off of an old Army bayonet. One Fillmore Macarthur, who lived directly across the street from me, was arrested and hauled down to the nearest precinct. I never cared for this odd duck of a man who was bigger than me and lived with his parents. However, I was glad to hear that he was spared the rubber hose treatment when another mysterious letter appeared on top of the chief's desk, arriving just in the nick of time. Once it contained the seal of the imprint of a red hand.

Citizens of Kenosha,

You are all circus clowns! The fat slob is not the Lincoln Park attacker; I am!

With bloody affection,
Crimson Druid of Wisconsin

MacArthur had been spared a brutal beating and the murderer had now brazenly given himself a nickname that would go a long ways to strike fear into the heart of the natives of Kenosha. The ghastly handle also drew suspicion towards the Irish and Welsh of the city; for hadn't the murderer been heading southward towards the Irish Prairie after the Simmons Field attack; and wasn't the killer wearing the outfit of an ancient druid who hailed from the ancient chronicles of the Emerald Isle, as well as Wales. A suspect with a name like 'MacArthur,' a highland Scottish name, neatly fit into the Celtic motif. The outcry, however, against the creepy Fillmore was perhaps mooted somewhat because he was a remote relative of the General MacArthur who had led the Wisconsin Black Caps brigade at the Battle of Gettysburg. Fillmore was also a veteran of the last war.

It was my duty to set-up a meeting with the massive man shortly after his release for an exclusive interview. I conducted the exchange with him inside of his father and mother's house where he had been shuffled off to a dusty room in the attic. He was reputedly a child molester and he had been sacked from his dispatcher's post at the Bain Wagon wheel Factory on 52nd Street to other allegations of sexual misconduct.

"We're Scot-Irish Protestants," said Fillmore, quickly taking my crowd off of the hook.

"Were you in Lincoln Park on the day of the third crimson Druid attack?" I asked.

"I was on my way over to Lincoln Park with my knife on Saturday, so what about it?"

"Don't act the town bully with me, mate."

"Okay, okay, keep your shirt on...mate! I had my trusty Union Army bayonet and I was off to hunt some squirrels. As you know Lincoln Park is filled with the critters and it is seen as a civic duty to polish some of them off. Anyway, I kept on walking until I reached Anderson Park where the pickings are more plentiful. I walked along the outer edges of Lincoln on Sixty-Seventh Street, but I never actually walked into the park itself. Some old farmer gave me a ride on the way homewards but I didn't pick-up his name."

"The tracks near the murder site were made by a big man wearing boots."

"So arrest every big man who wears boots and you have your man."

"Are you working...again?"

"The letter from the Crimson Druid cleared my name, Farrell. The police even compared my script with the handwriting in the letter. Ha! There was no match. Nobody has anything on me. I'm as clean as a hound's toot. I'm sorry I am not your man...neighbor."

"Do you ever wear smoked glasses?"

"Only when I go to baseball games on a sunny day.'

The fourth and final attack occurred on the far north side of town at the intersection of Washington road and 30th Avenue. A carriage had picked up a fare on a Saturday night in late October. In his logbook the cabbie had entered his last fare's destination: the Kenosha Theatre on Main Street downtown where the famous Mike 'Slide, Kelly, Slide' Kelly, the baseball player, was performing the famous *Casey at the Bat* routine. Irish Mike was the star catcher for the Chicago White Stockings, as well as a batting champion. So it was possible our 'Crimson Druid' was a baseball fan.

The horse had only clopped a half block when a shot rang out. It only took one solo bullet to rip apart the head of Andy Stinefast, the driver. The blood splattered the insides of the coach, and also splashed on the paved road. The poor fellow's coachman's top hat was filled to the brim with gore. The police speculated that the murder had fled the scene of foot and that he was swimming in blood.

Three teenagers had witnessed the entire assault from their upstairs bedroom window. Their father reported their testimony as soon as possible. Their descriptions matched that of the other sightings of the 'Crimson Druid': a stocky man wearing smoked glasses. However, this time the Halloween costume at been left behind. Oddly enough, two night watchmen on duty rushing to the location of a blasting police whistle passed a man on the street that was a complete replica of the suspect. The man had looked them full in the face and had nodded before heading northward. The officers on duty later stated that the man they passed was 'not' Fillmore MacArthur.

I had just galloped upon the crime scene, notebook and pencil ready for action, when Dick Andresen showed up on foot. He was being tugged along by his massive German shepherd who went by the curious name of *Zodiac*. I could recognize my friend and rival's stocky frame and trademark smoky glasses from a hundred yards off.

"Farrell, it looks like the Crimson Druid is back to having a good time here in Kenosha," said Dick.

"How did you get here so quickly?"

"Did you forget I'm a Pole from the St. Casmir parish down the street here on the right?" he asked with a laugh. "'Andresen' is my 'Mark Twain.'"

"Oh, it's you, the reporter," said one of the first night watchmen on the scene as he stepped around a street gaslight. He gave dick Andresen the once over.

"Are you addressing me, officer?" asked dick.

"Didn't I just see you heading north but a few minutes?"

"No, the mutt and I just got here….and we came from the east."

"I could swear I just so you going north….but there was no dog."

"It looks like you're a suspect, my Polish friend," I said with relish.

"Perish the thought, you Irish paddy," snapped back Dick, no longer amused.

"I'll have to look into this further," announced the beat cop.

"Don't forget I was with you all day at the Knights of Columbus shindig on the Saturday the Lonigan boy and Owens girl were sliced up at Lincoln Park. You're my alibi, Farrell!"

"He has a point there, officer," I reluctantly admitted.

The very next day I received a letter in the mail with a bloody piece of material stuffed inside. The police lined it up exactly with a missing piece from the bloodied hat of Andy Stinefast. The letter was addressed to me. This third letter also bored the signature of the red hand.

Farrell you fool,

This is the Crimson Druid speaking:

I'm sure you have heard of the good time I had over in Polack Town last night. Wait until Thanksgiving when I burn down a school house of bawling brats!

Kenosha hasn't seen anything yet!

Only a mere day or two before the arrival of Major Stuart O'Farrell in our city, a math teacher from Kenosha High School had been pulled in by Chief Gleason for questioning. The police had been tipped off by an anonymous letter that Marshal Pennyworth had a 'funny' way about him in his dealings with his pupils. It was quickly discovered that Mr. Pennyworth had a reputation of hating his female charges. He was certainly a dead ringer of the description of the killer. Furthermore, his handwriting was a pretty good match to the *Crimson Druid* letters on file. Unfortunately, the tubby crackpot had an airtight alibi of his own; for he had attended the popular Mike Kelly vaudeville act at the Kenosha Theatre with three of his high school students. I had it on good authority that all three of the boys walked with wiggles and spoke in shrill lisps. However, I was only interested in the wrong doings of the 'Crimson Druid' and not the shady private life of a possible sexual deviant.

"Either charge me or leave me alone!" Mr. Pennyworth had bellowed out at Gleason. "Is it a federal crime to share a penmanship style with a serial killer?"

"We are duty-bound to pursue all leads," protested the chief.

"I think you're trying to frame me for murders I had no hand in," shouted back the teacher as he grew more hysterical.

"You may go…for now….sir."

"Fine way to treat a veteran of the Union forces," the man sniffed as he took his departure to rejoin his cadets who had waited patiently for his return. "We'll be at the malt shop downtown if you feel like pestering me any further."

I felt very sad for my flustered cousin.

"It seems like every heavyset man in Kenosha occasionally wears smoked glasses and is a veteran of the blue uniform," I said with a shake of my head. "It makes them all suspects, including me and you."

"Get lost, Gerard!"

Now it is time to introduce you to the famous Irishman from New York City!

"Major O'Farrell, I presume; I'm Steven G. Farrell of the *Kenosha Port Daily*."

The man's handshake was firm, strong and manly.

"You must be an Irish cousin of mine," he blurted out.

Stuart was a massive hulk of a man whose face had seen kinder days. In spite of the numbers of his years he still presented an imposing and commanding demeanor. However, I saw no physical resemblance between us besides our size.

"We left Ireland eons ago," I mumbled, turning red with a blush.

"All members of the Farrell and O'Farrell clans are from the same tribe. We are all descendants of the first Fearghail chiefdom of Longford who helped Brian Boru, High King of Ireland, defeat the Vikings at the Battle of Clontarf in 1014."

"I'll have the porter see to your bags being delivered to the *Daytona Beach House* downtown," I said.

"Field always handles my luggage," announced O'Farrell.

At the mentioning of his name a sawed off giant with a very wide body and a massive hunchbacked peaked around the Major's broad back and leered at me with a devilish grin. I reeled a few feet backwards in disgust from the man's ugliness as he laughed at the alarm smeared across my face.

"I'm the Major's factotum."

We had no sooner reached the lobby of Kenosha's best hotel when a messenger boy rushed in with a telegram from Chief Gleason stating that another suspect had just been grilled. This time a vigilante group made up of Italian immigrants from the Columbus Park neighborhood had just dragged into the police station a fellow Italian.

"He's not one of us!" they shouted in harmony.

"What's this all about?" the sergeant manning the reception desk had barked out as the chief came barging out of his office.

"He's the wolf who is devouring the sheep!"

Lawrence Capone worked down at the docks as a roughneck. He was also a social pariah within his own community due to many unsavory incidences that none of them wanted to go into any detail on.

O'Farrell had the opportunity to meet the chief and the suspect at the same time. Lawrence immediately declared that he was an American citizen, as well as a veteran of the Civil War. He also was a singer of hymns who had joined the Hungarian congregation of Catholics at St. Stephen's Parish because they had a better choir than the Italians over at Mount Carmel and Holy Rosary. A cousin from Italy suddenly appeared and swore out a statement that his cousin had spent the entire previous December visiting other cousins in Buffalo, New York which meant he couldn't have possibly committed the first attack at Simmons Field.

"So is Kenosha full of Civil War troopers?" O'Farrell asked once Capone had been released.

"The city came out in full support of Lincoln and the Cause," I said with a sense of pride.

"I, too, served in the war as a captain," responded Gleason. "Farrell served beneath me as a first lieutenant."

"Did you encounter these men: MacArthur, Pennyworth and Capone."

"They served in our battalion but beneath our notice," I said.

"Speak on your own account, cousin, snapped Gleason. "I do remember that MacArthur and Capone were the best sharpshooters in Dick

Andresen's platoon. If I remember correctly, Pennyworth was in the Quartermaster division."

"Ah, is this the Dick Andresen you encountered in the death of the coachman?" asked O'Farrell.

"Yes, it is," I admitted. "He's now a fellow newspaperman."

O'Farrell began to put things into focus for us. All of the suspects were former soldiers with the knowledge of how to deploy weaponry. It was a good bet that they were all familiar with one another as former members of the same army outfit. Oddly enough, they were all portly men who wore spectacles and/or smoked glasses. Three of the four attacks had occurred in the neighborhood s of all three suspects. Then, too, one of the survivors had said his date was being bothered by a man by the name of 'Dick.'

"Every single one of the suspects has an alibi for at least one of the attacks," stated Gleason.

"Yes, chief, the alibis seem to fall neatly into place," intoned O'Farrell. "Perhaps the neatness itself is too pre-arranged."

"What are you proposing, Major?" asked Gleason.

"It is time for Field and I to load up and to capture one of our prey."

"You use the plural," I observed.

"Plural is correct."

"You suspect more than one 'Crimson Druid?'" asked Gleason.

"Cousin Gerard, you may assist us."

"Don't count out me and my lads," said the chief.

"We'll need you and three of your best men."

"I demand to know what's up your sleeve, Major."

"It should be apparent to all that the only thing we can logically deduce from all of the available evidence that we're dealing with a death squad of Crimson Druids rather than a lone gunman."

"That's outlandish!"

"I would also like to suggest that the hand emblem upon the Druid's outfit symbolizes a gang of five."

"It puts one in mind of the 'Bloody Hand of Ulster,'" Field said with glee. "It's the emblem of one of the four provinces in Ireland."

"You're both talking rubbish," charged Gleason.

"I would suggest to you that we have a quick look again at the letters sent by the Crimson Druid. I am certain Gerard mentioned that a red hand was drawn on all of the correspondence sent."

"It's waste of time, but I have no reason to object."

The three missives were retrieved from a vault in the chief's office. The Major pulled out a huge magnifying glass and examined the writings very briefly.

"The digits don't match."

"What in blazes are you on about, man?"

"The handwriting is the same on all of the letters, but the handprint changes considerably. If you observe closely the fingers and thumb are not in scale. The forefinger and the index finger belong to two different me. In fact, all five fingerprints belong to five separate men."

"Take a peek, your honor," challenged Field.

Gleason took a closer look and was convinced that O'Farrell's theory was correct.

"It's no trick on my part, cousin; I'm merely using some of the modern technology certainly under development by Scotland Yard in the detection of crime."

"Are you telling us five different men pressed down upon these sheets of paper to combine for one red hand?" I asked with disbelief. "This type of evidence won't hold much water here in Kenosha, I'm afraid."

"You'll be the giggle and gaggle of the community with all of your Celtic blab," predicted Gleason.

"For the benefit of your fair community we'll say only one man wears the mask: Dick Andresen!"

Our raid on the house of Dick Andresen produced no damming evidence but we did discover the primary suspect sitting in front of his fire where he was laughing hysterically. Gleason had no option but to have the man carted off to the nearby lunatic bin at St. Catherine's Hospital.

"Dick Andresen is bonkers, but it doesn't prove he's the man," scoffed Gleason.

"It was the shame that drove him batty," Field declared sagely.

"We found no evidence of a Celtic connection," I pointed out.

"Somebody no doubt cleared out the place of any artifacts and left dear Dick behind to take the blame," O'Farrell said quietly but with conviction. "It proves my hypothesis of a death squad is correct."

Gleason visibly shrunk after hearing O'Farrell's proclamation before sputtering out, "but isn't Andresen the face of the murderer?"

"No, chief," responded O'Farrell. "He is merely the index finger of a deadly fist."

"But the public demands a face," protested Gleason, adding, "and Dick Andresen shall be the face I shall present to them, mark my words."

The image of Dick Andresen being hauled off to bedlam haunted my dreams that night. He would immediately be confined to the notorious madhouse up in Mendota near the state capital of Madison.

I was eating breakfast with O'Farrell inside of the swanky O'Higgins Headquarters Restaurant on Pickering Road when a messenger from police headquarters rushed in to report to us that Chief Gleason had just blown his brains out inside of his office.

"There is the forefinger," O'Farrell said gravely as he finished his coffee.

"Andresen is Crimson Druid' screamed out every headline in the extra newspaper editions that afternoon.

'*Chief Gleason Commits Due to Depression'* ran other headlines beneath the fold.

"Is all of Kenosha going mad?" I cried with frustration as we headed over to the police station to get more information.

"The madness isn't finished yet, Gerard," said the Major.

The very next morning the police were summoned to the home of Marshall Pennyworth. Several rifle shots had crackled at dawn, smashing several and killing the early rising teacher. I knew where the blame went when I next met O'Farrell and he held-up three fingers.

"He was merely the middle finger who authored the letters but he was in on all of the planning," said O'Farrell.

"You can't take justice into your own hands, sir."

"Kenosha, Wisconsin will find that O'Farrell justice is swifter than any justice your legal system may ever administer in this case. My fate is in your hands, Gerard. Of course, you'll have to find your own proof without my assistance."

However, mob justice soon took over O'Farrell's when a group of men burst into a man's apartment near Columbus Park and roused him out of bed for his own execution. The man swinging from a tree immediately identified as that of Lawrence Perroto.

"That would be the pinky finger, Mr. Farrell," Field hissed into my ear.

"I imagine the thumb will be the last to be chopped off," O'Farrell said to me over a bourbon and water.

Fillmore MacArthur, in the far reaches of his parent's attic, was found performing a lewd act upon a fourteen year old girl only the day after the execution of Perotto. Speculation was rampant as to who informed the police of the impending situation. I had no doubts it was coins from the purse of the Major who had hired the lass to assist in the baiting of a criminal.

"You had no hand in my deeds, Gerard," O'Farrell assured me as I escorted him and his servant to the train depot. "If you're still a practical Catholic you can confess it to your priest."

"Otherwise it is a secret you carry to the grave with you, Mr. Farrell," field added with malice and menace.

"Kenosha made a bargain with me and I delivered," said the Major with a degree of satisfaction. "I found a group of men who addicted to blood after serving for four bloody years in the Union army. Why they decided to give in to their urges so many years after the war and how they reconnected is another mystery for you to figure-out on your own. Gleason was the only Irish one in the group, so I imagine he introduced the various Celtic themes. I think it is for the best is the public is never made aware of your cousin's part in the entire affair. It is best to let Dick Andresen to receive all of the credit."

"MacArthur and Andresen are still alive, aren't they?" I growled back, feeling as though I was being blackmailed into silence.

"The governor and the mayor will see to it that Mr. Andresen shall never walk freely again. As for MacArthur...that's your look-out now. They have nothing to gain by spilling the beans and being charged with murder."

"He'll get four or five years in prison, at least," said Field with a snort, "then you'll have to keep an eye on he's out."

"You could always send for us, cousin," jested O'Farrell.

"You both can go straight to Hell!"

"One day you'll put on your thinking cap and you'll see how all of the pieces fitted into place. It was a hardly a riddle at all for the Major here," said Field.

I left it that!

Years afterwards the natives of my village were quite satisfied with assuming that the 'Crimson Druid of Wisconsin' true identity was Dick Andresen. Since there were no more murders once he was locked up, it seemed only logical that he was the murderer. When the former reporter died as a mental patient people sighed with relief. Only I was aware of the fallacy in the public's thinking. The knowledge aged me considerably beyond my years. My stress level leaped even higher when Fillmore MacArthur was released after serving five full years for his misdeed.

It would be my duty to keep a close eye on the hulking man who moved back in with his parents who lived right across the street. I was fully aware that he knew I was tailing him, and that he liked to send me on wild goose chases around the city. His favorite spot was down by the boathouse near the lagoon in Lincoln Park. Sometimes he even turns around and smiles right back at me.

Steven G. Farrell

PAPER 3

OLUMHOR: LAKE MONSTER OF POWERS' PORCH, WISCONSIN

Olumhor's reptilian head merged from the cold and murky waves of Powers' Porch. The lake monster's eyes were an ugly orange, blinking wide open, large and vicious. The beast scanned the shores of its' Wisconsin domain before plunging back into the depths of the lake that bottomed out about 200 feet below the surface. There was plenty of wet room for Olumhor in Sheridan, a ten mile long lake that was mostly located south of the Illinois border with only a mere two miles of it on the Wisconsin side of the border. Sheridan, which was named after the great Civil War general, was six miles wide in Illinois but the bluffs of western Kenosha County jutted out on both sides to reduce the width to two miles once it swept over the state line: hence the name of Powers' Porch.

Olumhor, who was in a foul mood, was hankering for blood to appease the devilment surging inside of its seventy foot body. The creature's long but meaty tail gave him an additional bit of a stretch. He hankered for meat that was raw and bloody. His pointy Chinese dragon ears would also relish the screams of a victim in its death throe: a horse, a human, or even another lake monster of its own kind. He snapped his gigantic head out of the water and let out a mighty roar that shook the day when he spotted a canoe carrying the cargo of three fishermen. It was a mistake to fish at any time in Powers Porch, but in the summertime of 1903, when sea monster sightings were widespread throughout the state, it was especially foolhardy.

Widening eyes led to a widening mouth as Olumhor used his mighty claws to paddle his bulk to the boat. He skillfully employed his webbed feet and dinosaur-like legs to project him up into the air as though he were flying. A right claw ripped off one man's face; a swinging tail batted another one right out of the canoe; and then, as a finale, Olumhor picked the last man up and crunched off the upper part of his body. A crowd of swimmers and picnickers had flocked to the shore to scream in hopes of scaring the savage thing away. However, he enjoyed playing to the crowd by swinging the remains of the craft on to beach; his aim was deadly and hit its mark.

For good measure, Olumhor launched a land attack, and he was successful in outrunning several of his fleeing victims. A screaming fat woman, a tourist from Chicago, hit the sand with both of her arms missing. A brave but foolish lifeguard, a student at Bradford High, blew on his whistle for all he was worth and to no affect. The shrillness only brought him unwanted attention and his squashed remains soon became part of a nightmarish prehistoric footprint. At least now the newspaper men would have photographic evidence that the cheese heads up in Wisconsin weren't simply drinking too much Pabst Blue Ribbon in the hot July sun.

Olumhor pawed the earth before starting his rapid lurk towards the old Powers' mansion where the three Powers brothers, all eccentrics, lived. Ralph, the oldest, and Bibs, the youngest, raced outside their ancestral home clutching their hunting rifles in a bold show to stop the charge. Olumhor shook off the bullets with the black and green armor that was his skin. He sent Ralph flying with a swish of his tail that broke bones upon impact. Bibs heaved his useless piece of wood at the head of the beast. Bibs cursed in Irish, Italian, Polish, German and English as the rifle bounced off a thick skull. The thick skull then curled up into a battering ram that was used to head butt Bibs about fifty yards.

Olumhor then turned his evil attentions back to old crumbling estate that had housed the Powers' clan since their founding father's flight in 1837 from Waterford, Ireland. Their great-great-grandfather had started off the American branch of the family with violence and bloodshed. Old Poe Powers had cleared off the remaining Potawatomi tribesmen with a pike handed down to him from the 1798 Rebellion. He had then amassed his fortune by mining the bluffs of its tin and fishing the lake. There also were the persistent rumors of a tidy bootlegging business that serviced the dry puritan counties in Illinois. The people of Kenosha would later on pondered the possible feud that Olumhor had had with the Powers, but their tongues were set further a wagging by the monster's outlandish reaction towards his interaction with Professor Powers. The Professor was the middle one of the Powers brothers, as well as the most eccentric. He was an educated zoologist who had once taught at a small private college in the northern woods region of Wisconsin. It was rumored that the Professor had been a little 'too far out there' for the tastes of the dean and the uptight administration. He was also known to have published some scientific papers with arcane journals that were too technical and dry for the average person in the state of Wisconsin to comfortably tackle at their leisure. Later research by Farrell the reporter discovered two self-published book titled *Olumhor the Monster Still Swims Amongst Us!*, as well as *The Haunted Lakes of Wisconsin*. These massive tomes, published in 1895 and 1901 by Pickering Peanuts Press, lied unread on the book shelves of libraries throughout the Badger State until the slew of sea serpent sightings in Powers' Porch created a market for their insights. Farrell the reporter eventually unearthed an even earlier volume by Professor Powers published by Cara Press of Mayo, Ireland in 1892 titled *Olumhor the Monster Still Swim Lives Deep in the Irish Sea*. Farrell the reporter wrote in one of his many articles on the subjects of the Professor and the slaughter at Powers Porch that the word 'Olumhor' was an old Gaelic word from the County of Mayo that translated into the two words of 'Sea Monster.' So the monster from Powers' Porch was forever after known as 'Olumhor.'

Olumhor halted in his tracks just a few feet from the front porch of the Powers' place. Witnesses declared that the creature's agitation begun to subside when the Professor stepped out on to the porch and began to address him in a 'strange' language. Upon police inquiries the Professor stated that he had used a combination of Latin and Gaelic to sooth the savage beast.

"I think the Irish language actually did the trick," the Professor later told the police, adding, "no offense meant towards Father Warren of my parish."

Olumhor turned and made his way back to the lake. Only steps away from the water Sherry, another inhabitant of Lake Sheridan, took that opportunity to launch her own attack; her target being the left claw of Olumhor. The monster snorted at the loss of a limb before sinking sharp and pointed teeth into the neck of Sherry. Clap trap jaws twisted and broke the neck of female member of the species before being used to haul her down to her cold grave.

It took hours for the mess of the day to be cleaned up and for testimony to be written down by the men in blue and the gaggle of reporters from all over southeastern Wisconsin and Northeastern Illinois. Farrell the reporter had a field day when he located the eldest and the youngest of the Powers' brothers receiving first aid for the wounds inflicted upon them in battle.

"The Powers brothers are the heroes of the day," Farrell the reporter proclaimed to the assemblage.

Steven G. Farrell

Ralph and Bibs, alive but battered, were put in casts and released to the custody of the Professor, who was probably the real hero of the day with Gaelic mumbo jumbo.

The Professor capped off his day of triumphant glory by selling off a stack of his unsold stock of books. "The answer for today could be in these books!"

"What about the solution, Professor Powers?" asked Farrell the reporter.

It was only as the midnight hour approached that the three Powers were free to make their way down the wooden stairwell that lead directly to the great cavern craved out and hidden below their home. The stench of snarled flesh and drying blood became stronger as the three approached the tiny inlet they had chiseled out and where they had set up tanks of food and drink for their two pets of doom.

"Olumhor!" shouted Ralph, shaking his fist in anger at the repentant looking sea serpent.

"Leave the creature alone," warned the Professor. "No sense in stirring him up again."

"He's dragged home, Sherry, his mother," proclaimed Bibs. "He's done and killed and ate most of the poor girl."

"We need to kill Olumhor ourselves," Ralph said sadly. "Bringing that critter over from the Irish Sea to mate with Sherry and to breed a stronger beast was a bad idea indeed. We mixed an American sea monster with an Irish one and all we got was a venomous concoction that is a danger to everything around here. I'll have no more to do with scientific research!"

"Olumhor killed both of his parents and now he'll kill us," whimpered Bibs.

Olumhor lifted up his head as though he recognized his name. Then it groaned and appeared to pass-out from a loss of blood. His stump flooded up to the top and looked ghastly.

"Olumhor will die without our assistance," declared the professor, wondering.

"Good riddance," said Ralph.

"Amen," intoned Bibs.

"You two stooges were big cranks of Olumhor when my 'Frankenstein creation' was winning us bets against the farmers and

86

merchants all over the state. You won all sorts of doe when he defeated Pepie at Lake Pepin, Jenny at Lake Geneva, Bozho at Devil's Lake, and those other slithering things at Lake Ripley, Red Cedar and Lake Monona."

"Olumhor has now depleted the lakes of Wisconsin; now it's time for us to delete Olumhor before the coppers and that nosey reporter Farrell track things back here to us. We'll be sued for damages and the courts will hold accountable for all of the wanton bloodshed."

"What do you suggest?" asked the professor.

Ralph and Bibs stared back at their educated brother, letting him know by their stares that the burden of the cross was on his back. It would be him and him alone to solve the puzzle that he had created with his test tubes, electrical equipment and radio waves. There was only one thing to do and that was to inject the monster with a drug to keep it asleep until they could dispose of it. They had already constructed a huge crane to be used to lift of the sleeping beauty into a huge septic tank built on top of a sturdily made truck for the purpose of transport.

"It's your call," snapped back Ralph.

"We'll load Olumhor up and dump his body out in the middle of Lake Michigan. The creature will probably die in route. I'll pump something negative and poisonous into his wound to hasten his journey to Hell," said the professor, not relishing the idea of destroying his own laboratory son.

There were only a few hours left before dawn broke when the brothers were ready to roll on Highway 50, eastward towards the lake. The winnings had been plentiful and had provided them with their own sea-faring vessel that they had been using to go across Lake Michigan to find Olumhor new rivals over in the state of Michigan. The Powers brothers always traveled in the darkness.

It was no easy task to wrap around several nets to secure the beast to the back of the boat.

"Now all we have to do is toll the carcass to the middle of the lake where we can dump it," explained the Professor. "We want no traces of the beast left behind."

However, the vessel wasn't even out of sight of the harbor when Olumhor almost magically came to life and easily used all of the weapons nature and the Professor had bestowed upon it to break loose to the state of freedom. The three Powers all died screaming as Olumhor took his time to rip them all to shreds before sucking them into the bottomless pit of his stomach.

Olumhor turned all his attention to the swim back to shore. He felt in the mood for a romping rampaging that would make amends for any pain and injury inflicted upon his body. All mankind was his enemy and all warranted the death penalty. The hands of any clock in the city where still a long ways away from mid-morning when the slaughter began on Simmons Beach. The monster went from wanton murder to mindless destruction as he caved in the bridge that connected Simmons Island with the mainland of Kenosha with his battering ram of a head. He enjoyed hearing the sound of splattering wood and bending steel. When Olumhow reached 7th Avenue, he swatted down a horse drawn wagon before ramming into an approaching Ford Model T's. It was then the turn of a trolley car to be ripped off of the tracks. All of downtown Kenosha was soon crunched, chomped and crushed. It was now almost lunchtime when Olumhor stomped his way on to Sheridan Road, roaring a huge sour note of contempt at the helpless police officer whose bullet had no chance of penetrating the shell that protected his huge heart and other arteries.

The huge cross on top of St. Stephen's Hungarian Catholic Church became the bull's eye of the monster next target. Like a fascinated infant doddering towards a piece of dangling candy, Olumhor crouched forward with relish. He actually dripped spit from the anticipation of approaching satisfaction. The creature was so focused upon the cross high in the air that he never noticed the squad car that whirled around the corner of 5oth Street that spun out of control and literally drove up the creature's tail. The automobile jammed itself into the nape of Olumhor's neck and exploded, ripping out the back part his skull and forcing his brains to spill out all over his back and the ground. The explosive impact propelled Olumhor forward until its right eye was pieced by the cracking cross of the church.

Olumhor roared one last time as its belly was punctured by the downward fall on top of the crackling and buckling church. The monster did a final wiggle as death snuffed out the viciousness in those ugly orange eyes.

Kenosha had a lot of explaining to do to the outside world just as it had to do during the reign of the 'Crimson Druid' that had occurred not so many years before. It was the sort of international fame that no growing village would want on hanging over its head. Then there would be that Farrell fellow stirring up the hornet's nest, but never actually solving the case of Olumhor of Powers' Porch.

PAPER 4

KNUCKLEBONES

He was a big man who could move quickly for one of his immense size. He was an Irishman with bulging muscles, reddish hair and a gold chain containing an amulet of his god Lugh slung around his nick. The sparkling band symbolized that he was a Celt of high birth. He was able to get his legs walking rapidly more than most men, especially when he was in a hurry to get somewhere. On this occasion, on the road leading away from Jerusalem, he was making tracks to escape. No, he wasn't in trouble with the Roman legion who occupied the city in the name of Tiberius Caesar, and he hadn't upset any of the local authorities either. He wasn't even running away from a bad gambling debt, or the arms of a all too willing young village damsel.

Jerusalem had depressed him. Land of milk and honey or not, the city was a depressed speck on the face of a dismal desert as far as Fearghal Scotus was concerned. It was a place he vowed he would never go back to even if there was Roman money to be spent to witness his prowess as a wrestler in the pit of the Gladiator Arena in the Greek sporting stadium. He would always follow the promise of gold to Gaul, Syria or Egypt, but never again would his shadow darken the gates of the sacred city of the nation of Israel.

Fearghal was no politician or colonist or a thief. He was only a honest man plying his trade wherever there were crowds that appreciated the ancient art of self-defense thrown in with large doses of Germanic brute force and Celtic mayhem. He didn't care if the natives didn't like him, but this lot was one that needed sorting out for their sour demeanor and their disdain for the outsider from the western fringes of the known world. Adding insult to injury, somehow they pulled him into their world of injured pride, rebellion and messiahs written about in their ancient Hebrew language. It was all well and good but he had his own demons to wrestle with. Wasn't he on the run after getting chased out of Ireland by a land greedy relative who happened to have more clan members on his side than he had on his side?

He hadn't liked the first of this tribe that he had met on the road from Nazareth to Jerusalem. He happened to be at a rest stop where he realized he had plenty of wine but not enough bread. A group of unfriendly travelers had stopped near him and gabbed away in the tongue of their King David while they ignored his presence. Outright hunger made him approach where he was clearly unwanted.

"I'll exchange wine for bread," he said three times: once in Latin, once in Greek and once in the argot of the region. He gestured and pointed to indicate his desire. He received only odd looks for his efforts.

"Do you mean you would like to trade?" asked a handsome young man with very light features and almost blond hair. He was the first Jew to ever smile at him. His Greek was understandable and crisper than his own.

"I am happy I can understand you," said the Celt.

"Please join our fire and our repast."

His companions were not pleased with the offer but the Irishman decided to accept just to irritate them. Besides, there was something pleasing and gentle about this man that made him take a shine to him immediately. Fearghal remained silent as he followed the others in their eating rituals. He listened to words he could not understand, but he was impressed by the passionate manner of his new friend in his chanting. He accepted the broken bread and the goblet of wine that made the way around their circle. The dusk began to settle in and he got up to move. He was beckoned by a big man who spoke to him in the messy lingo of the region.

"The Master bides you to stay in our camp as it will mean more protection for you against lions and bandits."

The young man bide me to unroll my blanket close to him. He was flattered.

"You're not a Roman or a Greek," he prodded gently.

"Master, surely you can see he's a barbarian German from beyond the Rhine. Ask the Caesars what their opinion is of his race," said a tiny dark man with shifty eyes.

"I'm from Scoti as it is labeled in Latin. We call it Eire, or Ireland. I am from the clan of Fearghal. It means 'men of valor' in my tongue."

"Relatives of mine operate a tin mine in Cornwall."

"Aye, a stone throw away from us. They are Celts too."

"My mother was born there to a Jewish father and a ...."

"Master, it is late."

So that explained his fair skin and his light hair.

"I have an uncle there by the name of Stephen," said the young man.

"In my tongue the Greek name of Stephen is Stiofan. My name is Stiofan Fearghal," proclaimed the foreigner in a boasting mannerism that was common among his people.

"It is a fine name, Stiofan Fearghal."

In the morning they all marched together into Jerusalem where Fearghal parted company to find the quarters of Longinus and the other Celts in the pay of Caesar for the protection of Pontius Pilate, the hack who ruled Palestine in the name of the Empire. He was more than a little sad to wave his farewells to the half-Cornish wanderer.

There is no written record of how many matches Fearghal won or lost during his stay in Jerusalem to entertain the Roman centurions who patrolled Palestine for pay, room and board. There is a good chance that he had more than a few friends, who wore the gold plated armor and wore the red capes of Rome, were Celtic Irishmen or British: one of them was Longinus, a captain of the guard. Oral legend has it that whatever winnings Fearghal had raked in he immediately lost to wine drinking, as well as to the curious dice game known as knucklebones. It was reverses in gambling that wound up with the Irish wanderer carrying the tool box of a one of the carpenters on the Friday that three Jewish outlaws were to be crucified on Calvary, known as the 'Hill of the Skulls', the location set aside for public executions.

Fearghal found himself in the middle of the procession that weaved its way through the city; his throbbing head and the growing heat of the day making him indifference to those who struggled with their own wooden crosses, the soldiers who whipped and prodded, or the crowd of natives who lined the pathway and heckled at all in the procession with equal venom. It was only when the peak of the hill was reached and crosses, ropes and nails were spread out upon the ground for the victims that the grossness of the occasion began to dawn upon the wrestler.

"Fetch me my hammer, Fearghal Scotus!"

"Be quick there, my Celtic cousin!" joined in Longinus, all business now.

Steven G. Farrell

He was approaching the cross spread upon the ground when he suddenly recognized the man being readied for his punishment. The man, beaten and bloodied, looked up into his face.

"Why is it you, my friend?"

"Stiofan Fearghal?" the woeful man whispered for his ears only.

The Irishman turned his back from the outrage and faced the mighty crowd that attempted to surge past the Roman shields and spears to get a better look at the torture of this one man. Their energy was wasted as his companion of the road was lifted high in the air for all to see. He was soon joined by two other suffering prisoners: one on each side of him. Conversation was carried on between the crucified men but Fearghail couldn't hear the words for all of the braying of the crowd and the crude jokes of the Romans.

"Get in on the action over here, Fearghal!" Longinus shouted to me at the pierced feet of my friend. "Maybe your luck will change with this roll of knucklebones."

He was not sure how it transpired, but he chanced to become the winner. He scooped up his winnings and walked away with the robe that had been stripped from the man's body. It would be the only wages he would walk away with in his sojourn in Jerusalem. Before he moved away, he looked up at his friend on the cross with pity and compassion. The look was returned with the same level of grief by the crucified Jew. The wanderer was almost relieved when Longinus approached the cross and pierced the man with his long spear.

"It is high time to bring this to an end, me boy!"

Fearghal wanted to help take the man off of the cross but he was discouraged by his fellow Celts, who said that the Jewish friends of the man would view it as an act of pollution. The body would be attended to in the strictest of privacy and in accordance of their religious laws. There would be an anointment and then a burial in the nearby Garden of Olives.

Fearghal slept in the barracks of his friends that night as a huge thunderstorm crashed in the sky above and pelted the parched earth below with rain and hail. It was remarked upon how none of the seasoned veterans had ever witnessed such an upheaval in nature in all of their long years of service in the Orient. The Irishman was too numb and confused to pay much heed to the uproar all around him. However, he was relieved to find that the morning was fresh, clean and sunny. He made haste from the city with the intention of reaching a friendlier place like Lebanon or Syria.

There are several written accounts of how wanderers upon the road outside of Jerusalem encountered a man whom they recognized as an old friend and teacher; one that they only recognized after seeing the damage that had been done to his hands and feet. Fearghal Scotus never came across these writings accepted by church authorities as testimonies of proof. He wanted no more to do with the place or the people. He only stopped his walk northward to rest for the night and to build a fire for his lonely repast. He was looking off into the sunset when he felt a presence behind him. He jumped to his feet and pulled out his long knife. However, it was only the visitation of another lonely wanderer. Fearghal pointed to the cooking fish on the fire and waved his visitor over. The man was mostly silent except for some softly spoken prayers as he and Fearghal passed the meal and wine back and forth. On the last pass of the wine the man let his hand linger long enough in the flare of the fire for the Irishman to see the gaping hole.

"You poor fellow," said Fearghal, immediately making a connection between his guest and his recently executed friend.

The Celts have always been a people acceptable to miracles and myths.

"Stiofan, you have something of mine."

Fearghal was confused until the man nodded toward his pack. The first thing that was rummaged out was the robe of the crucified man. The visitor calmly put his hand out and the wrestler handed the cloth to him.

"I was holding it for you, my friend."

"I knew you would preserve it for me." Curiously the recovering man reached over and kissed Fearghal. Then he lightly touched the golden chain wrapped around the wrestler's bull neck. "When you arrive back to your fair Ireland in the west tell them about me."

The next thing Stiofan Fearghal Scotus was aware of was that the sunrise had replaced the sunset and that his fire had gone out. His friend had vanished without leaving behind a trace or a track. He immediately checked his luggage for the robe but it was missing to verify that he hadn't been dreaming or drunk. If he needed any final proof of identity of the rambler Fearghal found the amulet of his foreign god Lugh had been replaced by a figure that resembled a cross.

Steven G. Farrell

Like the *Odyssey* of the Greek Homer, the mostly forgotten book of *The Annals Of Annally* testify that Fearghal Scotus voyage homeward took him many years and rewarded him with many adventures. He was an older man of almost sixty when he was granted permission to return to Ireland by the High King of Tara. He built himself a home on the moist and rich soil of his ancestors almost exactly in the center of Ireland in what is now called the County Longford. The rumors circulated that the drifter had returned with pouches full of silver and gold coins. However, it was the returnee's tales that attracted more attention than his alleged treasure. The Celts are a race enchanted by stories, and Fearghal was chocked full of them. There was one glorious story, in particular, that became the most popular of all of his yarns: it included a chance encounter on a dusty road, a crucifixion, a toss of knucklebones and the return of a robe.

"Let this serve as proof!" he would conclude his long, rambling take as he held up the golden cross

PAPER 5

DOES HE BLAZE?

oes he blaze?"

"D "Socrates Poe Raven is reckoned the best classical scholar Trinity College has ever produced," I said to my sister in a rather peevish manner.

"Does he blaze?"

I had very little time for my sister's obsession with the dueling fad that had swept our native land in recent years. I suppose my darling sibling was in good company; for the entire land was swooning in the passion of challenges, wounds and funerals. All was well as long as a gentleman acquitted himself with honor. I was rather relieved that I was just a shade too old and mature to be caught up in the frenzy.

"Master Raven is counted among the most handsome young bucks in all of the County Clare," Miss Bowen, a lovely maiden from Donegal, put in for my benefit. I think this northern lady had set her sights in my direction.

"Does he blaze?" was said a third time.

"He is a most worthy squire with estates, livestock and gold galore," said my brother Robert in a jesting manner.

"Does he blaze?" was said for a fourth time.

"Such talk, young lady," scolded my father. "We want a suitor for you who is worthy of your rank, dowry and beauty."

"I agree with Father," I seconded.

"For once, Henry," laughed my brother.

"Many an Irish gentleman of good stock has proven to be a wastrel once they came into the family fortune. Too much wine, gambling and dueling will bring ruination upon a house quicker than war or treason," lectured father.

My sister's blazing eyes of defiance was her answer to us all. The old man decided to turn his attention to the refilling of Shaw, McCartney and Wilde's cups. It was a duty that received at least a measure of appreciation and gratitude.

So there you have it, my readers: sister wanted a blazer: a duelist! A 'man who blazed' was a sensitive soul who would put out a challenge under the merest of excuses and pretenses. It was a pistol and twenty paces at dawn. Regardless of the pain, injury and death, it seemed as the entire Irish nation was swooning with the chatter of dueling. It wasn't like Ireland had ever had any shortage of violence raging through the four provinces.

"Even the lower orders are copying the ways of their bettors," put in Miss Murphy, the daughter of a mere papist squire who could just barely afford a mount and a pair of riding boots. "They duel with their walking sticks."

"The butchers of Belfast are chopping one another up by the fountain in the town square."

"The peasants of Wexford are running one another through with homemade pike sticks for the price of a pint of stout."

"Many a lord, knight, squire and farmhand lie dead here in the west of Ireland because of the current rise of interest in mayhem," put in Sir Wayne Sexton. "The English stand by and gloat as we murder ourselves with glee."

"We Irish are a violent race of madmen," my sister said with gusto. "You know of our folklore, don't you?"

"Yes, Queen Maeve, Finn McCool and all of those bloody hands of Ulster." countered Sir Wayne, adding in a pious manner, "and all of our warring is our Celtic curse before the time of Christ."

"Whatever happened to our time honored Irish custom of settling our differences with our bare knuckles?" questioned Robert.

"Like a caveman," one of the ladies jeered. "We want our menfolk to use weapons like Kelly and Grimes and their notorious duel up in Tyrone. It's true the Papist defeated the Orangeman, but it was a jousting match for the ages."

"Sister, if you want a blazer so much why don't we set the wedding date with our cousin, John?" I teased.

"Does this John duel?" asked Miss Bowen.

"The 'blow in' doesn't know who 'Fireball McNamara is," chortled Miss Murphy in the uncouth way of her stock.

"Our cousin John is champion of all champions here in Ireland," said my sister, all puffed up with pride.

"The 'Fireball' has over sixty bouts to his credit," acknowledged Robert, impressed with the figure in spite of angering our father.

"Unfortunately our cousin John has had almost as many wives," jested my sister.

"The blackguard refers to his pistols as 'Bas gan Sagart," observed Robert.

"I never learned the language of the Gaels," confessed Miss Bowen to the delight of Miss Murphy.

"It translates into 'death without a priest.'"

"I must have a man who blazes," insisted my sister.

"Such bloody talk for the Yuletide," I chided as I took my leave of the merry little group of bloody-minded females. It was time to seek-out my young friend, Socrates Poe Raven. I found him brooding by the great fireplace, claret in hand. His disposition brightened when I approached. He was a pleasant enough young fellow, who held a Master of Arts from Trinity College in Dublin. I was more impressed by the castle he resided in near Ennis.

"Did you get in a word edgewise in my favor when you were among the hens?"

"She'll only have a man who is ready to march off twenty paces for her amusement," I admitted, patting the lad on the back.

"I have danced the waltz in Berlin, drunk the best wine in Paris, and study the statues of Athens, but I have had very little practice with the trigger, I'm afraid."

"This fad is all stuff and nonsense, Poe. This too must pass."

"Perhaps if I somehow staged a duel....one without any real bloodshed...it would be enough to make her quiver and we could proceed from there."

I shook my head with grave misgivings. Such things were never mere illusions inked by the quill of Shakespeare or Sheridan.

"I'd leave off with such fanciful notions, boy o."

The doorman came into the grand hall of our holdings and proclaimed at the top of his Welsh lungs: "Sir John McNamara of Quinn Castle!"

Bagpipes, flutes and whistles ushered my grand cousin into the gaiety of the holiday spirit. He still presented a well cut form although he was balding and becoming heavier with age.

"This McNamara is more infamous than even the notorious Captain Blood had been during the Restoration," Somebody nearby said for everyone's benefit.

I swear I saw Poe's ears perk-up with interest.

The midnight hour was approaching as was the very last dance of the evening. It was a time when the young sought out their favorite. I caught Miss Bowen's eye and knew that I would have somebody to embrace as the servants began to put out most of the lights to provide the privacy for brief kisses, whispered promises and poems of adoration. I was not pleased to see Sir John leading my sister out to the middle of the floor. My displeasure grew as my friend Poe Raven briskly approached the couple and abruptly brushed 'Fireball' aside as he offered his arm to my sister. Poe's actions were unwise, as well as unpardonable.

"The young lady is already engaged for this last spin around the spinning wheel," proclaimed Captain McNamara, a smile barely masking his peevishness.

"I declared earlier this evening before your arrival," protested Poe.

Poe Raven hadn't gotten far navigating the lovely damsel towards the dance floor before the Captain struck him across the face and, without further ceremony, took up my sister's arm. The hall of dancers gawked in astonishment as Poe impulsively reacted by decking the Captain with one mighty vulgar punch. My father, brother and I quickly intervened and fruitlessly tried to restore order before the chaos could set in and ruin our affair. However, there was just enough of an interlude for the Captain to issue a challenge to Poe Raven. The young and naïve gentleman rapidly accepted and proposed pistols at twenty paces. It was done.

"Satisfied?" my father hissed at my sister after the castle was cleared of all visitors.

"You just signed Poe's death warrant," added my brother.

"One of them shall die, or be seriously wounded," I noted sagely.

"We must put a stop to it," insisted my sister, her eyes finally opened to the sheer terror of a violent duel between two determined Irishmen.

"I'll try the Captain in the morning."

My approach was rebuked with a harsh laugh.

It was then decided that I was to reach out to Poe and persuade him to issue a formal apology to McNamara. However, I did not find him at home to receive my warning and my sister's plea. Later, we heard the rumor that my friend had hired off to Dublin to be trained in the art of firearms with a professional duelist now retired and passing on his knowledge of pistols, swords and fists to young gentlemen with packs of gold to spend and beautiful ladies to impress.

I was one of the few spectators permitted to attend the field of honor in a remote and rocky corner of Mayo. Dueling had been declared illegal years before by the monarchy and all participants in one were technically outlaws. Poe Raven, along with a second, was waiting there with the judges when I arrived with my younger brother. It seemed like ages before the glittery coach bearing the McNamara illustrious family crest along with the infamous Captain and his backers.

"Is there no turning back on all of this with a handshake?" asked the referee as pistols were loaded and examined by all parties.

"Not on my part," the captain snorted with contempt.

"Let's continue, please," said Poe; his face pale and his brow wet with sweat.

The Judge began the long count: 1, 2, 3, 4, 5, 6, 7, 8, 9, 10, 11, 12, 13, 14, 15, 16, 17, 18, 19…..20!

Captain McNamara, with his many years of experience, was the first to stand and deliver. His shot crashed mere inches from the right boot of Poe Raven.

"I'm satisfied that this man is a true Irishman," announced the captain, handing his pistol to his second.

Now all there was to do was for Raven to squeeze off a poorly aimed shot and he would have acquitted himself in the eyes of Ireland. Captain McNamara had successfully demonstrated that he had spared the life of the young man. However, by the determined look on the face of Poe Raven we could all observe that he was lining up his target with extreme care. Even the smile on the captain's face appeared to freeze up seconds before the finger was squeezed on the trigger.

"Damn you, Raven!" I said out loud at the discharge of a bullet and smoke.

The shot ripped across the top of the captain's shirt shoulder, leaving a rip but no blood.

"I'm satisfied that this man is a true Irishman....and I hereby announce my permanent retirement from all dueling in the future," said Poe Raven, handing his pistol to his backup.

We then repaired to a nearby pub to relive our glorious battle.

"Sir, you shall be my best man one year from today," Poe said to the captain at the end of the evening.

One year later, my sister was wedded to Poe Raven, and Captain McNamara served as the best man. As a wedding gift, the chieftain of the McNamara clan gave the newlyweds two fine horses and a set of silverware from Toledo, Spain. I always suspected a greater gift had been delivered on that field of honor a year before when the captain spared a life, my friend proved he had mettle and my sister had finally had enough of those who blaze..

PAPER 6

THE AFTERMATH OF THE ST. VALENTINE'S DAY MASSACRE

PART ONE: *THE GHOST OF JIMMY CLARK, GANGSTER*

A l Capone, Chicago's number one kingpin since the demise of the Bugs Moran Irish North Side mob via the St. Valentine's Day Massacre, was sitting all pretty and secure on top of his syndicated throne as 1929 headed into the spring. He had ventured back northward to his kingdom in the American Midwest once the machine gun smoke inside of the garage on Clark Street had cleared and the Cubs were once again playing baseball in the green confines of Wrigley Field over on the corner of Addison and Clark. Hack Wilson, Gabby Harnett and the rest of Big Al's friends on the squad looked like they were all set to easily cop the National League Pennant. Big Bill Thompson, a corrupt Republican deep inside of Al's vest pocket, was once again calling the shots for the Mob inside of the mayor's office. Life was good for an Italian-American thug from the mean streets of Brooklyn. Sure, that federal agent punk, Eliot Ness, was getting his picture in the newspapers for capturing, and destroying, a few cargo loads of Old Log Cabin Whiskey sent down from Canada courtesy of the Jewish lads in Detroit's Purple Gang. Let the pretty boy haul down a few headlines as Frank Nitti thought of an idea of getting him out of the way.

"Chicago, Illinois!" proclaimed the conductor as the train reached its' final destination at Union Station. "It's our last stop and all off!"

"We're finally here, chief!" said Jack McGurn as he fussed with his own tie before reaching over and straightening out Big Al's tie.

Mae Capone, the hoodlum's pretty Irish wife, shot the torpedo a dirty look before turning her attention toward the needs of the couple's only child, Sonny. So the Capone clan was back in sunny springtime Chicago, and plenty of the old gang was on hand to greet them on the platform:

Murray Humphries, Screwy Maddox, and Willie Heeney. Another welcoming committee was on hand to cheer their hero's return in the lobby of the Metropole Hotel, Al's armed fortress at 2300 S. Michigan Avenue on the near south side of the city. The most important members of the Syndicate, as well as the most discreet, fat Jake Guzik and Frank Nitti, were the last of the big shots to greet the kingpin, and they were waiting for him inside of the boardroom. There were financial statements galore: booze, dames, numbers, protection, loan sharking, gambling, speakeasies, payoffs and such. The large numbers in black at the bottom line of the ledger indicated that 1929 was off to a big, big start. You had to love Herbert Hoover as president... even if it meant voting against a fellow Catholic New Yorker like Al Smith?

"Have there been any recent sightings of our old pal, Bugs Moran?" Al finally ventured as Frank held out a match to his cigar.

"The big Mick was last seen headed for Montreal, Canada," snorted the man known as 'the Enforcer.'

"I have it on good authority that the Irishman is still in hiding over in Paris, France," added the man known as 'Greasy Thumbs.'

"Isn't that somewhere over in Europe?" sniffed Al.

"Yeah, but he doesn't know that," said Jake.

The three big dogs enjoyed laughing at the expense of George 'Bugs' Moran but they all knew full well that he was too tough, demented and war-like to stay out of Chicago for long. It was just a matter of time before the Big Mick had all of the little micks and krauts on the north side back in fighting order and, then, the ten year war for the liquor business in America's second largest city would start all over again. For all of his lack of an education, Al Capone still had the astuteness and acumen of any Wall Street investor. One could never underestimate the opposition, especially if the opposition included people like O'Banion, Weiss, Drucci, the Gusenberg brothers and Mr. Moran.

"By the time Moran drifts back into Chi-town, we'll have most of the North Side under lock and key," boasted Frank.

Al wasn't so certain.

The rest of the day and evening was spent with old friends, bottles of the best bootleg hooch, and the most beautiful swinging dames on the loose that money could buy. The world could not have been better until the next day when he awoke with a mammoth hangover and to the sounds of rustling curtains opening and closing. Who was dense enough to disturb the sleeping beer baron by admitting and omitting the morning sun by pulling the blinds up and down? The racket was grating.

"What's the heck!" shouted Al, cupping his eyes to peer into the outburst of brightness.

The shades were mercifully closed but a room light was snapped on. It took Al's bleary eyes a moment to adjust in order to see the solid shape of a well-dressed man standing at the foot of the bed.

The flunky was puckish enough to only stand there with a sneer smeared across his ugly mug instead of greeting 'Snorky' with a 'good morning.' Instead, the man muttered the nickname Al hated the most: "Scarface Al Capone!"

With that one dreaded word Capone was out of bed and screaming, "Jimmy Clark! Jimmy Clark!"

In a few short moments the room was full of bodyguards with drawn-out weapons. However, Jimmy Clark had vanished into thin air.

"I saw somebody slip behind the curtain," said one of the galoots.

"You can run but you can't hide," said another thug.

Al lingered in the background; his shaky hand holding on to his favorite 38 snub-nosed Smith and Weston. He carefully watched as his entourage inched their way to the still vibrating curtain. Nobody fired as one big yank revealed....nothing. Jimmy Clark wasn't there! Then it rapidly dawned upon them all that Jimmy Clark had been one of the eight Moran soldiers who had perished beneath a hail of machine gun bullets on St. Valentine's Day.

"Jimmy Clark has been dead and buried for months now, boss."

"You sure it wasn't Moran himself," somebody started to say before receiving a sharp elbow to the ribs.

"It must have been a bad dream, Mr. Capone."

However, Mr. Capone knew it wasn't a bad dream when Jimmy Clark began to pop up all over the place in his daily life. Once he even sat on the toilet while Al was taking a bath. Al saw him walking behind a peanut vendor at Wrigley Field. There was Jimmy standing in line to put down a bet at the race track. Any given night of the week he could be seen casually strolling by Al's residential home on the south side. Of course, only Big Al was able to see Jimmy Clark in the solid flesh and blood; others only caught glimpses of his head or his receding shadow. Al humorlessly wondered if Jimmy Clark had a key to every single room in the Metropole, as well as to Al's backup fortress at the Lexington Hotel in Cicero. Snorky' even fled up to Kenosha to hang-out with his with his bosom buddy, Ellie O'Hara, the gambling czar of Wisconsin. One time at sunset, Al could see Jimmy Clark walking on the nearby sandy shores of Lake Michigan's from Ellie's back porch. Jimmy Clark was even nasty enough to flip Al the bird before being absorbed by the summertime heat.

Needless to say, the mob thought their peerless leader was going batty. Maybe he had picked up a dirty disease from one of his many lady friends. There was speculation that he had had one too many shots of turpentine-tainted moonshine. The boss had also been under the strain of North Side attack for years now. Dodging bullets from the gats of Moran and the Gusenberg boys would rattle any man's nerves. Al grew silent about the appearance of Jimmy Clark, realizing that the sightings of a ghost weren't to be believed by anybody, especially by the cutthroats and pirates he employed. It was better to 'dummy up' than to be perceived as a dummy.

Only Klaus Kressin, Al's personal valet and a stodgy German from Berlin, seemed to believe the big boss and his blab about the ghost of Jimmy Clark.

"As I live and breathe, Mr. Capone, one morning when I came in to air out the master bedroom I saw a man standing by the window and looking out on to Michigan Avenue. He was smoking a cigar."

"It was probably one that he lifted from my private stock," gripped Al, growing hostile.

"When I approached him he gave me the shock of my life by hiding himself behind the curtain."

"He's done that to me as well!" exclaimed Al.

"I was even more puzzled when I checked behind the curtain and there was nobody there," concluded Klaus.

"So I'm not nuts," said Al, stuffing a hundred dollar note into the butler's vest pocket.

"The cook saw him too once down in the kitchen, but he was told to shut his trap because they didn't want to alarm you," said Klaus, ratting out Nitti and McGurn.

"Feed the chef this C note," said Al, stuffing another bill into the servant's pocket, "and tell him to keep his eyes peeled."

"I got you, Mr. Capone."

"You both shall report directly to me if you get a load of the ghost of Jimmy Clark, see?"

The sightings of the dead gangster abated from that moment on for a few months. However, Jimmy apparently decided to make a cameo appearance on the very afternoon that the Cubs had dropped the decisive World Series game to Connie Mack's Philadelphia Athletics. Jimmie Foxx, Al Simmons and Lefty Grove had shown up the mighty Cubbies, costing Al a big bundle in lost wages. A dejected Al retired to his bedroom in no mood to be pestered by man, beast or ghost. When the curtains began to dance Al didn't hesitate to pull-out his piece and squeeze the trigger six times. This time he audibly heard a body drop to the floor, and on this occasion he saw very real and red blood gushing all over his expensive Persian rug. Now he had all of the physical proof he needed to wipe away the stench of having a reputation as being a nut case.

"I took ole Jimmy Clark for a one way ride!" Al exclaimed with pride as he waved the boys over to the fallen body of his foe.

The unraveling of the gore filled drapery revealed a still warm corpse.

"Hey, boss, isn't this Klaus Kressin?"

It was Klaus Kressin!

Now the ghost of Jimmy Clark was joined in his haunting of Al Capone with Klaus Kressin, who was as snarly and sneering as his new partner. The two spirits even followed the convicted racketeer to the federal pen in Atlanta and, later, to the lonely rock off of the shores of San Francisco known as Alcatraz.

Al Capone didn't complete the sentence handed down to him by a judge in a 1931 Chicago courtroom because he was deemed mentally unfit due to the encroachment of a virulent strain of a venereal disease. People in the inner circle of the Chicago Outfit begged to differ: it was the two ghosts who had driven him loony.

The once mighty overlord of the American Midwest spent his last few remaining years as a recluse on his estate in Miami, Florida. Sometimes Al Capone got in some good fishing at his swimming pool while he daydreamed about his childhood in Brooklyn and his salad days in Chicago. Oftentimes he could be heard screaming in terror and panic, "for the last time leave me alone, Jimmy! Klaus, you know it was an accident! Scram, ghosts, scram!"

Steven G. Farrell

PART TWO: *BUGS MORAN'S REVENGE*

I t was a safe bet to any thinking American that Prohibition would be on the way out as soon as Franklin D. Roosevelt won the presidential election from Herbert Hoover in November of 1932 which was only a few short months ahead. George 'Bugs' Moran had mixed feelings about the ending of an epoch that had made him a very rich man, as well as the second most important man in gangland Chicago. Some newspaper reporters even speculated that Moran would become *Public Enemy Number One* now that Al 'Scarface' Capone was safely behind federal prison bars. Bugs Moran didn't like the publicity. However, those in the known knew that Frank Nitti, Jack McGurn, and the rest of Chicago Outfit were nibbling away at Moran's fiefdom from four different directions. Ole George was one tough Irish mick who wasn't going to go down and out without one hell of a donnybrook. Years as an illegal business man on Chicago's North Side had filled him with enough business savvy to go along with his native street smarts to clearly be able to read the writing on the wall. He had gradually started to move the primary focal point of his liquor and gambling interests from his old haunts on Clark Street on the Near North Side of Chicago to Waukegan; and even further northward into Kenosha, Burlington, Racine and other destinations in the southeastern corner of Wisconsin. The great exodus of the North Side Mob from the confines of Chicago had begun after the bloody but successful ambushes of O'Banion and Weiss a few years before, but the move had picked up momentum after the notorious day now known throughout the country as the *St. Valentine's Day Massacre* occurred on February 14, 1929.

Moran had been so unsettled by the slaughter of seven of his friends and associates that he had taken it on the lam for about a year, hiding out over in Paris, France as he regained his bearings. Upon his return to Chicago, he was shocked to find that his re-appearance didn't even faze the Syndicate in the least bit. As far as the Capone gang went George Moran no longer cast a very long shadow in the bootlegging affairs of the Windy City. Their indifference was a sign of utter contempt. George had to learn to live with being considered a minor leaguer as he retrenched himself. He felt that with the help of Leo Mongoven and the leftovers from his old gang that he would make a dramatic comeback.

However, there was something else bothering the dangerous Irishman: he needed to get his own back against Al Capone for the St. Valentine's Day Massacre. It was something that everybody expected of him although nobody but Leo voiced it. The fact that the Syndicate was giving him the ozone was because they assumed that he was too afraid to stand-up to them now that he had lost the better part of his shock troops. It was adding insult to injury to the notorious Mr. Moran.

'Bugs' had hired sleuths of his own to investigate the mystery of identity of the gunmen who were responsible for the bloody operation. Everybody knew that Big Al, Nitti and McGurn had been in on devising the blueprint for the attack: two vehicles painted up like police squad cars, two torpedoes disguised as men in blue, two machine gunners, and two getaway drivers also dressed as Chicago cops. Of course, there were numerous look-outs, decoys and messengers involved in the battle tactic, but Moran was only interested in the death squad of six. Who were these hired galoots, and how could paddy whack them? Moran was dead certain they weren't Italians from the Outfit or Sicilians from the Mafia; for the Gusenberg brothers and Jimmy Clark would have gone down shooting before they would have allowed any of those greasers into their hideout on North Clark Street. But Big Al's organization employed all sorts of Irish, Polish, German and Jewish hoods. Scarface even had working alliances with Egan's Rats, an Irish gang from St. Louis, and the Purple Gang from Detroit, whose members were exclusively Jewish.

A gumshoe began to compile a list of possible suspects, and the list narrowed down with each passing day until there were six primary suspects who filled the shoes of the death squad that pulled off the Massacre four years earlier: Fred 'Killer' Burke, Gus Winkler, Fred Goetz, Raymond 'Crane Neck' Nugent, Claude Maddox and Bob Carey. Burke was already serving a life sentence for killing a cop out of state. Nugent had suddenly disappeared off the face of the earth with no help from Bugs. Winkler, Goetz and Maddox were all still very entrenched in the Syndicate's Chicago scene. He'd have to get to them when their guards were down. For the moment that only left Bob Carey to reckon with.

A tip from a member of Manhattan's West Side Irish mob put George Moran and Leo Mongoven on an eastward bound train from Chicago to New York City. The two did their utmost to pass themselves off as businessmen trying to drum up business with their sample cases.

"Carey is small potatoes, George," said Leo, looking out at the flat terrain of northern Ohio.

"Carey is a start, Leo," retorted George. "One down, four to go. I suspect somebody already paddy whacked Nugent."

"Bumping them off won't bring back the boys, you know?"

"I think the boys would appreciate the gesture," answered Moran, adding: "We both know we have to go through with this hit."

"I'd rather we were hitting Nitti or McGurn or even...."

"Don't wreck my mood by mentioning that behemoth by name."

The two Irish-American mobsters hailed a taxicab at Grand Central Station. The address they gave was to a dive bar in Hell's Kitchen, right in the heart of Own Madden's territory. 'Owney the Killer' had just survived two drawn-out wars with 'Legs' Diamond and 'Mad Dog' Coll. However, he currently was tangling with Dutch Schultz and his Bronx and Harlem based company in an even bigger feud. However, Owen had decided to do another mick a favor by passing on the word about Bob Carey's whereabouts.

"He's going by the alias of 'Sanborn,' and he's living at 220 West 104th Street," whispered the informant like the stoolies in those IRA movies, hat pulled down low over his eyes.

"Anything else, bud?"

The rat pushed a hundred dollar bill across the beer-stained bar towards Moran, nodding his head in a downward motion.

The Chicago kingpin examined the note in the dim light of the barroom before tossing it back with a growl.

"It's funny money!"

"Precisely," jeered the Judas. "Sanborn is playing the counterfeiting game these days."

"We can use it as bait," suggested Leo.

"The Duke of the West Side, as Damon Runyon has coined him, had the exact same idea."

"You mean Owen Madden?"

A raised forefinger served as a warning not to bandy the overlord's name so freely.

Another taxicab took them to the Upper West Side. It was easy as pie to find the correct apartment number. The two men had their game plan coordinated and all set to deploy.

"Who's there?" asked a muffled voice of a man from behind the door.

"We're in the market for more of these nice pieces of paper," called back Leo as he slipped the counterfeit hundred dollar bill beneath the door.

"Who sent you?"

"The Duke himself highly recommended you."

The sounds of a deadbolt being opened could be heard. Leo stood there smiling like an expectant merchant as the door slowly opened and he came into view. A Chicago Bears' forward thrust by the hefty shoulder of George Moran crashed in the door all of the way. A startled Bob Carey had no time to react as Leo Mongoven heaved him to the floor. Moran closed the door behind them.

"What's the rumpus about?" asked a woman as she approached behind the fallen Carey. A speeding bullet headed for the space between her baby blue eyes was the last thing she saw before she was engulfed by the eternal darkness.

"Rose!" cried out the fallen man as 'Bugs' snuggled his eager rod up against the temple of his skull.

"This is for boys back in the Clark Street garage," hissed Moran.

"You're Moran?"

"I'm Moran," snorted back Moran. "Isn't it just too bad for you that I didn't show-up at the garage like my boys?"

A piercing slug crushed its' way through the man's brain before he had the time to utter a comeback to the last remark. The two hoodlums barreled their way down the back stairway as other tenants rushed to the scene of the crime. Nobody there would be able to identify two gunmen from the Midwest when the police arrived. At any rate, the New York authorities were glad to be rid of yet another red hot for hire, so they ruled it a suicide. Within a few hours the boys were on a train heading out of Philadelphia for Cleveland. They would shake-off any would-be posse before they were home.

A few nights later George Moran was inside of his favorite Irish pub on Sheridan Road in Kenosha, Wisconsin where he was tossing back Old Log Cabin Canadian Whisky with Ellie O'Hara, the gambling czar of the immediate region. Ellie and George were friends from way, way back, but the Kenosha racketeer started to get antsy when Moran's tongue began to loosen with each passing highball.

"I just got back from New York?"

"Did you run into Owen Madden and Frank Costello?"

"I went to pay a visit to my old pal Bob Carey."

"I don't think I know him."

"He used to dress-up like a cop in Chicago in order to worm his way into the strongholds of other people."

"He dressed like a cop?"

"He did just that, Ellie, and so did his pals. It was a decoy in order to get into a certain garage on North Clark Street back on St. Valentine's Day…"

"I don't want to know, George."

"….in 1929."

"I'm deaf tonight!"

"They were hired by one Al Capone."

"I guess I'll be going George."

"It was revenge."

"Be seeing you, George."

"Bugs Moran's revenge!" roared out George the gangster.

PART THREE: *MCGURN IS PAID BACK IN FULL*

After the St. Valentine's Day Massacre was successfully pulled off in the winter of 1929 Jack McGurn, Al Capone's third-in-command, thought the world was his oyster and , furthermore, that he would one day even become the number one tribal chieftain of the Chicago Outfit. Although it hadn't been 'Machine Gun' Jack who had operated one of the two choppers used inside of the garage on North Clark Street seven years earlier, the entire scheme had been hatched by him. The Gusenberg Brothers, Jimmy Clark, Adam Heyer and the others were all dead and gone and out of the Outfit's hair, as well as the North Side, for good due to the blueprint Jack had put on the table in front of 'Scarface,' 'the Enforcer' and the other conspirators at the lonely resort in the green woodland of northern Wisconsin.

Jack had even been the one to recruit and instruct the hit squad: all former members of St. Louis Egan's Rats, an Irish gang that had migrated northward to Chicago to carve out new kingdoms for themselves. Nitti always referred to the Rats as 'the American Boys' to show his contempt for the outsiders, but Big Al always had welcomed them with open arms. It could always be said that Capone was a man without prejudices who was willing to hire muscle from outside of the Italian and Sicilian communities. In fact, Big Al had immediately agreed with Jack that it was wiser to use Irishmen in on a massive hit on an Irish gang rather than blow the cover with using gangsters that had dark complexions or were ethnic-looking. Jack, himself, stayed tucked inside of a hotel with a beautiful blond on that fateful winter morning when the bloody Valentine's was delivered to Moran's door. Jack's 'Blonde alibi,' as the newspapers termed his moll, kept him out of prison as a gunman; however, people in the know knew he was the mastermind of the entire operation.

Now the Death Squad of six who invaded the Moran gang's fortress on North Clark Street was virtually extinct itself. Fred 'Killer' Burke was serving a life sentence in prison for the murder of a police officer in Missouri. Raymond 'Crane Neck' Nugent had been missing for years and was believed to be dead. Bob Carey had shot himself in the head out in New York City. Fred Goetz had been 'paddy whacked' by the South Side O'Donnell brothers gang for an indiscretion. Gus Winkler had been machine gunned down after inheriting much of Bugs Moran's north side territory. The Outfit itself was the primary suspect in the destruction of Winkler.

That only left Claude 'Screwy' Maddox of the original six left to tell the tale. The hefty Irish hillbilly was a tough nut to crack because he could handle himself with his fists or a gun. He was one tough mick who also kept his own counsel and wasn't one to spill the beans. Maddox had also taken the added precaution of brown-nosing Frank Nitti. It was a wise decision on the part of Claude, for Mr. Nitti because the top cat once Capone was sentenced to eleven years in the federal penitentiary for income tax evasion. And there was the rub: Jack McGurn could never stomach brown-nosing to Frank Nitti.

What were to be the makings of a new gangland king had only served as a launch pin to his gradual demise. Once Big Al was shipped down to Atlanta Jack had found himself persona non grata in the daily structure of the Syndicate. Gone were the plush days of Prohibition, and the new venues of slot machines, numbers and gambling had been rapidly sealed off to him by you know who. He wasn't even invited to the corporate sit downs in Nitti's boardroom of directors. Murray Humphrey, Jake Guzik and Willie Heeney routinely failed to return his telephone calls and telegrams. Even the once friendly Ralph Capone, Al's brother, was giving Jack the cold shoulder. He was now as hard-up and as down-at-the-heels as many another American slob during the Great Depression that was ushered in after the stock Market Crash of October, 1929.

Steven G. Farrell

So there it was in a nutshell: the St. Valentine's Day Massacre, the Stock Market Crash and the ending of Prohibition had reduced the once rolling-in-dough Jack to a now a nickel and dime punk without a Mob. Life had just not treated him fairly. He often wondered if he had cursed himself when he had had his boys knife-up the famous singer Joey Lewis when he had wanted to bolt from McGurn's night club for a try-out in Hollywood. Joey had survived the attack and was now a popular night club stand-up comic while Jack's once hot spot was padlocked for good. Maybe the Jew had put the hex on him for the dirty deed.

If Jack McGurn didn't have enough problems on his plate to digest, he knew that Bugs Moran still nourished a strong grudge against him for the paddy whacking of seven of his disciples in 1929. Never mind that the Guseneng brothers and Jimmy Clark had richly deserved their just deserts after they had tried to assassinate him at least three times. Once they had even cornered him in a telephone booth. Irish Micks! It was sure as shooting that no Irishman alive ever saw the whole picture of things. The Celtic people were a race of madmen who acted on impulse alone without putting deeper thought into their actions. Jack had never been given to being paranoid. One could argue that it was his sharp instincts and street-wise intellectual acumen that had kept him alive on the mean streets of Brooklyn, and the even meaner streets of Chicago. He had survived and prospered during the bloodiest days of the beer wars fought between the North Side Irish and Germans and the Italian dominated Outfit on the South Side. He had displayed better footwork than Fred Astaire and Ginger Rogers when it came to dodging bullets and out-running gunmen on their missions for the enemies. It was still a creepy feeling to know that the burly bulk of Bugs Moran possibly lurked in every shadow in every alley throughout Chicago ready to leap out at him at any moment. The Irishman was taking his own sweet time like a Bengal Tiger stalking his victim and enjoying the psychological torment he was inflicting upon his fleeing victim.

"Moran wants me bad!" Jack had reminded himself hundreds of times every day since February 14, 1929. Seven long years was not long enough to cool off the hotter than hot Jack.

Jack was also fully aware that Bugs wasn't going to turn his head on a platter over to his hired galoots. No, the Big Mick wanted to do the job himself. McGurn's first thought was to get Moran before Moran got him, but the word had been sent out from the top (Capone and, later, Nitti) that Moran was to be left untouched. The stay of execution itself was a clue to Jack, the former prize fighter, that things weren't okay with him and the big shots. One could be of two minds about the saving of Moran: first, the Outfit was displaying its utter contempt by not fussing with him anymore

112

or, second, it meant that somebody upstairs in management was counting on Bugs to pay Jack a return on his St. Valentine's Day investment. The good-looking man by the Chicago crime media as 'Machine Gun' Jack was partial to the second explanation. He now had to hop from sleazy hotel to sleazy hotel in order to keep his whereabouts unknown. He changed his barbershops and diners as often as he changed his shorts in order to remain a man of mystery. The only point of contact he kept for the public were a string of bartenders strung-out throughout the North, South and West Sides of Chicago. It was Joe Gleason of *Finn McCool's Cool Spot* that had relayed the *Kiss of Judas* message to him in February of 1936.

"Ellie O'Hara is in town, Jack."

"Is he bored with the action up in Kenosha, Wisconsin, or what?" asked Jack.

"He's hanging around Chi-town with Burt McNamara and Mayo O'Brien."

"Three Wisconsin hicks in from the sticks to paint the town," laughed Jack, doling out his loose change for a scotch on the rocks. He no longer could expect the drinks to be on the house like in the rare old times.

"The word was dropped that they'd be bowling a few games at the Avenue Recreation Bowling Alley over on 805 North Milwaukee," said Gleason, adding, "Do you know it?"

Jack was immediately suspicious. Could it be a set-up by Nitti, or Moran?

"What of it?"

"Don't get frosty with me, Jack," said Gleason, offering up a free drink as a peace offering. "Ellie spilled the beans and said that one of his rivals up north was stepping out of line and robbing his bookies. The goon is an Italian and Ellie thought you could persuade him to lay-off in his native tongue…as it were."

"So it's business?"

"Mr. O'Hara must have meant business, for he paid me a sawbuck to pass the word on to you."

"Ellie has always been free and easy with his bankroll."

Jack had to think about it. After all, O'Hara, McNamara and O'Brien all had known links with Bugs Moran and Ralph Capone. Then, too, the Wisconsin mugs tended to avoid violence at all cost. Cash and negotiation was more their speed. It was just like those farmers to hire a wop to deal with another wop. The name of 'Machine Gun' Jack McGurn could be just the right tonic to scare-off a Kenosha greaser. He wondered what it would be worth for his time. He was going to ask for $1,000 but he'd settle for half of that amount. Who was he kidding? He'd settle for a tenth of that and a ham sandwich.

"They'll be there around midnight," said Gleason. "I'm off of my shift by then if you want me to tag along. You know, I'm related to McNamara and O'Brien?"

"Nah," huffed back Jack "I don't need a babysitter. Thanks just the same, Irish. Midnight, you say?"

"That it is, lad"

Jack McGurn took a long walk in the Loop to clear up his head in the frigid night's cold. He even ducked into a greasy spoon for several cups of hot coffee and the blue plate special. He wanted to be absolutely stone cold sober when he met the Mickey trio at the bowling alley. Never trust the Micks! He also wanted to come across as rough and ready for any muscle job that might be in the offering. He was down but not completely out. A decent paying job would warrant a visit to a tailor for a brand new suit. A sparkling pair of new shoes for his feet would be grand as well. Dang, he was starting to think like an Irishman. It felt even grander to once again be a force to be reckoned with. Jack would be the comeback kid of 1935.

"805 North Milwaukee," Jack barked at the taxicab driver who had looked long and hard into his mirror to size up his customer.

Jack enjoyed being recognized, but he patted the revolver tucked away beneath his winter overcoat for a sense of security. He normally avoided venturing into the north side of the city because it had the reputation of being the most violent section in all of Chicago. It was better to avoid any turf the Irish felt belonged to them.

Jack McGurn felt relieved to find that the bowling alley was still jumping with a horde of customers. There were bowlers galore, and the bar was still jammed packed with drinkers. He hustled a bottle of legitimate beer and then proceeded to hunt down his three friends. They were too engrossed in their own pin-whacking to notice his approach. Considering how late it was none of them was the worst for wear.

"Jack!" greeted Bret McNamara, whose main claim to fame besides his immense size was that he was sitting next to Willie Marks, one of Bugs Moran's bodyguards, on the night Willie was paddy whacked in a Wisconsin speakeasy.

"Take a load off, Jack, and join us in the next game," cajoled O'Hara, forever the glad hander.

Beers were drunk and business was discussed as the bowling alley trade grew sparser with the approach of dawn. Jack still had his wits about him, but he certainly was feeling mellower than when he had first walked into the dump. He was also feeling at the top of his game after bargaining with Ellie to a price of $750.00 to have a 'stern' talk with one Greg Chapelli of Twenty-Second Avenue and Columbus Park in Kenosha.

Jack's triumphs continued as he got off a perfect strike. His moment of jubilation was short lived as he turned around on the heels of his rented shoes to find that his sporting partners had vanished into thin air. His surprise escalated into downright panic when he viewed the two masked gunmen approaching him on tiptoes. He immediately recognized the stocky figure of his number one enemy. Moran had finally treed him. He had no time to react as several slugs ripped into him and sent his spastic figure flying onto the polished wooden lane. A friend and a brother of the slaughtered Pete and Frank Gusenberg gloated over the body for a moment before one of them, the huskier one, tossed something on top of the riddled chest of the corpse.

It was a gag card that read:

You've lost your job,

You've lost your dough,

Your jewels and cars and handsome houses,

But things could still worse you know…

At least you haven't lost your trousers.

Bugs Moran, ever the Irish prankster, had finally gotten the last laugh on 'Machine Gun' Jack; and James Gusenberg could now rest easily knowing that the boys who had died in the garage on North Clark Street on February 14, 1929 were finally avenged seven years and one day later on February 15, 1936. A good gambler could also receive good odds that Frank Nitti, the inheritor of Big Al's throne, wasn't sorry to see his one-time rival finally out of the picture. Some even speculated later on that it had been Frank who worked hand in hand with Bugs to set it all up.

"So long, Jack McGurn!" one of the gunmen called over his Irish shoulders.

Steven G. Farrell

PAPER 7

MERSEY BOYS
(BEATLES' STAGE PLAY)

DRAMATIS PERSONAE

Al Moran: A college professor from Chicago. He is roughly about 30. He is good-natured but can be tough if pushed. He is popular with the English because he is laid back and easy going. He is of a generous heart. He likes women and they like him, but he doesn't chase them except for Ginny Browne.

Ginny Browne: A student who is around 20 and is beautiful. She is tall and has a great body. Her hair is reddish brown. She is walking sexuality, but she isn't trashy or vulgar. She loves life and people. She is working class and speaks her mind. She loves Al but enjoys leading him on. She is such a powerful figure that even the four Beatles are in awe of her. Oddly enough, they back off of her for Al's sake.

John Lennon: A sassy college student who is a born rebel and troublemaker. He can be awfully rude. He is talented and has a good voice and he is proud of his abilities to write lyrics of songs and poems. He lost his father when he was young so he has a very conflicted view of adult males. Al is father figure, sort of as well as a mate. He insults Al but likes it when Al fights back. John wants success but he wants the Beatles to be their own men and independent. He calls Al Proffy Mo.

Paul McCartney: A teenager who is good looking and talented. He likes nice clothes and pretty girls (in that order). He is wants to make money and will do anything to make it big. He will compromise quicker than John. He is respectful and rude at the same time. He views Al as an elderly mate but one to be discarded if need be. He admires John but will stand his ground with him. He cheekily refers to Al as Uncle Albert (later a hit song).

117

George Harrison: The youngest one in the group. He is a bit naive but he is very confident because he comes from a stable family with a father, mother and siblings. He has a healthy respect for Al but also very warm. Paul is his equal but he is afraid of John. He is loyal to the Beatles above all. He refers to Al as Our Albert.

Ringo Starr: The oldest of the group and the last addition. He is respectful to everybody and very easy-going. He is a pleaser because he is unsure of his status within the Beatles. Al knows him the least of the 4 Beatles. He usually refers to Al as Professor or Doctor. He is noticeably shorter and homelier than his three band mates.

Gerry Marsden: A happy-go-lucky rock n roller and an art student. His group, Gerry & the Pacemakers, are a distant second to the Beatles in popularity but he doesn't care. He and Al like one another but they both pursue Ginny Browne.

Alan Williams: A middle-aged hurly-burly businessman of questionable moral and ethical character. He's very much a scouse stock character: sassy, kind and tough. He's not even remotely impressed by the Beatles of their chance at success. He likes them enough to find them the rare paying gig. He is axed completely from the Beatles scene as soon as they make it big.

Cynthia Powell: An art student who is a beautiful blond. She is very polite, formal and demure. She likes feel the glow off of her best friend Ginny. She is protective of John but she feels put upon by him. He doesn't completely respect her.

Brian Epstein: A record shop owner who is around 35 or so. He is handsome, refined, well-dressed and softly spoken. He is a homosexual and Jewish. He is the outside trying to fit in. He has a very strange relationship with the Beatles. He is protective and will spare no expense for success. There is an underlining current of sexuality between him and John.

Clancy Bartender: Should be Irish and charming. He's ready with a pint and a bit of the gab.

Waitress: She is still pretty and a little trashy. She warms up to al quickly. She likes to put down Alan Williams but she likes him. Alan claims she used to be a stripper.

Ferryboat Woman: A working woman, kind and talkative. She enjoys talking to Al the American tourist.

Errand Girl: About twenty and sexy. She'll even have sex with Al to get her hands on the Beatles.

Bob Wooler: The famous local DJ and the Emcee of the Cavern. He is the editor of *Mersey Beat*, the magazine.

Mrs. Lampkin: Al's attractive landlady who has her heart set on him. She calls Al 'Albie' and she likes to make him tea.

Florrie Hagen: A student at the Art College and a friend of Cynthia Powell and Ginny Browne. She's a bit of a suck up. She is Gerry Marsden's sometimes girlfriend. She has a childish competition going on with Ginny for the attentions of Gerry and, at times, Al.

Miss Hayes: Brian Epstein's personal assistant and factotum. She's very protective of Brian.

French Model: She earns extra money by posing in the nude at the Liverpool Art College. She speaks in French. She laughs at the English for their immature attitude about the naked body. She enjoys herself.

Pigtails: Another cute groupie who is willing to settle for Al if she can't have any of the Beatles.

Mersey Boys starts in Liverpool, England circa 1959 and finishes in the same city circa 2010, so the main characters like Al Moran and Ginny Browne visibly age.

ACT 1 SCENE 1

Setting: Liverpool 2009 flashes across the screen. A battered and old manuscript *Being a True Account of my Life with the Beatles' by Professor Albert Moran is below the date.* There is a cut to the Beatles playing at Shea stadium. On the stage, Steve Farrell is handling some letters.

Voiceover: Dear Uncle Adam, Uncle Al passed away in his sleep. He had been anticipating his death long before I arrived here in Liverpool, England to assist him in his final arrangements. His final days were peaceful. I have found a trunk-full of old black and white photographs from the Fifties and Sixties. One curious side note is that Uncle Al bequeathed to us his autobiography. It is mostly about his time spent with John Lennon and the Beatles. To me it reads like a secret history of the famed Beatles and the Mersey Beat days of the 1960's. I recall my mother, God Rest Her soul, bragging about how her brother was a lecturer of John Lennon at the local art college in Liverpool. However, I had never known that the relationship had gone much deeper. I wonder how much of his book is true. After all, Uncle Al was a master of that Midwestern cracker barrel style of humor. You know, all pulling your leg with a serious expression on his face, and then some hardcore facts popping up to the surface out of all of the myths, tall tales and Irish blarney. Anyway, I have an old Wisconsin Irishman to bury. I'll be back to Chicago in about a week.

Sincerely yours,

Steve

ACT 1 SCENE 2

Setting: Liverpool, 1959: The interior of an Irish pub. Young college students sit at tables while a more working class clientele lines the bar. A middle-aged American, **AL MORAN**, makes his way through the crowd to find a stool at the bar. He is a college professor by trade and a new arrival in Liverpool. He considers himself hip and with it. **AL MORAN** is listening to the strange accents all around him. He is newly arrived from Chicago, USA. **CLANCY THE BARTENDER** is at a bar.

AL: Could I get a draft beer?

Clancy: Wot's that, then, whacker?

AL: I can't understand a thing you're saying.

Clancy: Just using the Scouse on you, mate. It's the local lingo here in Liverpool. It's a pinch of Welsh, a dash of northern English, and several scoops of Irish thrown in for good measure. It'll grow on you, mate. Here you are.

Al: Thanks. It all sounds interesting.

Clancy: What brings you to our old port city, sir?

Al: I'm going to be taking up a professorship at the Liverpool Art College. My name is Albert Moran.

Clancy: I say, do you fancy C and W, old man?

AL: Is that more of the Scouse talk?"

Clancy: It's what we call Country and Western music. It's right gear to all of us Scousers.

AL: C and W is more of a southern thing; I'm from Chicago. We like jazz and blues music.

Clancy: We Scousers must be hillbillies, yokels and hicks, then, for we're daft for the sound. Slim Whitman and Ernst Tubbs, both Yanks, are top billers all over England.

Al: Southerners hate being called Yankees. I doubt if they'd be third billing even in Nashville.

[Al feels bad because he realizes he has hurt his new friend's feelings. He makes amends by ordering a fresh round.]

Al: Lemee get another, please.

[His attention is drawn to two pretty young women who have approached them at the bar. They are **GINNY BROWNE, CYNTHIA POWELL**, and **FLORRIE STAUDINGER,** three lovely students at the Liverpool Art College. One of the ladies attracts his attention. She must be the most beautiful woman has ever seen.]

Ginny: Two bitters, Squire Clancy.

Clancy: Well, well, well, are you all behaving like proper English ladies?

Ginny: Calling me English is a stab to me proper Irish heart.

Florrie: And my people are from Vienna, Austria

Clancy: Professor Albert Moran, I am pleased to introduce you to Cynthia Powell and Ginny Browne.

[Al can't take his eyes off of Ginny Browne.]

Al: The pleasure's all mine.

Ginny: You're a Yank!

Florrie: Oh, and he has such big shoulders just like a Yank.

Al: I'm direct from Chicago, Illinois.

Clancy: Yanks are very much in!

Cynthia: Do you swing to R and B?

Al: Is that anything like C and W?

Ginny: It's rhythm and blues, professor.

Al: Don't you like rock n roll?

Cynthia: Ah, roll over Beethoven. We heard of it.

[Ginny pulls Al to his feet and drags him by the hand over to juke box in the corner. Buddy Holly's *That'll Be the Day* is playing. Al is delighted as well as flustered when she drags him out on to the dance floor. She has some good moves. He's a bit awkward and clumsy. Others join them. Afterwards Ginny pulls Al off to a quiet corner, for she wants him to herself.]

Ginny: Did you bring any discs with you, like Elvis, Little Richard or Buddy for homesickness?

Al: I have stacks and stacks of them.

Ginny: Would it be dodgy of me to request if I may have a listen sometime?

Al: You're welcomed at any time.

Ginny: Fancy buying me a black and tan before the music starts?

Al: I could use one myself. Where's Clancy, is that his name?

[Ginny collars a passing Clancy.]

Ginny: Clancy, Squire Clancy, that is, two pints of Black and Tan. It's the Yank's first pull of the stout.

Al: I have had a Black and Tan before, on St. Patrick's Day.

Clancy: Will you be of Irish blood, sir?

Al: I'm half Irish.

Clancy: Half Irish! Well, you're about as close to Ireland as you can get without actually being there. Most of the people here in Liverpool are Irish. We call Liverpool the capital of Ireland.

[A young man with greasy hair and a defiance attitude slouches his way into the pub. He is carrying a guitar inside of a case. He spots Ginny and heads towards her.]

Al: It looks like Bob Dylan is here to liven up the barn dance for us.

Ginny: Who? You mean Johnny? He's a cross between Jesus Christ and Buddy Holly.

Al: The glasses explain Buddy but how does the Good Lord factor into it?

Ginny: He's a terrible lad that one but really he's a sweetie pie. Be wary of him, Professor; he's one of your students at the Arty and he eats instructors up with his kippers....that is if he shows for class.

[JOHN LENNON stares at Ginny, up and down. She returns the stare. John gives Al a dirty look and approaches them.]

John: Who is the old gaffer, luv?

Al: Should I buy you a brew?

Ginny: A brew! Oh, how Yankee. Yes, please do but you'll not be able to shake him after. He's a sponge.

[John takes the pint of beer out of Ginny's hands and drains it. He dares Al to say something.]

Al: You're pretty cocky if you ask me.

John: Who's asking?

Ginny: Give him time to warm up to you, sir.

John: Ginny here bestowed a majestic knee-trembler upon thee yet for services rendered to Her Majesty?

Al: Huh? Should I order another round, Miss Browne?

Ginny: At the college I'm Miss Browne. The rest of the time I'm Ginny. And I'll call you Al.

Al: Maybe I shouldn't be doing this, if you're my students and all.

Ginny: Don't be a square!

[Al tries his luck with John.]

Al: What sort of stuff do you play, man?

John: I don't do any of me own stuff, granddad. Not yet, anyway. I play the standards: Elvis, Buddy, Chuck and such.

Al: I hope you put a kick in your licks.

John: Are you a Yank?

Al: I'm an American, yes.

John: So you're just off the bloody ship?

Ginny: Guess again, darling; he's our new instructor over yonder at the college.

John: What's your game, Ginny?

Ginny: Let me introduce you to Professor Albert Moran.

John: So you're Al Capone from Chicago.

[Al is beginning to sour on the young man; but he doesn't want to appear weak before Ginny.]

Al: Don't say it if you can't spit it out correctly.

John: Wasn't Moran another gangster in Chicago who put in the boot to Capone?

Al: Yeah, you're talking about Bugs Moran. He was my great-great uncle.

John: Well, I'll be. Mr. Bugs Bunny. You're a bloody rabbit. Do you like your carrots cooked or raw, doc?

Al: I like my carrots far away from drunks who can't hum a tune, much less sing or play a guitar.

[Gin burst out laughing but John only glares a long moment before slamming down his empty glass and storming back to the stage. Al attempts to make peace by sending a fresh drink up to the angry singer.]

Ginny: Round one goes to the Yank!

[John, in a snit, makes his way to setup on the tiny makeshift stage. Cynthia and Florrie join Al and Ginny).

Cynthia: What's wrong with, John? He didn't even say 'hello' to me.

Florrie: Something is always eating that one, Cynthia. He's so moody.

Cythia: Have done with it, Florrie.

Florrie: And, Ginny, quite hogging the professor. I want to get to know him too.

Ginny: Go ply your trade on the docks, luv.

Cynthia: Ginny, you're so rude.

Florrie: That's just Gin being Gin.

[Ginny glares at Florrie as steers Al away.]

Al: Do you like that Johnny?

Ginny: He's just in a snit. John Lennon is a lovable swine. He'll grow on you.

Al: Warts grow on people too.

Ginny: I suggest we retreat for tonight and let him simmer down. He'll try to knacker you when he's up there.

Al: To hell with the punk!

Ginny: He likes you, Al. You're both cut from the same cloth.

Al: I don't know about that. By the way, what is a knee-trembler?

Ginny: John is a terrible, terrible lad, really.

Al: Now I'm dying to know what it is.

Ginny: You'd already be dead if you knew exactly what it is. I'll show you if you promise not tell a soul.

Al: You have my sincere promise.

[Ginny takes Al by the hand and leads him outside. She guides him to a secluded spot in the night. They are safe in the dark of an alley.]

Ginny: Get up against the wall, Al.

Al: What? Like this?

[The sounds of unzipping and heavy breathing can be heard.]

Ginny: Are you knees trembling yet?

ACT 1 SCENE 3

Setting: A rather rundown hallway, day. It is the first day of classes so students and professors rush to their assigned classroom. A visibly nervous **AL MORAN**, a briefcase in hand, watches the students entering the room. He steps in to address his new students. The buzzing stops as he approaches the lectern. He spots **GINNY BROWNE** sitting off to the side. She is next to **CYNTHIA POWELL**. She smiles at him and lowers his eyes. **FLORRIE STAUDINGER** waves to him.

Florrie: We're here to see you off to a good start, professor.

Al: Good morning, class. I'm Dr. Moran and I will be your lecturer in Art History for this term. Oh, by the way, if you think I'm talking funny it's not because I'm from Birmingham.

[There is delighted laughter.]

Al: And I'm not a Cockney from London. I'm an American from Chicago and I'm certain you'll soon get used to my Midwestern accent. And who knows?—Maybe in time I will acquire some of your diction. I recognize Miss Ginny Browne and Cynthia Powell.

Cynthia: Oh, Professor Moran, I am so eager to take this art history class with you!

Ginny: My knees have been trembling ever since I found out your teaching this class, Al…er…Dr. Al….Moran.

Al: And where's Mr. John Lennon? John Lennon is not here for his first day of class?

[Cynthia puts up her hand. Al nods to her.]

Steven G. Farrell

Cynthia: Johnny, I mean Mr. John Lennon will probably not be here today, Professor Moran. Headache, I should think.

[Several snickers greet her remark. **GERRY MARSDEN,** a popular student at the college and another rock n roller, decides to get involved. His classmates anticipate him to be flippant.]

Gerry: Our John will probably have a headache the entire week.

Florrie: But Gerry and I shall always be here on time. Right, Gerry?

Ginny: Oh, please, get your nose out.

Al: And you are…Mr. Gerry Marsden.

Gerry: At your service, sir. The entire term is more likely for our Johnny.

Florrie: Gerry is me fellow.

Ginny: Lucky Gerry.

Al: So Mr. Lennon is a slacker?

Gerry: Maybe you'll eventually smell the rotter, sir. He smells like fish n chips, that one does.

Ginny: It hangs all over him, that.

Cynthia: You're all terrible liars.

Gerry: Cynthia loves our John, you see?

Al: He may be a slacker but he can sure rock and roll; but don't tell him I said that. Now let's continue with the roll call, not rock and roll, shall we?

[A voice can be heard singing outside of the classroom.]

John: Sugar in the morning, sugar in the evening, sugar at suppertime.

[Some of the students are aghast; others are amused. The door opens and in walks **JOHN LENNON.**]

John: Bless me soul if it isn't Mr. Al Capone from Chicago, relative of Bugs Moran, he is.

Al: I'm pleased to see you again, Mr. Long John Silver.

John: I'll just have a seat, if you don't mind.

Al: Ah, but that's only on Saturdays when we're off duty, but for the rest of the week you're Mr. Lennon the serious student and I'm Dr. Moran the serious lecturer.

126

John: I can't be certain of all that.

Al: Please join the rest of the class and please listen with attention to my lecture. Now that we are all settled, let's begin. We are going to start with *in media res*, as it were, with Vincent van Gogh.

ACT 1 SCENE 4

Setting: In the hallway after class, day. The class is exiting.

Al: Lennon, your presence has an electrifying effect on the rest of the student body.

John: Does it now, Dr. Moran?

[Gerry approaches from the classroom.]

Al: Yes. It'd be great if we could have you in earlier so we can savor your presence a bit longer.

Cynthia: Let's go, Johnny, and get some lunch!

John: I'm coming, you go on ahead.

Ginny: Johnny, you leave the professor be now.

John: Earlier it is. Ten minutes, certainly.

Al: Five minutes before the bell rings would suffice.

[John Lennon exits, after the girls.]

Gerry: He won't keep his word, mate.

Florrie: John is in an open stage of rebellion. He thinks he's a Teddy boy.

Al: I can see that, thanks.

Gerry: If you fancy an earful of home grown American music have a listen to Radio Luxembourg. It's a radio station for your fighting lads over in Germany.

Florrie: We'll always keep you company, professor. Right, Gerry?

ACT 1 SCENE 5

Setting: Outside of the college, day. It is about the fourth week of classes and Al is walking down a street with his briefcase when he sees **JOHN LENNON** up ahead. He is wearing a black leather jacket and smoking a cigarette. He is accompanied by young men who are also clad in black

127

leather jackets and they have cigarettes dangling from their lips. The two youngsters are **PAUL MCCARTNEY** and **GEORGE HARRISON**.

John: Dr. Moran! Over here!

Al: John, long time, no see! Your attendance is lacking and I want to see some of the items required for your portfolio straight away.

John: Sorry about that, guv. Me auntie has been sick and on me hands these past weeks.

[The two boys twittered at John's rudeness. One is dark and handsome and the other is rail thin and has an elfin look. They are both respectful and disrespectful at the same time.]

Al: Oh, I hope she's on the mend soon for we all miss you at the Art College.

George: Hon, mister, his aunt, that'll be Mrs. Mimi Stanley, this autumn time. Doctor Roberts, most respected in Woolton, has announced her fit only just this after.

Al: Oh, I see, I guess. Are you two art students?

George: I'd be lucky to earn one O level much less get into any college in England. Me auntie doesn't have the influences and pounds to get me into the arty like Jonny's auld one.

John: Have done with it, son. It was me bleeding natural talents that battered down the castle door. The Professor hasn't seen art like the stuff me pencil wheels to life.

Paul: My name is Paul McCartney and I'm at the Liverpool Institute for now but soon I'll be under your tutelage at the Liverpool Art College. My father, Jim McCartney, wants me to read literature at Oxford.

John: That one won't be happy until he has you working at the Cotton Exchange with him. Stick with the song writing and leave the art to me. There is only one bloody painter per group.

Al: Group as in gang?

John: No, mate, we are a Band. You know, with guitars and such.

Al: Yes, right.

George: I play lead guitar. My name is George Harrison.

John: This is Al Moran and he's just off of the boat from America so don't slag the poor man until he gets his footing here on foreign soil.

Al: It's nice meeting you, Mr. Harrison.

George: Mr. Harrison is me Da and I'm just George.

Paul: It was our pleasure, professor. We're sorry to rush but we have to catch the number seventy-one.

George: Me da is at the wheel and we ride for free.

Al: Just a moment. I want to invite you all to a session we're having in our drawing class next Monday. We have a live model. It's a nude.

Paul: I'll be there, sir, and I'll show you I can draw too.

John: It's not a peep show, Paulie. Bring a regulation drawing kit or you'll get the boot.

George: I'll just be off then. Ta, lads.

Paul: Bye now, Professor Al.

Al: Nice guys.

John: They're gear in me band, Johnny and the Moon Dogs. We used to be the Quarrymen, named after me old school. We're floating the idea around of Long John and the Silver Beetles.

Al: That name is way too long. The word Beetles stands better alone. Maybe you can have fun with the name by changing the second 'e' in Beetles to link your name to the Beat Generation.

John: Sod bloody Jack Kerouac and the Beatniks. We're a right proper English band, not American.

Al: Ah, well, I'm off because I have drawings to grade.

John: Bloody Beatles with an 'a'. That's just a crazy!

ACT 1 SCENE 6

Setting: College classroom, day. Al is trying to control a mob of students inside of his classroom. Students are giggly and others are shouting. The word has gotten around campus that there was too be a nude model in Dr. Moran's drawing class, so he is contending with a full house.

Ginny: You're going to put Allan Williams and his nudie nightclubs out of business, professor.

Al: Very funny, dear.

Cynthia: Oh, how immature people are acting. They should all grow up. Professor, we must clear the entire area for only the serious students. Here, I will help.

Al: Thank you. That goes over there.

Gerry: I put on clean socks for the occasion, Professor Moran.

Florrie: You'd never do that for me, Gerry.

Al: Your socks are different colors.

Gerry: Well, you know, it was, ah, early.

Ginny: You could have washed up as well, Gerry.

Al: This is a madhouse. Class! Class! Remember you're getting graded on this assignment, please.

Gerry: Let's sic the dogs on them, Dr. Moran.

[The uproar grows louder when a pretty young **FRENCH MODEL** walks into the room wearing nothing but a robe. She is followed by a lecherous John and a trembling Paul. Paul clutches his drawing kit. The two take empty seats behind Cynthia and Ginny. The French Model is offered a stool by Al.]

MODEL: (In English) Thank you, doctor. (In French) My, how horny your class is.

Al: I really thank you for modeling for us.

Model: (In English) It is my pleasure to serve the world of art anywhere in the world, including Liverpool.

Al: Make yourself comfortable and we'll start in the moment.

Model: (English) You may start anytime, professor. (French) At least you American; these English stink to high heaven!

Al: Quite right.

Paul: Dr. Moran, I'm here. Just see how I draw. I am quite good, you know.

John: You mean drool, not draw.

Paul: Shut up, mate, you're no better.

Al: Good to have you, McCartney. Find a seat. Some of these people are just leaving.

John: I'm about to get the first A of me entire collegiate career, Professor Al!

Cynthia: John, grow up! Have a little class for this project.

Ginny: Oh, he's growing...up....they all are, including our professor.

Cynthia: Ginny, don't you go encouraging them any.

Florrie: What are you on about?

Al: Attention! Attention, everyone! If you're not on the roster for this class get out of here before I throw you out. Let's go, now!

John: That's telling them, Proffy Mo.

Al: I'll handle this, Lennon. Out! Out! No idle onlookers. This is a small screening for my select students and guests only, that's it!

[Paul reluctantly stands up.]

John: He doesn't mean you, Paulie. Dr. Al invited you here, didn't he?

Paul: Yeah, I guess you're right there, Johnny. Thanks, Uncle Al!

[The room is cleared pout of the thrill-seekers and Al starts to confidently take control of the situation. He points to a stool in front of the classroom for the model. She smiles, takes her place and disrobes. The room is silent but nobody says anything.]

Gerry: Blimey!! I forget me specs!

Florrie: you don't need them, mate. She's getting enough eye as it is.

Al: All serious artists must first learn how to draw the basic outlines of the human body. I'll be going around checking to see how you're faring.

Cynthia: I think I'm feeling a little ill.

Ginny: You're a little ill at ease. Just relax and draw.

John: Just be happy we don't have to draw Moran in the buff. That would make me bloody sick to me guts.

Cynthia: You're not helping matters, John.

Ginny: Look at Paulie. He's beet red!

John: His hands are shaking too.

Paul: I'm just fine, leave me alone. I'm trying to concentrate on me work.

Cynthia: He's doing fine.

Al: Less chatting from Lennon and Browne and more drawing would be what the doctor orders.

Steven G. Farrell

Ginny: I know the doctor's orders for that randy Yank.

John: Oh, professor, will your take a peek at what I'm peeking at, please?

Al: Lennon, how did you ever get into an Art College?

Paul: It was his auntie's money

Gerry: Why to put the boot in, Paul?

Al: Silence is golden.

John: But my eyes still see.

Model: (English) Fag.

Al: What?

Model: (English) Smoke, please

Al: Anybody have a pack of cigarettes on them? And some matches.

Gerry: Coming right up, sir.

Florrie: Stay right here. I'll do the delivery.

The Model puts a cigarette and blatantly ignores a light from Florrie. She faces Al.

Model: (English) Fire, please. (French) Merci.

Al: Sure.

Model: (French) You talk like a man but tremble like a school boy.

Ginny: She's making the professor's day.

[Paul starts to breath heavily and finally stands up and rushes out of the room.]

Paul: I'm not ready for the art college yet. I'm off and running.

John: He's off and running….to the toilet.

Ginny: He's hard all over.

John: He's glad all over.

Cynthia: You two are sickening and you're making me ill again.

Al: If this nonsense doesn't stop this very instance I'm going to send her home and start lecturing again.

[The students let out a collective groan.]

Gerry: Why punish us for another bloke's erection?

Al: Marsden!

John: Professor, I need to go to the toilet for ten minutes meself....make that five.

Ginny: That'll be closer to one minute, I should calculate.

Cynthia: This isn't anatomy class.

Model: (English) How truly amazing it is what a pair of naked breasts can do in this sex-crazed land.

Florrie: Can somebody please tell me what's going on here.

Model: (French) Dismiss the class, you fool. We can make love like animals, my American grizzly bear.

ACT 1 SCENE 7

Setting: Classroom, day. A few weeks have passed on by since the notorious live nude session in the classroom. AL MORAN is watching the clock as well as grading papers. There is a gentle rap at the office door. Al frowns before responding.

Al: You may enter.

[Ginny Browne slowly opens the door and slowly curves her head inwards with a cautious look. She then smiles.]

Ginny: Dr. Moran? Al!

Al: Miss Browne. Ginny, if we're not on a professional basis just now.

Ginny: Johnny wanted to remind you about the Beatles gig at the Jac Coffee House tomorrow night. It'll be absolutely smashing! The scene will be happening, even if he and the lads are off tune.

Al: Didn't you promise me I could paint you?

Ginny: Maybe I'll sit with you myself or maybe I won't sit with you. I'm asking myself why I should worry over your comforts; do you know what I mean, Al?

Al: I'm sorry I asked.

Ginny: You sound like a bloke who has big ideas.

Al: A simple "buzz-off buster" will get me to back-off if that's what you want.

Ginny: Really, Al, I like you but let's have fun and not get ahead of ourselves. Is that okay by you?

Al: Fine by me.

Ginny: It's a wee bit early but I could go for a drop and I'd be civil if you were to suggest one.

Al: Maybe you can sit for me today.

Ginny: Why not ask that French tart to sit for you.

Al: That's uncalled for, gin.

Ginny: Another time, mate. Never mind, then. You'll see me bare soon enough and we won't have any canvases to get in the way.

[Ginny Browne exits.]

ACT 1 SCENE 8

Setting: A Pub, day. Ginny and Al walk into the same pub where they had been the night John had been playing up on the stage. The same **IRISH BARTENDER** waits on them.

Bartender: Ah, the Irish-American gent and the lovely tart from the neighborhood.

Al: We'll take two bitters, Clancy, my bold man.

Clancy: Well, now, haven't you taken to the place.

Ginny: Do you have a copy of the *Daily Worker* somewhere about the place?

Clancy: Coming right up, luv. It's a good issue, been reading it meself.

Al: Is that a dirty commie rag?

Ginny: You Yankees don't cotton much to Marx do you?

Al: We sure don't. Joe McCarthy and the Red Scare has driven any American Communists underground. I'm a Democrat myself; but no Communist. Besides, it isn't likely there's ever going to be any workers' revolution in the States since the Russians cocked theirs up.

Ginny: Don't be such a sourpuss of an industrialist.

Al: I'm a realist. As long as the workers have their beer, sex and television they'll continue to pop out babies for the factories and the salt mines. Most people are destined to be laborers.

Ginny: You're not in the lecture hall, luv.

Al: I can't help myself.

Ginny: Be a dear and rub my shoulders for me.

[The bartender arrives with two pints and a newspaper and he smiles at Al who has begun to massage Ginny's back.]

Ginny: If you must know, I am looking for articles about the Beat and Jive scene here in Liverpool. The *Daily Worker* is the only paper in town who writes about the musical scene. Save the political talk for your professor friends.

Al: Do they ever write about John Lennon's band?

Ginny: They wouldn't waste their time on that lot. Beatles, my foot! What a dreadful name. He's just trying to rip-off buddy Holly and the Crickets. They'll not travel far with a name like the Beatles.

Al: At least the Beatles is an easy name to remember.

[Gin looks over her shoulder and gives Al a gentle look before kissing him. He is startled but pleased.]

Ginny: John and his lads have never rated very high with anybody in Liverpool. They just don't fit in very well, always rebelling and all. Only you seem to care....and maybe me a little bit. Rory Storm and the Hurricanes are the big headliners in this old port city.

Clancy: Don't forget about Gerry and the Pacemakers.

Al: Who?

Ginny: Al, you know Gerry Marsden, the daft lad with the goofy smile in my morning class. He sings ballads while Rory screams and hip hops all about the stage like a mad man!

Al: Is Gerry a close friend of yours?

[Ginny flashes him and angry glare before choosing to ignore his question. Instead, she buries her head in the newspaper.]

Al: What?

[Al stops rubbing her back and sinks back into his seat. He is upset at his own envy.]

Ginny: Listen to this, Al: "The Mersey sound is the voice of 80,000 crumbling households and 30,000 people on the dole." It sounds like Liverpool sure enough.

Al: Tell me about the Mersey Sound.

Ginny: The named it after our dirty Mersey River. It's English R&B mixed with American C&W. It's Irish too. You'll get an earful of it tomorrow night if you show-up at the Jac. I'll be there by your side for some of it.

Al: Do you want me to show up, Ginny Browne?

Ginny: Suit yourself, luv.

Al: Why do you have to be so hardboiled?

Ginny: Clancy, another Hodgson for me. Make it a small one, please.

Clancy: Sure thing, luv.

Al: I'll take a Guinness, Mr. Clancy.

Clancy: Yes, sir, Mr. Yank.

Ginny: It's high time that the paper is noticing our rocking lads from Liverpool. We haven't had much good news around this port since the 14-18 war.

Al: You mean World War One? That's what we call it.

Ginny: Leave it to the Yanks to change the name of a bloody war.

[Clancy delivers the drinks.]

Clancy: So the guv here is into "Scouse Swing."

Al: If that's another name for the Mersey Sound you can put me down for a 'yes.' I didn't realize there was a whole unique sound.

[Ginny pulls Al close to her. She kisses his ear before whispering.]

Ginny: Talk only to me, my sweet, or you'll have a major conversation going with Clancy and the crowd. You're the American here.

Al: If that's the way you want it.

Ginny: You're a proper gent when you have a mind to be. I'll always have you remember that I'm not a Rutty Judy. I go my own way!

Al: What is a Rutty Judy?

Ginny: I'll wise you, mate; it's a bar whore.

Al: Oh, well. You're a nice girl, Ginny.

Ginny: Am I, now?

Al: Yes. You're jumping down my throat for no reason.

Ginny: Ach, now, sweetie pie, I didn't mean to hurt your feelings.

Al: Give me another kiss, luv.

ACT 1 SCENE 9

Setting: Day time, outside. Al is walking aimlessly around to kill some time. He sees a sign that reads **ALBERT DOCKS**. The daylight starts to fade and he decides to take a ride on the ferryboat that works the Liverpool-Speke's line. He watches the rolling waves of the Mersey and approaching shore of Birkenhead. The musical version of *This Boy* can be heard in the background. He sits down next to a woman sipping tea from a paper cup. She has on a working man's cap and Al thinks it makes her look cute. She is in her early twenties and he wonders what she does for a living.

Al: Gray day, huh?

Ferryboat Woman: It is indeed. It's Liverpool weather.

Al: I have gotten to where I like it…the Liverpool weather, I mean.

Ferryboat Woman: Are you on holiday, sir?

Al: I'm a professor at the Art College.

Ferryboat: Fancy that. I wanted to go to college but a job is a job. I guess this old river has gotten me hooked.

Al: You work on this ferryboat?

Ferryboat Woman: Anything wrong with that, mate; it's honest work…and I'm good at it.

Al: I think it's cool. I had expected the jobs to be held like older guys like myself.

Ferryboat Woman: Oh, you're not as old as that, luv.

[She reminds him of Ginny. She gets up to get back to work. He doesn't want her to leave.]

Al: Do you normally work this shift?

Ferryboat Woman: Maybe I do, maybe I don't.

[The ferry lands at the dock.]

Ferryboat Woman: Not going ashore, sir?

Al: No, I'm just on broad for the ride. I'm just a tourist. I'll glad to pay extra. I'm going back across to Liverpool.

Ferryboat Woman: No need to trouble about it, sir. Enjoy your stay with us. Beneath all of the dust it's a grand place. I've been here me entire life. But if they ever stop this old tug's run, I'll pack me things and head over to Detroit in the big parish across the ocean. I have a brother in Detroit, Michigan.

Al: I enjoyed speaking to you.

Ferryboat Woman: Likewise, sir. This is Speke and Speke is where I stop.

[Al is disappointed when she gets off at the stop. Al stays on his bench.]

Al: See you, miss.

Ferryboat Woman: Ta, luv. I wouldn't mind see you too. You caught me at the end of me day. Next time try getting on this ole tug earlier. We can have a longer chat.

Al: Yes, you can tell me all about Speke.

[She is off and leaves him with a sly wink.]

Ferryboat Woman: And you can tell me all about Amerikay.

Al: I'm a professor at the Liverpool Art College.

Ferryboat Woman: So you teach all of our young painters and such. How charming.

Al: Could I interest in you in sitting for us some day?

Ferryboat Woman: Would I have to shed me clothes?

Al: Not necessarily. The last time we went that route I had to call in the riot squad.

Ferryboat Woman: I'd do it... for some, others no.

Al: Here's my card.

Ferryboat Woman: Ta, Dr. Moran.

[He wistfully watches her walk away. He feels better about life until he starts worrying about Ginny.]

ACT 1 SCENE 10

Setting: Coffee Shop, at night. Al is walking down the street. He finds the correct entrance and enters. The place has some younger, college-aged students. Al recognizes several of his students who wave and call out his name. Up on a tiny stage he sees **JOHN LENNON, PAUL**

MCCARTNEY and **GEORGE HARRISON** huddled together in a discussion. Al approaches the group.

John: Get in tune or I'll thump you.

[Paul visibly flinches but he recovers when he sees Al.]

George: Professor Moran.

Paul: Hello, Dr. Al. Take a seat as I play a smashing opening chord on *Twenty Flight Rock.*

Gerry Marsden: Dr. Moran, we're over here.

[Al feels pains stabbing inside of him as he joins Gerry and Ginny at a table.]

Waitress: What's your pleasure, handsome?

Al: Stout!

Gerry: It isn't a boozer, sir. Only coffee, tea, orange juice and such served on the premises. Join Ginny and I later for a real nightcap.

Florrie: I'm so delighted to join in on the fun.

Waitress: And what's wrong with a cup of good English tea?

Al: English tea it shall be, my good woman.

Gerry: Mr. Williams, over here!

[**ALLAN WILLIAMS**, the owner of the coffee house, joins the table.]

Williams: What's all the shouting about, Marsden?

Gerry: I want to prove to you that we're attracting a tonier crowd these days. Let me introduce you to Professor Moran of the Liverpool Art College. We're cleaning up the naughty 8 district that gives our fair city such a black eye.

Williams: Glad to hear it, lad; now if we could only class-up the Beat and Jives bands around here we'd be on a roll.

Al: I like your place here, Mr. Williams.

[The two shake hands.]

Williams: I own several clubs in the area.

Waitress: Strip joints, he means.

Williams: Hush, darling.

Steven G. Farrell

Waitress: Tell the nice gent about your nudie dive over on Steel Street.

Williams: Well, luv, you don't mind taking off your clothes, now do you?

[Everybody shares a laugh. Williams pulls Al off from the others.]

Williams: Would you happen to have any ties with any American record labels back home? We have a good thing going here and I rather think I'd like the Yanks pick-up on it before the Germans.

[Gerry pops over Williams shoulder to listen.]

Gerry: Are you getting all of the lads a record deal, Mr. Williams?

Williams: I was thinking of Rory Storm and the Hurricanes, not about the rest of you dole boys. Just listen to their noise when they are playing!

Gerry: We all have talent.

Williams: You boys all have talent for painting the walls of me shithouse.

Paul: George will now play some raunchy 5 note blues riff from Arthur "Guitar Boogie" Smith. Let's have a nice hand for George Harrison.

John: And let's have a nice handout for Lennon and McCartney.

[Ginny decided to get Al's goat by kissing Gerry all over his face. Al responds by moving to another table filled with his students including Cynthia who greet him with open arms. A livid Florrie chases after him.]

Florrie: a want a kiss right now, professor.

Cynthia: What's gotten in to you?

Florrie: Her! Ginny Browne is stealing Gerry away from me.

Cynthia: Children, behave.

[Florrie kisses Al and glares back at Ginny and Gerry. They laugh at her.]

John: Tommy Moore, our drummer, shall now start us all marching to the beat of *Blue Suede Shoes.*

Williams: Get professional before I put in the boot!

[John troops his band over to Al's table. John notices Ginny with Gerry.]

John: Is the tart doing you wrong, Al?

Al: She's a big girl, John.

John: Let's march over there and punch them both out. Marsden needs his ears pulled for him.

140

Al: What if we lost?

John: I fought the Brownie and the Brownie won.

Ginny: Have done with it, Johnny, you swine.

Paul: Mr. Williams, have you meet the great Dr. Moran from the windy City of Chicago, Wisconsin in the USA?

Williams: I just met the bloke. Nice and all but he doesn't have any pull in entertainment like Lew Grade.

Paul: He's a scholar and I wager he speaks German.

John: And how would you know that, son, if you're not even a college student?

Paul: That doesn't mean anything.

George: Our Dr. Albert is full of manuscript reading and arcane knowledge.

Williams: I'm planning a trip over to Hamburg, Germany to pitch the Mersey sound to the krauts.

John: That'll learn the buggers for World War Two.

[Ginny pulls Al away.]

Ginny: Don't have any of it. Al. Williams is the local bullshit artist. He's filling the lads' heads with impossible dreams.

[Williams pulls Al away from Ginny's hold.]

Williams: Can you speak German natural and in a conversation?

Al: My grandparents were from Berlin and I served in the Army over in Stuttgart for two year.

Williams: So you know a thing or two about the Rhineland, then?

George: Our Albert was a short-haired squaddie like Elvis was in Freidberg. He can do more than order a lager.

Williams: The Christmas holiday will be upon us soon. We could set up something for then.

Al: It might just work. Let me think about it. I think that the Beatles are a talented group.

Ginny: Come with me, luv.

Al: Now? But I just got here! What happened to your friend?

Ginny: I said right now!

Al: I'd conducting business. I think Mr. Williams is on to something. We might just take John's band and if Mr. William's has a gig in Germany then we can start a tour. It seems like all of the pieces are in place in this City and the time is right for a big change. I got a feeling...

[Ginny forcefully drags Al out of the pub. In the night air she begins to kiss him. A foghorn can be heard in the background.]

ACT 1 SCENE 11

Setting: College Classroom, day. **FERRYBOAT WOMAN** is posing in front a very select group of advanced students. **GINNY** is sitting between **JOHN** and **AL. CYNTHIA** is next to John.

[**Florrie** is next to Al. They are all painting including Al.]

Ferryboat Woman: This is chillier than riding the Ferryboat in January.

Al: We appreciate your visit.

John: And we appreciate your...

Cynthia: Don't get anything started, John.

John: I was only going to say we appreciate her bravery in facing the cold.

Ginny: We're all business today. You'd think you never saw a pair of well-formed...

Cynthia: Don't encourage him, Gin.

Gin: I was only going to say we appreciate her well-formed eye lashes.

Ferryboat Woman: Your college is full of music hall comics, professor.

Al: I ignore most of their nonsense.

Gin: And we ignore most of your lecturing.

John: Ah, put the boot in, Gin, luv.

Florrie: Why can't we paint naked men for a change?

Ginny: For once Florrie has asked a brilliant question. I'd like a bloke with a right big...

Cynthia: Ginny, you're being cheap.

John: Well, Al is as cheap as they come.

Ferryboat Woman: So much disrespect for a fine professor.

John: Never you mind, luv, we all love our proffy mo. Gin loves him the most.

Ginny: I'll batter your teeth out, one by one, mate.

Al: Focus on your canvases. John I need to see some substantial improvements in your work. Thus far I haven't been impressed.

John: If you don't fancy me works then you mustn't be much of a Greenwich Village rebel intellectual. I don't think you have a real understanding of it.

Al: I'm from the North Side of Chicago, not New York. But regardless of locale, I am indeed not digging your scene.

John: I'd think a real American beatnik would have more appreciation of the sublime.

Al: You need more substance to be sublime.

John: Maybe I need more drawings of naked men with huge dicks?

Ginny: I hate you, John Lennon, with all of my might.

Al: This is a college, John, and not a pub.

[She storms out of the room.]

Cynthia: Can't you leave off tormenting her, John. You know how she feels about the professor.

Florrie: Oh, fill me in on the gossip. I always felt he was rather sweet on me.

Ferryboat Woman: I think our professor can set his sights higher than mere school girls.

Florrie: Are you addressing me?

Ferryboat Woman: I'm addressing the good doctor.

Cynthia: Come on, Florrie, let's find Gin before she jumps into the Mersey.

Cynthia and Florrie leave. The Ferryboat Woman is obviously happy but John and Al talk around her as they paint.

Al: You're obsessed with the vulgar, Lennon. Why is that? Ginny is a sweet gal.

Lennon: I know what her obsession is with, mate.

Al: Oh, so now you're a regular Sigmund Freud?

John: It bothers you, Al. Her, I mean. It's serious, mate, I can see it before me very eyes. Don't tread on me, son. We're mates to an extent. Own up to it! She's daft but she'll come around. She likes you, too. She isn't all that sweet, but you're right, she is something special. Now, I'm off to Teddy's Life Session in Room 71. Some bird is painting me portrait. I should charge her for me services.

Al: Cheeky, John.

John: The lads and I are playing one of the local strip tease clubs, but we'd rather you didn't drop by unless you're desperate and you want your Uncle John to fix you up with one of the talents. Otherwise, you can find us over at the Jac on any given Sunday afternoon. We go there in hopes that Allan Williams has booked us a date. Later, mate!

[John exits.]

Al: Now I can fully concentrate upon you.

Ferryboat Woman: And I can fully concentrate upon you.

Al: You are the most fetching of women working the Mersey line.

Ferryboat Woman: And you're the smoothest talking Yankee roamer working the Mersey line.

Al: Can I see you more of you.

Ferryboat Woman: Gladly.

[She stands up and spins around for Al.]

Al: I mean can I take you out for a pint?

[She abruptly sits back down.]

Ferryboat Woman: Aye, and that too.

ACT 1 SCENE 12

Setting: Coffee Shop, day. It is a bleak winter's day. Al, in a winter overcoat, enters. **ALLAN WILLIAMS** is tending the cash register.

Williams: Good to see you, professor.

Al: It's getting colder.

Williams: Those dole boys, the Beatles, are here and taking up valuable space. Can't you find them jobs mopping up floors at the Albert Docks?

Al: They'll do just fine.

Williams: What can my girl get you? It was the waitress that you found appealing. She gave Al a warm smile.

Waitress: Hello, darling.

Al: How about a coffee and a bacon sandwich?

Waitress: Java and and butties coming right up, honey.

Al: Make that a round for me and the Beatles.

Williams: If you like, sir, but I wouldn't encourage that lot of loafers.

Al: They'll buy me plenty of bacon butties and coffees in the future, I'm sure of it.

[The Beatles' ears pricked up when they heard the mentioning of food.]

Williams: Professor, I took the time off to go to Germany with a tape recording of what I thought was music. Instead, it was Lennon and his lot yodeling, farting and making a din. They deserve the gallows. But I'll let them explain to you.

[Al takes a seat next to the 4 Beatles.]

Al: Where's Tommy Moore, your drummer?

John: He's 36 and in a nursing home where he belongs.

George: He means Tommy took his drums and went home because John insulted him.

Paul: I'm telling you, Johnny, we have to get Ringo Starr, the drummer of Rory Storm and the Hurricanes tagged for the ride.

John: Yeah, maybe.

Paul: Can you play the drums, sir? We need one that badly. You're American and still cool.

Al: How's life treating you, Lennon?

George: His auntie gave him the boot over his grades.

John: There's no shame in it. I'm an artist and artists suffer all of the time.

Paul: You're so noble, John.

Al: You can stay with me until you other digs.

John: Thanks, whacker, but I have already taken up lodgings on Percy Street and Gambler.

George: He means he's freeloading off of Stu now.

[The food arrives and the Beatles tear their food apart like ravished wolves.]

Al: More beacon butties, miss.

John: Did the Arty finally give you a pay increase, Al?

Al: Speaking of the Arty...

John: Don't start, mate. I'm out of that can at the end of terms.

Paul: Leaving without his certification.

John: Bugger the piece of paper, Paul. I'll only regret losing the grant money.

Al: I'm sorry, John.

John: Don't be sorry, Al. We're off to Germany. There are plenty of American and British soldiers and tourists over there.

George: We'll make plenty of dosh!

Paul: Too blinking right!

Al: I thought Mr. Williams said he didn't have any luck with the Fatherland.

George: Germany's only the first stop.

John: And where are we going, lads!

The other two shout in union: To the top of the pop!

Williams: We'll have none of that shouting in here.

George: We're ready to go to Germany, Mr. Williams.

Williams: You didn't much appreciate the last gig I found for you at the Garston Bath.

George: The Blood Baths, you mean.

Paul: The bloody tiger Boys almost castrated us for chatting up their birds.

George: We're lucky we got out alive.

Williams: How's about the Blue Angel?

John: No more nudie places.

Williams: Now I can't very well book you lads if you're too high and mighty to play the usual fare in Liverpool.

Paul: We're ready for the Krauts

Williams: I sure hope you're right about that. Make me some money, boys!

Al: Let's go listen to my records before we all get in a Donnybrook.

George: Sometime, you should come over to for tea with me parents. They'd like you, I'm sure.

Al: Thanks for the invite. I might just do that. What's the address?

George: 25 Upton Green in Speke.

Paul: Sir, we're off to Germany soon. We have been slotted in a three month engagement at the Indra Club.

Al: That's great! I wish you all lots of luck.

George: We want you to visit us, Professor. We'll be lonely for a friendly face.

John: Let's get out of here, fellas.

George: Where we going, Johnny?

John: Where we going, boys?

The other two shout in union: To the top of the pop!

John: Try and catch up Al or you'll get left behind.

ACT 1 SCENE 13

Setting: Railway Station in Liverpool, day. Al is waiting inside for his train. Two bags sit beside him. He hears somebody call out his name. He is shocked to see **GINNY BROWNE** running towards him.

Ginny: Al!

Al: Ginny!

Ginny: Are you leaving us, Al?

Al: I'm off to Germany to see the Beatles. I figure you'd never miss me as I never see you around much.

Ginny: You're a very foolish man., my American Joe.

[She pulls him to her for an embrace and a kiss.]

Al: Want to come?

Ginny: Not here and now, sweet one.

Al: I mean Hamburg.

Ginny: I know what you mean. I'm off to Scotland to see some cousins of mine. I'd rather go to Germany.

Al: I'm seeing Lennon and the boys play in front of the Germans.

Ginny: Stay out of the German rain.

Al: I have more than enough for another ticket. Why don't you come with me?

Ginny: Upon your return I shall permit you to paint me…in the raw.

Al: Ginny, I—

Ginny: What, Al?

Al: It's that you're a very nice girl.

Ginny: Oh, am I now? Is that what you mean to say?

Al: No, it isn't.

Ginny: Well, what then? Have out with it.

Al: It's that…John Lennon and I were talking and, well…

Ginny: Oh, that's just grand!

Al: No, no, we were just talking about you. It doesn't matter. What I mean to say is that I really dig you. I think that you're just wonderful, with your soft hair. You smell nice. And you feel nice. I love to kiss you.

Ginny: I do too.

[They kiss.]

Al: You're like a teddy bear.

Ginny: That's sweet enough, I suppose.

Al: But it's, well, maybe, something more.

Ginny: I thought I told you to just take it easy. Don't you listen to me, Yank?

Al: Sure, I listen fine.

Ginny: Then do as I say.

Al: No, I think it's time you listen to me.

Ginny: Go ahead, I'm listening.

Al: Come with me, baby, let's spend some time together.

Ginny: I won't Al. I'm sorry.

[Ginny begins to skip away like a school girl.]

Al: Don't leave me like this, Ginny.

Ginny: Stay away from the German whores and don't drink too much German beer.

[Ginny exits.]

ACT 1 SCENE 14

Setting: The Beatles' living quarters, day, Hamburg, Germany. The five Beatles are suffering from hangovers and moving around, drinking coffee. The quarters are stark and ugly. John picks up a half empty bottle of beer, considers, and then takes a long drink. There's a knock at the door.

Paul: Someone's knocking at the door.

John: Piss off, you kraut bastard.

Paul: Do me a favor, open the door, let 'em in.

[The knocking continues.]

George: Make it go away, John.

Stu: Please, John, listen to Paul.

[John finishes the beer and approaches the door with the bottle in his hand as a weapon.]

John: Bloody Germans are it again. This time we're ready for you, bastards!

[John opens the door to find Al standing there with his bags.]

Al: Excuse me but is this the Beatles residence.

John: Al, we never thought you'd make it! The prof is here, fellas! Get up, everyone!

[The Beatles rush to greet Al.]

Al: It's great to see you, boys!

John: You too, me mate! I'm glad you made it!

George: Our Albert is here at last.

Paul: We'd thought you'd be a no show, Uncle Albert.

John: The cheap bugger, Williams, has us staying in squalor.

George: Yeah, and we are not happy about it.

Paul: Tell him we said so, huh, Uncle Al?

Al: Who's this?

Paul: That's Ringo Starr, our new drummer.

John: How are things at the Arty and in the Liddypool?

Al: Everything is as you left it, John.

John: How is Ginny Jenny Henny Penny Boone Boomer Brownee Browne?

George: Did you put the ring on her finger yet, Al?

Al: She saw me off at Lime Street Station. No ring, though.

John: Go on now, brown cow.

Al: Ginny Browne has a mind of her own.

John: And a brilliant ass, eh, Al?

Paul: And you'll call me gaffer, Uncle Albert?

John: When you get back, will you be telling Cynthia that I'm keeping fine?

Al: I send all of your loving to her, John.

Stu: We're off for our breakfast, professor. Please join us.

John: Come on, then, Al.

George: We can only afford grotty cornflakes.

Paul: It's not like the larder back home.

Stu: We're reliving the Irish famine here in Germany.

John: Moran, you've triggered a rebellion among me troops.

Al: I'm vacation and I expect to be well-fed. And I fully expect to feed my mates too.

[The Beatles begin to dress and talk excitedly. John winks at him and smiles.]

John: If Ginny doesn't have a lock on your trousers we'll find another bird for you.

George: It's rather early in the day for that sort of chat.

Paul: He only just got here.

John: Listen to the saints a go marching in.

Al: I hope that you have some castles and cathedrals to show me, lads, in this lovely country.

John: We're more interested in the whores than in history.

Paul: You're a swine, Lennon!

John: Bloody weather here is worse than home!

Al: Stu, you should really come back home when I leave. I think you're failing at being a rock n' roller.

John: He'll stay here with the rest of the Beatles.

Al: Stu is more artist than bassist. He should be finishing up his studies at the college.

[A fight is ready to breakout so Ringo steps in diplomatically.]

John: Listen, here Moran! This is my group and I make the decisions here.

Ringo: What do you think of Hamburg, skin?...I mean, ah, Professor Moran.

Al: Ringo, you should jump the Rory Storm and the Hurricanes and join the Beatles. You'd fit in better with the Beatles than Pete Best. Pete is just an average drummer and too crabby to be one of the group.

John: Pete Best is a Beatle too, Al. What's gone wrong with you? Ringo is just filling in for him.

Paul: Pete Best is a wanker, John!

John: Moran, go form your own group and stop messing about with the Beatles. Better yet: go back to the Arty and tell me old mates to get on with their blessed studies and to stop sniffing the paint.

Al: Sure, I'll just leave with my thick wallet, and you'll be back to eating cornflakes.

Paul: He's got a point, Johnny, I sure could use some thick German sausages for breakfast right about now.

George: Yeah, let's leave the retched cornflakes. Bloody German weather!

Stu: Come on, then, let's go, Johnny.

Paul: After breakfast, let's see come cathedrals with the Uncle Al.

John: Lead the way, prof, we want to leave this oppressive place.

Al: Follow me, lads!

INTERMISSION
(15 Minutes)

ACT 2 SCENE 1

Exterior: ENTRANCE TO THE CAVERN-NIGHT. It is night and Al is standing in line outside of a nightclub. A sign, *The Fabulous Beatles Are Back,* is hanging across the entrance. Many of the fans appear to be teenage girls who are bubbling over with excitement to see their heroes back from Germany. Al is taken back by the ruckus. A very pretty girl approaches Al and tugs his arm.

Errand Girl: Are you the famous Professor Al Moran?

Al: I don't know about the famous part but I am Professor Albert Moran.

Pigtails: We have been keeping a watchful lookout for you, sir.

Errand Girl: Are you really a mate of John Lennon and the Beatles?

Al: Best mate.

Errand Girl: I think Paul is gorgeous.

Pigtails: George is more my speed.

Al: The German frauleins felt the same way. Boys will boys. I'm talking about boys now. But the boys have plenty of girls. Paul doesn't need a date, but I do.

Errand Girl: So I'll be your date…starting tonight. I've been instructed to wait for you to show. A former student of yours as well as a good friend wants me to direct you to his office.

Pigtails: I say you move ever so fast.

Al: My friend has an office?

Errand Girl: Right this way, sir.

[The girls lead Al next door to a pub. They exchange sexy looks.]

Al: This friend has an office in a pub?

[John Lennon and he is at the end of the long bar. He is with Paul and three or four girls.]

Errand Girl: Just follow me, Professor Moran.

John: Hey you, Dr. Moran. I'm surprised to see my old proffy woffy from the arty farty trying to get into the Cavern.

Paul: It's our truest friend, Uncle Albert.

[Handshakes are made all around. The girls are impressed by Al's connection the Beatles.]

Al: Bugger off, rocky and roller coaster, cocky and diddily squat.

John: Leave the Lewis Carroll bit to me, Al.

Paul: Do you have a disc, Al?

John: If not go and buy it now. Some of the shops carry it but if not they'll order it for you.

Al: What are you guys trying to tell me?

Errand Girl: The lads recorded a single over in Germany called *My Bonnie*.

Pigtails: It's gear!

Al: Who sings it: John or Paul?

John: You're wrong on both accounts.

Paul: Tony Sheridan belted out the lyrics but we played the instruments. We took it to help plug our career.

Al: That's great, a real break! Good work, lads!

Errand Girl: I can go around the shops with you to help you find it, Dr. Moran... Al.

Pigtails: Why not propose marriage to him, dear?

John: Careful there, luv, another one has a lock on his zipper.

Paul: We'll be a thanking you, sir.

Errand Girl: She may have a fight on her hands.

Steven G. Farrell

John: He'll have a fight over his trousers.

Paul: It's time we we're off to the salt mines of the Cavern Club, Johnny.

Al: I was sorry to hear about Stu's death. It was so sudden.

Paul: A medical situation of some kind.

[An uneasy quiet sets in.]

Errand Girl: You don't have to leave do you, Al?

Paul: Easy there, now, girlie, this is our Uncle Al. You're just here to fetch the beers.

Errand Girl: I think he's sexy!

John: The Beatles will all be back here directly, Al. Keep her warm for us. I know you liked Stu a lot, Al, but we just don't talk about it right now. He just dropped dead from an old head injury. I have lost so many in my life. My life is sad. Ta, mate.

Paul: You take care of him.

Pigtails: I would if I had a crack at him.

[The errand girl embraces Al as the Beatles leave.]

ACT 2 SCENE 2

Setting: A record store, day. Al and Errand Girl enter to look for the record. They are holding hands.

Errand Girl: I thought there'd be a cue for the boys' hit record by now.

Al: There will be, soon enough; have a little patience and you'll see.

Errand Girl: It's so exciting!

[A distinguished looking salesman approaches the two. He is smiling and respectful. He has a name tag that says *Brian* on it.]

Brian: May I be of service to the two of you?

Errand Girl: Yes, you can!

Al: Perhaps; but I rather doubt it.

Brian: Despair not, sir. If we don't have it in stock we'd be happy to order it for you. (Calling out) Miss Hayes, I require your services. Bring your pad.

MISS HAYES, Brian's personal assistant approaches eagerly.

154

Miss Hayes: Another order, Mr. Epstein.

Brian: Hopefully we can tend to this charming young couple's order.

Miss Hayes: Things are really rolling in the world of records.

Al: This record maybe hard to locate.

Miss Hayes: Mr. Epstein and I are the experts of locating the hard to find.

Errand Girl: Hush, Al, don't be so negative. We're looking for a hit recording from Germany.

Brian: The Germany location should pose no major obstacle if you're willing to do some waiting.

Errand Girl: Waiting?

Miss Hayes: A two week wait is standard.

Al: The record is on a German small label.

Brian: You say it's a small label, sir?

Al: I mean that the recording was released by a very small German recording studio.

Miss Epstein: German, is it? Why not Italian?

Brian: They call it a small label, eh? I shall remember that in the future. For at Epstein & son we aim to please every single customer. Is the recording classical or opera?

Errand Girl: It's rock n roll, mister!

Miss Hayes: For goodness sake! Isn't that the same thing as jazz?

Brian: Do you recollect the title, sir?

Errand Girl: *MY BONNIE.*

Brian: Would that be by Tony Sheridan and the Beat Brothers?

Errand Girl: Yes!

Al: That's it! Very good, sir. Their real name is the Beatles.

Errand Girl: Do you have it, then?

Brian: Not yet, I'm afraid. But I have ordered a limited stock direct from overseas because I have had at least a dozen requests for it in recent days, just like you two, walking into the store and asking for that record. It has baffled me why so many people are asking for such a rare find. I wonder if it is not some kind of marketing gimmick.

Miss Hayes: It could be a novelty song of some sort.

Al: Brian, please, I assure you it's the real thing.

Errand Girl: If you have ever heard the Beatles play and see how they turn on the crowd you'd realize that they're going to be bigger than Elvis, Chuck Berry or Buddy Holly. They're taking England by storm! Read the newspapers and listen to the radio, man!

Al: They're catching on in a big way, sir.

Brian: Are you an American, sir?

Al: One hundred percent.

Brian: Is the record catching on, as it were, in America?

Al: Not yet, but soon. The Beatles will soon lead a British Invasion of rock n' roll to my country, for it's not Tony Sheridan and the Beat Brothers who are going to do it but the Beatles.

Brian: Yes, now that you say the name Beatles, an oddball name, I recall that they play in the clubs around here. British Invasion sounds quaint.

Miss Hayes: Aren't they insects?

Errand Girl: They mostly play the lunchtime session at The Cavern.

Brian: And you have seen these Beatles perform live, sir?

Al: I have seen them perform many times here in Liverpool and several times over in Hamburg, Germany. They're all close friends of mine, especially John Lennon.

Errand Girl: John Lennon was a student of Professor Moran here.

[Brian is visibly impressed by the title.]

Brian: Are you Professor Moran?

Al: But you can call me 'Al'.

[They shake hands.]

Brian: And you may call me Brian. I'm Brian Epstein of Epstein & Son. This is my factotum, Miss Hayes.

Miss Hayes: He means I do all of his dirty work.

Errand Girl: I'm glad you two are best of friends.

Al: Why not join me at the Cavern tomorrow at twelve noon for their show? It'll be fun.

Brian: Shall you introduce me to these wonderful Beatles?

Al: Why, certainly. So we'll see you then, Brian. Come on, luv.

Errand Girl: Bye, Mr. Epstein!

Brian: Yes, goodbye. Right. Well met, I am sure. Be safe. Keep warm and dry. Don't let the bed bugs bite. What a strange world. You just never know, do you? These Times are indeed special. It's amazing who you can meet in a record store.

Miss Hayes: Good day to you both.

Brian: Aren't they a charming pair, Miss Hayes?

Miss Hayes: He's too old for her, I daresay.

ACT 2 SCENE 3

Setting: Exterior, The Cavern, day. **AL** is standing outside of the cavern at noon time. He is hesitant to enter; until he sees **BRIAN EPSTEIN** and **MISS HAYES** rushing down the street. He is waving his arms and calling out Al. Today Al is with **PIGTAILS**.

Brian: Hello, Al! Hello!

Al: How are you doing, Brian?

Brian: I am fine, thank you. It's good to see you again.

Al: The same here.

Miss Hayes: Another young lady, professor?

Pigtails: Another day, another bird jay as they say.

Miss Hayes: The Liverpool art College is certainly the place for a robust American professor to teach at.

Pigtails: Our professor teaches us ever so much.

Miss Hayes: I imagine he does.

[The Two shake hands like old friends. Brian is relieved that Al is with a date. The two exchange idle conversation as they make their way into the club and are ushered up to the front. The Beatles are rushing up to the stage to thunderous applause.]

Brian: I see you're quite important, my professor friend.

Al: You're going to love this.

[The Beatles begin to sing. Brian is enthralled. Al looks over at Brian and he is struck by Brian's reaction to the Beatles; especially John Lennon. Al realizes that Brian is homosexual.]

Brian: These chaps have something tremendous here, Al!

Al: They're heading to the top of the pop!

Brian: Smashing! Utterly smashing!

Al: They're going to fill Elvis' boots.

Miss Hayes: And this is all the rage?

Pigtails: Quite so.

Miss Hayes: It's so loud!

Pigtails: Beat and jive is supposed to be loud.

[During a brief pause Al notices that Ringo is waving at him with his drum sticks.]

Al: Let's go, Ringo! You're a Beatle now!

[An announcer announces the Beatles by name. The audience applauds when they hear Ringo's name; but there is a smattering of boos.]

Brian: Why the rudeness? What is the reason for that?

Al: Ringo is the new drummer at the Beatles and a few people are upset that the Beatles sacked their former drummer, Pete Best. Pete was too moody. The Beatles are upbeat!

Brian: I love the leather and the boots!

Al: The girls like it too.

Miss Hayes: They're about as charming as Huns.

Brian: I want to manage them, Al. Do you hear me? Do you think they'd even be remotely interested in my representation? Are they spoken for, in terms of a professional manager?

Al: I'll pass on the word right now that I want to meet them today, after their show. You can ask them yourself. I'll introduce you to John Lennon. However, then you're on your own, Brian. They're good lads; but rowdy. Keep your wits about you.

Brian: Oh, I most certainly will, don't you worry about that.

Miss Hayes: They have a rough look about them, Mr. Epstein. Are you sure they're proper for the store?

Pigtails: They're proper enough if you want to cash in.

[Al stops Errand Girl.]

Al: Excuse me?

Errand Girl: Hey you!

Al: Do you remember our friend, here?

Errand Girl: Yes, of course, hello, Mr. Epstein.

Pigtails: What she's doing here?

Miss Hayes: Now the Yank has two in hand. Lucky American.

Brian: Yes, hello. Please, Al, send the message at once.

Al: Okay, okay. Listen, cupcakes. Tell John and Paul that Uncle Al has someone he'd like them to meet right after the show, in the dressing room. You got it?

Errand Girl: I got it, Yankee man.

Al: See you later, then.

Errand Girl: Bye!

Pigtails: Break a leg!

[During a song Errand Girl rushes up to Paul McCartney and shouts at him. Paul turns to John and points out Al and Brian. John speaks into the microphone.]

John: Calling Moran! Calling Moran! Please see Lennon and McCartney shortly here after!

John: You two old chaps in the back with suits!

Paul: But not you, Uncle Albert!

Brian: We're getting in to see the Beatles! We're getting in to see the Beatles!

Al: Try and be cool, Brian.

Brian: Right, yes. The Beatles are cheeky as well as musical, the naughty rascals. How shall I ever tame him and them?

Steven G. Farrell

Al: Let's make a break for it now, Brian!

[Al and Brian shoulder their way through the crowd as the Beatles also fight their way into their dressing room. Miss Hayes and Pigtails wait behind]

Al: Lennon, it's me, Moran!

John: Hello there, Al Capone of Chi-shitty town. Who's the quality in tow?

George: Good to see you again, Dr. Al.

Al: I have to speak to you guys right now. It's all business.

Paul: Be polite, Johnny, we've a visitor.

Al: I want to introduce you to Brian Epstein of Epstein and sons.

Brian: Epstein and son, there's just one son, me.

[George slowly shakes Brian's hand, suspicious. The other Beatles hang back.]

George: What brings Mr. Brian Epstein of Epstein & Son here among the savages and peasants?

John: George, don't you know how this sort works? They can sniff out a quid from 10 miles off.

[John sneers and sticks out a nasty had for a nastier handshake.]

George: Is that so, Mr. Epstein?

[Ringo decides to make a move. He offers his hand.]

Ringo: Any friend of Al Moran is a friend of mine.

Al: Why not hear the guy out before acting like a scouser lout?

John: So, Al, you put great store by this parley then I guess we should go along for old time's sake. So you're a friend of our Uncle al, eh, Brian? Welcome you are, sir.

Brian: Gentlemen, I have a business proposition to make to the Beatles!

George: You do, have you?

John: It doesn't surprise me, we're the Beatles!

Paul: What is your proposal than, sir?

Brian: I want to be your manager! I want to take you to the States. What do you say?

John: Oh, well, that is something.

160

Paul: We say yes!

George: Goodness, gracious me.

Al: Shake the man's hand, gents!

[Brian shakes hands with all of the Beatles.]

ACT 2 SCENE 4

Setting: Inside Al's Apartment, Day. Al is working on a manuscript and listening to the radio. His ears perk up when he catches what the DJ is saying.

DJ: Well, lads and lassies, you all thought Liverpool was only the northern port city that is home to all of those funny talking dancehall comics and unemployed Scousers, but here's a new twist for you all to dance to…no pun intended…so let's all have a nice listen up to what the north has offer us cockneys here in the south. I think you're going to lose your mind over this spin.

The Record Plays:

> Love, love me do
>
> You know I love you
>
> So please love me do, woo ho
>
> Love me do.

Al: The Beatles are on London radio!

DJ: Are you ready for the flip side, rock n rollers?

[The radio plays *PS I LOVE YOU.*]

DJ: So there it is, kiddies. You heard it right! The music is straight out of the old port city of Liverpool itself. I've heard it through the grapevine that it is called the Mersey Beat sound. Did you like it, eh? As for myself I'm not too much of a staid southerner to admit that I love both numbers! Good show, lads! Ladies, you'll grow to love the Beatles. Lads, you'll grow to wish you were the fifth Beatle. These young scousers write their own music. No Yanks need apply! Yes, once again they're England's very own Beatles. Remember the name. The old island is dancing for the first time since Hitler's invasion. It's the Beatles or should I say the Beat All. I think they're going to beat all to the top of the pop.

[The announcer's voice fades as the telephone begins to ring.]

Al: Hello?

Ginny: Did you hear them, Al?

Al: Just now and they're great!

Ginny: They're off and they'll soon leave us behind forever.

Al: Don't say that, Ginny. Oh, how my heart breaks.

Ginny: Forever, but we shall see, we we're a part of it for now.

Al: It's beyond belief.

Ginny: Al, I'm burning hot. Can I come over to your place right now?

Al: Ah, well, yes, you can.

Ginny: It's just you and me and your bed.

Al: Hurry up then, I'm burning too.

[Al hangs up and moves about the room, looking for something in panic.]

Al: Ah, ah, ah…

[There's a rap at his front door. It's too early for Ginny to have arrived with her overnight bag. He opens the door to find his landlady, **MRS. LAMPKIN**. She is carrying a pot of tea on a tray.]

Mrs. Lampkin: You're cloistered up here in this stuffy old apartment and I thought you could do with a spot of tea.

Al: Wait! Today is rent day, right. I should have brought it down to you.

Mrs. Lampkin: Oh, professor, the thought never entered my head, seeing how you're always so punctual. The very idea, Dr. Moran!

Al: I have it all filled out for you.

[Al hands his rent to Mrs. Lampkin and she stuffs it into her blouse giving him an eyeful of her ample bosom.]

Mrs. Lampkin: I must say that an intelligent scholar should do much better than teaching that scruffy load of long hairs at the Liverpool Art College. You should be at Oxford or Cambridge, at the very least. You should be teaching English finest and not their failings.

Al: I am quite content here in Liverpool at the Art College.

Mrs. Lampkin: Professor Moran, you lack ambition. May I call you 'Albert?'

Al: I go by 'Al,' Mrs. Lampkin

Mrs. Lampkin: Nothing snobby about you, Albie.

[Al keeps on looking at his watch to tip-off his landlady that he wants her to bugger off. But she keeps on pouring him tea. When he heads over to the phone she follows him. She starts to circle him. He starts to setup his canvas and ready his brushes.]

Al: Well, I guess I had better get ready.

Mrs. Lampkin: Ready for what, my bold American?

Al: My work, Mrs. Lampkin.

Mrs. Lampkin: All work and no play will make Albie a very dull Yankee boy. I have seen you glancing at me with quiet appraisal and approval. I'm a bit past me prime as a first place mare but I still can trot with those tarts you have to look at over at the Arty.

Al: You're certainly worth checking out but now is a very awkward time for me as I'm expecting...

Mrs. Lampkin: Nonsense, Albie! There's no time like the moment as the poet like to proclaim.

Al: I have engaged a model for this afternoon for a very important assignment...it's the dean's daughter.

Mrs. Lampkin: Oh, do tell. Is it to be a nude, you nasty lad? I expect somebody's knickers will be coming down, and I don't mind if they're mine.

[Al is virtually ready to crawl under the door when there's a loud rap at his door. He is visibly relieved and Mrs. Lampkin is not happy about the interruption.]

Al: Who is it?

Ginny: It's the girl who is going to give you a jolly good rodgering.

Al: Come in, Miss Brown. By the way, Mrs. Lampkin, this is my model.

Mrs. Lampkin: She's the dean's daughter?

Ginny: Oh, I'm a lady of many parts. I'm also Professor Moran's model. Today shall I pose as Sir Francis Drake or as King Charles 11, doctor? I have me costume right here in this overnight bag.

Al: Today I just need you to pose as a student from the art college.

Mrs. Lampkin: In the nude?

Ginny: Oh, yes, in the nude. It's the only way I can get this bloke here to concentrate on his work.

[Mrs. Lampkin, in an attempt to regain her dignity, straightens herself out and decides to act casual about it. She hastily gathers her tea pot and cups.]

Mrs. Lampkin: Of course, dear, after all we've progressed somewhat here in the sixties.

Al: Thank you for the tea, Mrs. Lampkin.

Mrs. Lampkin: Next time would you be so good as to save me time by bringing the rent downstairs to me, Albie? Dr. Moran, I mean.

Al: I will do so.

[When Mrs. Lampkin leaves the room Ginny throws herself into Al's arms.]

Ginny: Oh, Albie, are you shagging every bird in Liverpool between the ages of 18 to 48?

Al: Don't start on me, Gin. I just survived a terrible ordeal.

Ginny: Or a terrible temptation? Let me cool you off, luv.

ACT 2 SCENE 5

Setting: Inside the pub next to the Cavern, at night. Al expects the Beatles to pop in. He is sipping a pint when John, Paul, Pigtails and Errand Girl enter.

Al: Here the Beatles are now.

Errand Girl: Our favorite Yank is here.

Pigtails: Put out the porch light, luv.

Paul: Hello, Dr. Moran.

Al: Loved the record, Paul. Good work, gents.

Paul: It is really gear, Al.

John: So you're still following our struggling career, Al?

Al: Not so struggling anymore. It's like a big dream.

John: Make that a big wet dream.

Al: It's our collective big wet dream.

John: Speaking of such things, I'm going to introduce you to Leslie.

Al: Who's that?

John: A sexy redhead. She's just over there.

Paul: We treat our Al well. He's our number one fan.

John: Wasn't the man my very own Proffy Mo…at the arty. He was my inspiration and my major guide. He is the Plato to my Aristotle.

Paul: We've missed you, Uncle Albert. Everything is crazy right now. I can't even explain it to you. Come around more often. You introduced us to Brian; now we'll do some introducing of our own.

John: He's too busy chasing after Ginny Browne, around the town and how.

Al: I dig your classy threads. You guys are cool now. I guess you're buying dinner.

Paul: We're quite trendy.

John: That Eppy's doing.

Al: Do I know this Eppy? Is she some magical lady? Is that the redhead?

[The boys chuckle over the remark.]

Paul: Eppy could be considered a lady of certain sort.

John: Come now, Paul.

Paul: Right.

John: Eppy is bloody Brian Epstein. You pawned the guy off on us, Moran! And a right fine move, that.

Paul: Actually, Al, we're forever grateful to you, sir. Brian got us the recording deal and the dosh is rolling in. We can afford cool Italian sports cars now.

Al: So it was Brian who transformed you into a business concern. That's amazing. What a lucky break. I am happy for you.

Paul: I have no complaints on that score.

John: Eppy knows his numbers and percentages but he sticks to marketing and packaging. The Beatles still create the sound and the beat. I take me regular baths and change me socks until the cows come home as long as the music isn't compromised for the sake of the music.

Paul: Yeah, well, that's John talking, Uncle Al.

Al: Showbiz is showbiz!

Steven G. Farrell

John: Sod showbiz, Al!

Paul: Our Johnny can stick with his Marxist blab but I'm all set to make the capitalistic cash!

John: Are you free for lunch tomorrow, Al?

Al: We haven't had a chat in a spell. Why not? When and where?

John: Tonight, Leslie can have you but tomorrow I want you all by your lonesome.

Al: Sure, why not? I don't think I've ever had a redhead before, come to think of it.

Paul: Good luck, mate.

Errand Girl: Stand me a pint, Al.

Pigtails: And me as well, professor.

[John and Paul exit, arm in arm.

ACT 2 SCENE 6

Setting: Inside of a Diner. Al and John are digging into lunch and they're enjoying their time together.

John: Can you pay-off the slate today, Al?

Al: Now that you're a hotshot recording artist one would think that you'd fork out the dough for me for a change.

John: If your pay envelope can't cover the price of the feed then it's the scullery for the likes of me. Do you fancy scrubbing a pot, mate?

Al: So you're still skint?

John: I'm skint but beautiful.

Al: Sod it, Lennon. It looks like it's on me again. I shouldn't have come here together with you. You sure put on a good show, I was hooked there.

John: Come together right now over me.

Al: Pass the sugar. I guess I'm glad to see you again.

John: Glad all over as the Dave Clark Five would sing. And here is the waitress just now. Tip her generously, Uncle Albert.

[The two made their way out to the street.]

166

LAST PAPERS

Al: Brian should polish-off those mooching ways of yours, John Lennon. Still and all, I must admit we miss you over at the Arty.

John: I can't believe you've stuck it out this long. Good for you, Yank.

Al: It's a job. I like Liverpool too. And Ginny.

John: I find it odd that you'd fancy Liddypool over Chi-town.

Al: I like what I like. Love and money, I guess, moves us all.

John: I can't wait to make tracks from here. I'm bloody sick of the whole lot of it.

Al: That's because you are from here. Someday, you'll look back with much fondness on Liverpool.

John: I think Paul and George would agree with me. Ringo is the truest scouse of us all. He wants to marry and have children.

Al: He's an adult and that's what adults do.

John: Tell me about your dad?

Al: What's with the serious question all of a sudden?

John: Me father ditched me when I was a wee lad.

Al: My dad is a quiet guy. He is a serious Catholic and he always votes Democrat.

John: Did he drink...I mean really drink?

Al: Oh, he drank a few beers on the weekend. He drank dark Irish beers on St. Patrick's Day. We had ten children, so there wasn't much left over for beer. The man was plenty busy.

John: Where there any birds larking about?

Al: My Ma would have horsewhipped him for that. She's tough German dame.

John: Al, me father, was a cook on a ship. He sailed the seven seas like Sinbad the Sailor. I have heard talk that he was a very easy-going chap but that he lacked common sense. He's been gone so long I'm not certain.

Al: What about your mother?

John: Dead.

Al: I didn't know. I'm sorry.

167

Steven G. Farrell

John: She was hit by a truck. I saw the life crushed out of her with my own eyes. Let's change the subject, Al.

Al: Sure thing. How is the record selling?

John: Fab!

Al: Excited about it?

John: Only a start, isn't it?

Al: Don't be hard, be honest.

John: Okay, mate, I'll do me best to answer your curious inquiry. I love the music, the pounds and the birds. The screaming birds scare me at times, though. They want me cock because I'm star. It is really sickening. It beats the dole and the Arty.

Al: Are the Cockneys buying the record?

John: Eppy assures us that our record sales are brisk and that we're surging to the top of the pop.

Al: That Brian Epstein. Amazing.

John: Our album *PLEASE ,PLEASE ME* will blow the Londoners over for keepers. We'll show them what for.

Al: You're on a roll, Beethoven.

John: Roll over, Beethoven.

Al: Here's a pub just now. Fancy a lager, mate? It's still on your quid.

[John and Al enter and get a beer. They begin to sing later, after a few beers.]

John and Al:

Last night I said these words to my girl

I know you never even try girl

Come on, come on, come on

Please, please me like I please you

John: Good sound, that.

Al: Thank you.

John: I bet the American gent here wrote that ditty.

[Lennon and Al roar-out in laughter.]

168

John: Will they buy it in the States?

Al: I predict it'll be on the charts soon.

John: Do you really think so, skin?

Al: Rock n' roll has been stale since Buddy Holly's airplane crashed in an Iowa cornfield.

John: Is Iowa a city or a state?

Al: It's an entire state.

John: The Beatles shall never play in Iowa State in revenge for the death of Mr. Holly.

Al: Better tell that to Brian Epstein and he probably won't approve.

John: Don't talk to me about that patsy. Did you know that about him when you introduced him to us?

Al: I don't ask people about those kinds of things. Besides, who cares?

John: He's all right, I suppose. I won't lie to you, mate, he does have it for me.

Al: Is that right?

John: It makes me a bit uncomfortable.

Al: I'm so sorry about that. We can't help who and what we are in this life, John.

John: It's like how Al Moran can't help being a bore of a professor.

Al: Professor Moran recognizes the abilities of the Beatles. He understands his place and time and he'll do his part in your success story.

John: Abilities, me arse. He only recognizes the size of me...

Al: John, please, now, lad! It is better Brian as your manager than dear old Mr. Williams.

John: Or you, Al Moran. Paul, George and Ringo all wanted you as our manager but I put me boot down, and hard.

Al: I would have kicked ass and taken names. You should have listened to them.

John: Stick to your oil and brushes, Al. We would have all followed you to Hell and back but we knew that as an Irish Mick you'd have no business for the cash register.

Steven G. Farrell

[John is getting gloomier as the pints continue to flow.]

Al: What's bugging you, John?

John: Oh, nothing. Women are on my bean.

Al: You get all the women you want and yet you're downcast.

John: Keep your filthy thoughts to yourself. I am a respectable, church-going young man lately.

Al: Is that right? Since when have you've gone back to the Catholic Church?

John: I'm back in the pews since I married Cynthia Powell.

Al: Well, well, I had no idea. Congratulations! Sorry for my levity. You know I have a high regard for her.

John: We tied it up nice and legal in some governmental office. It was a dreary affair, mate. Bloody hell, Al, she's having our baby very soon. I won't run off on her the way Alf ran off on me and my Mum.

Al: I envy you all around, John. You're a good man.

[John punches Al in the arms.]

John: How about another round for the happy husband?

Al: I haven't seen Cynthia around campus lately.

John: She's in hiding. It's Brian's idea. He thinks it'll hurt our popularity if it comes to light. Fandom is fractured in the skull.

Al: I don't like that one bit. You're old enough to be married. Three of the other Beatles are eligible bachelors.

John: Don't forget how the fans turned on Jerry Lee Lewis when he got married.

Al: Didn't he marry his fourteen year old cousin?

John: It was marriage that did him in.

Al: Now you're talking through your hat!

John: I think Brian knows the business world more than you, Al, with all due respect.

Al: At any rate the Beatles are off and running. You're going to big. Bigger than what the world has ever seen before.

John: So you know that for sure? Explain your theory, professor

Al: The Beatles are fun, sexy and wild. The time is right, and ripe. The Beatles are the average person's fantasy come true. We'd all like to pick up a guitar and join you. The girls all desire you. It's all on the TV now, and the radio, everything is hitting at just the right time, and you are the ones to capitalize on it all. Replacing Pete Best with Ringo Starr was the master stroke of genius.

John: Tell that to some of our rioting fans. Poor Ringo got a black eye. We really only gave Pete the sack because Paul was suffering from the green-eyed monster. Only one pretty boy per group.

Al: What's the 'green-eyed monster'?

John: What? You're joking, right?

Al: No, really, I've never heard that term before, what is it?

John: Let's get out of here, mate. We have big things happening. Green-eyed monster, me arse!

Al: Come on, now! Don't just walk out like that! I have a right to know the truth! I am your professor or former professor, Lennon, get back here now and answer my question!

[John exits. Al follows him.]

ACT 2 SCENE 7

Setting: Outside of the college building, day. Al Moran is leaving the building with his briefcase. Many of the students smile at him or wave as he passes. He is a very popular professor at the college. He is known as an excellent professor, but he also known as the close friend of John Lennon who is now a campus legend.

Paul: Al! Professor Al Moran! Uncle Albert!

Al: What's all the shouting about, bhoyo?

[The two shake hands and then embrace.]

Paul: I didn't want to miss you, mate.

Al: I'm glad to see you.

Paul: Have you heard about it, then?

Al: You mean about John and...

Paul: Sssssssh, don't say anything about that. No, I mean about me twenty-first birthday party. It's very important, like.

Al: Congratulations, Paul. Now you're a man.

Paul: I'm trying to render you an invite to the grand affair. Your Johnny's favorite arty proffy mo and you're one of our dearest mates.

Al: I'd love to attend.

Paul: Ginny Browne will be there.

Al: I see. Well, I have not seen her for a spell. It will be good to get caught up again with her. You know, and everything.

Paul: Oh, just cool it, mate. She's working with Bill Harry and the *Mersey Beat Magazine*. She's quite the photographer and journalist at that rag these days, getting quite a name for herself, she is.

Al: I didn't know that. Things didn't go according to my plans, in general. I guess it is bad luck.

Paul: Are you still pining away for Ginny, my dear friend *Pliny*?

Al: Ginny is still sinning and I'll win because I'm without sin, if that's what you mean.

Paul: You can't always get your bird to sing.

Al: Have you tried, Paul, you swine. You know how I feel.

Paul: Tried and failed, mate. Me and half of Liverpool have gone down that road unsuccessfully. She does what she wants to do. Fancy you being so jealous, Uncle Albert, and your advanced stage of life and all.

Al: I'm glad that one lady in this old town has some taste and some standards.

Paul: George, Ringo and Cynthia want to see you. I want you to meet my family. They're Irish like you're family in Chicago. Ignore the tart.

Al: Regular Americans, they are. I'll be there.

Paul: This Friday, then, you know the place. About noon, don't be late, mate!

Al: Okay!

[Paul runs away.]

ACT 2 SCENE 8

Setting: The backyard of a house, at night. Paul McCartney's birthday party is a large family affair. Many of Paul's closest friends have been invited.

There is plenty of beer and food to go around. A large *HAPPY BIRTHDAY PAUL* sign is draped across the yard. John and Cynthia are sitting off by themselves. John looks like he's in a foul mood. Al shows up with Errand Girl. She is dressed very well and looks good.

George: You better forget this one, Dr. Al.

Al: I have already taken the precaution of sleeping with her, George.

Errand Girl: Al, really, must you?

George: You're still the naughty professor.

Al: I'll confess it to Father McKenzie the next time I go to confession.

George: Are you going to become a devout Catholic like me mum?

Al: No. I think this one is after Paul, anyway.

Errand Girl: I am not!

George: She's a cheeky tart. Here's the other tart just now.

Pigtails: You're spending time with me tonight, aren't you, professor?

George: You're worse than Paul, Al.

Pigtails: Al is better than Paul and I know what I'm on about.

[Paul is the center of attention.]

Paul: Al Moran! Come over and meet me Da and brother!

[Errand Girl is beside herself and she kisses Al with passion. Ginny pulls Al away.]

Ginny: That's a fine way to behave in the public eye, Professor Moran.

Errand Girl: Hey there, now! What do you think you're doing with me man?

Ginny: You just hush, now, little thing.

Errand Girl: I think I was told about you already, you tramp.

Ginny: Oh, was you now? And how's that?

Al: Just a minute. Let's not have a cat fight here. I'll just be talking to Ginny here, for a moment.

Errand Girl: A 'cat's fight', ha! I've not heard that term before, Al.

Ginny: He is the professor.

Errand Girl: I am quite aware of that fact.

Pigtails: You're both tramps if you ask me.

Errand Girl: Stop shadowing me.

Pigtails: I saw him first.

Al: Ginny, it's good to see you again. It's been too long.

Ginny: This is Bob Wooler, the famous local DJ and the Emcee of the Cavern. And he is the editor of *Mersey Beat*, the magazine!

Al: Oh, it's, ah, nice to meet you, Mr. Wooler. You guys are doing a wizard job of getting the word out about the Beatles and all of the lads.

Bob: So you're the famed Professor Moran?

Al: I'm only John Lennon's former lecturer.

Bob: Ginny never stops talking about you.

Al: Is that right?

Errand Girl: Yes, and I am...

[Ginny gets flusters and starts looking for a diversion. Al is thrilled.]

Ginny: Paul!

Paul: Yes, luv?

Ginny: Over here!

Paul: Coming now!

[Gerry Marsden and Paul McCartney and George Harrison approach. Florrie rushes over to claim Gerry's arm.]

Bob: I say, professor, perhaps we can get you to write a piece about your experience with John in the classroom at the Liverpool Art College?

Gerry Marsden: And our professor can indeed write as well as lecture.

Florrie: And Gerry is his star pupil.

Bob: That's great, then.

Al: Gerry Marsden! Bob, this is Gerry. He's another one of my wayward pupils of yore.

Gerry: Me band, Gerry and the Pacemakers, are doing are utmost to keep the pace with the one and only Beatles. This is my steady Florrie.

Florrie: We're almost engaged.

Paul: You'll flounder for sure if you continue turn out rubbish like *How Do You Do It?*

Al: Wasn't that a Lennon and McCartney original, Paul?

Paul: We'd never pen such cotton candy tripe.

Gerry: No need to take that tone, whacker. The Beatles reign supreme. That's a true fact.

Paul: You're too bloody right, Marsden.

Florrie: Why so cruel, Paul?

George: Cut the sermon, Paul.

Bob: Gilbert and Sullivan, the lot of you!

Al: I could use a drink.

Paul: Right, you are. I'll fetch the doctor a pale ale.

Florrie: Good riddance, mate.

Al: Is that all you got?

[Al wanders over to John and Cynthia.]

Al: Need another refill, Mr. Lennon?

John: Only if you have the strength, proffy mo.

Cynthia: John, he's a professor of art at the college. Can't you show anybody any simple respect? He's not proffy mo. He is Professor Albert Moran.

John: And can't you leave off nagging me for one moment, me darling?

[Bob Wooler approaches, alone.]

Bob: So, Johnny, how was the honeymoon?

John: Right, thanks for asking. We'll go on a good and proper honeymoon when I can afford it and we have some holiday time off from the music.

Bob: No, no, no, Lennon. I don't mean your legal honeymoon with your wife. That's plenty scandalous enough news and more than we can take here in Liverpool. I mean the illegal one you took in Spain with another person.

John: Wot's that, then?

Bob: You know what I'm on about. Stop larking about with me. All of Liverpool knows you went to Madrid with that queer Brian Epstein. The newspapers all wrote about it. You were in the room together. What did happened there, pray tell?

[In a flash, John flattens Bob with a wild punch. He is not content to leave it at that. He begins to batter that fallen man. Al steps in and pulls John away. However, with an incredible show of strength John breaks free and falls upon Bob again.]

Jim McCartney: Is that Lennon fellow at it again?

[Several hands pull John up. One of them is Al who receives a clout to the nose. John breaks away and returns in a moment swinging a shovel.]

Jim McCartney: Hey now, what's happening? This is a private party! I wish me Paulie would stay clear of that bloke. He's a nutter!

George: I think you broke the professor's nose!

Ringo: John, put down the bloody shovel and calm yourself!

Paul: And Al with his Glen Ford good looks.

Ringo: You did break up the professor's Roman nose, John. You better step down now.

Ginny: What have you done to my sweet Al?

Errand Girl: That's my Al, you bitch!

Ginny: You can just shut up your mouth then, missy!

[Ginny and Errand Girl wrestle. Ringo Starr tries to break up their fight.]

Paul: Ginny isn't the only bird who worships him.

Ginny: Go to hell, Paul!

Ringo: Can't you see the man is after dying on our hands.

[A towel is provided and people try to piece the party back together again. Bob is taken off by Gerry.]

Ginny: Al, call me soon. I miss you.

Errand Girl: Shove off, grannie.

Ginny: If you want to keep him, tickle him beneath his right ball.

Pigtails: Hey, I know that one.

[The women are about to square again off when John and Cynthia come over.]

John: Don't drop me over this, Al. It was just a mistake.

Cynthia: John loves you, Professor Moran. He really does.

John: I was out of me head but it wasn't you I was enraged at.

Al: It's okay, Lennon. My nose isn't broken. It's been broken before, believe me. I still love you. We all love you, in fact. We always have. Just try your best to love us back some, from time to time, if you don't mind. It really won't hurt you any to do that, I promise. You're all that we have in this cruel world, Lennon, you just don't see it yet.

John: I'll try, then, for your sake, prof. You're a good friend, a suppose Yank would say.

Cynthia: I'll make you a grand supper tomorrow night. Bring Ginny Browne. You two are meant for each other.

John: Nobody else can tolerate the two.

Errand Girl: Don't I have a saw in Al's affair of the heart?

Cynthia: Stop this nonsense, you two. You're the scandal of Liverpool. And, professor, dump these two; they're beneath your dignity.

[Before John departs he impulsively hugs Al.]

Pigtails: Some crazy people here.

ACT 2 SCENE 9

Setting: Inside a pub, day. John Lennon, now a big success with the Beatles, is waiting for Al Moran at a table. He pushes a pint towards Al as he takes a seat.

John: This pint is on John Lennon of the internationally known Beatles.

Al: Thanks for the pint, Beatle, but what's with the royal summons?

John: Sorry, whacker, but it really isn't me ordering you about. No, it's me coming to you on me bloody hands and knees and begging you to help out a friend in need.

Al: You never had to beg me in the past, John. What's changed, now that you're famous?

177

Steven G. Farrell

John: We are not famous yet. But Eppy signed a deal with some major studio to make four feature-length films over the next few years.

Al: Sounds like a cool thing. So what gives?

John: It isn't cool if you have no screenplays and nobody to pen the movies for us. Get my drift here, professor?

Al: Spit it out, John. Where's your usual Hunnish bluntness.

John: Al, you know the Beatles, so right up some cracking Hollywood atmosphere for us. How hard can that be? We're really in a bind here. It's hard to find good writers these days.

Al: I have never written a film script before.

John: And we've never been in a bloody movie before, so we're equal. But you are a writer!

Al: That's all you wanted to meet me about? I smell a rat. What's wrong with you, mate?

John: Nothing, really. That's it.

Al: I don't buy it. Speak the truth to your old mate.

John: Oh, all right. I just want to say goodbye, I suppose.

Al: What? Goodbye?

John: Let's be real here, Al. It's not going to be much longer. The days are changing. We all see that. The old life is all gone now. Just the future awaits us. It's scary but very real. I am ready for it. I wish you could come with me, God, how I wish you could. But you can't. So we're alone in this, the lads and me.

Al: All right, then, Lennon, goodbye, and good luck.

John: Thank you, mate. We won't be forgetting you. But my old professor should get a good gig out of it, while I still have a chance. We'll do it for old time sakes.

Al: Wow, you're a wonderful person, John.

John: Let's not get saucy, now, please.

Al: Nobody wants to see the Beatles act, John. Let's be honest here. People just want the Beatles on the silver screen.

John: Then it'll be Simple Simon. Who said anything about acting, anyhow?

Al: Well, I suppose I could take a whack at it. People will want something like those American Frankie and Annette beach blanket bingo flicks. Now, mind you, it's not going to be *Gone with the Wind.*

John: So write it just that way, Moran. And leave out the bloody beach. I hate sand.

Al: I suppose I could do no worse than most Hollywood hacks.

John: There you go, son. You can keep Annette but put in the boot with Frankie.

Al: I could substitute the Pacific Ocean with the Mersey River. We can swing Fabian, Troy and Bobby Rydell with Paul, George and Ringo.

John: Now you're cooking with gas! Write a scene where Ringo gets Bridget Bardot off with his huge honker.

Al: Nobody would like it; but maybe Ringo would.

John: You know the Beatles speed in life better than any Grubb Street writer. You had better sign on before Eppy finds his own scribbler for the task. Just make it halfway decent.

Al: After this pint, I'm off.

John: I have purchased you this one pint, Al. I want to fill you up good and proper.

Al: Well, now, how about that, too? Oh, how things have changed. Well, I suppose I always knew that they would. That's what I said, all along, anyway.

John: I would like to talk to you about things.

Al: I want to find a bookstore to track down a book or two on screenplay writing. What's that?

John: London is grand but phony and not so friendly.

Al: London? I guess I've never been there. And I've been in England now for a fairly long time. I've no excuse for it!

John: Yes, and there is even talk about going to New York. Al, what are us four chaps going to do in New York?

Al: New York? New York is great, be sure to visit the Statue of Liberty. You know, it's funny, no one ever does. They all say they are going to see it but then they never make the boat ride. Johnny, sometimes you have to just take a boat ride to get a good perspective on life. It has a way of refreshing your spirit, you know what I mean?

179

John: I guess you're right. It'll be an American ferry boat ride.

Al: But look, I at least need some format to work with.

John: Invent your own bloody structure. That's what I do these days.

Al: I better get back home.

John: Home?

Al: Not home, per se. Ginny and I are back on track these days. I have to catch up with her.

John: Good for you, mate. I told you.

Al: Don't look so glum. Remember, you're John Lennon. It doesn't seem like much to you right now, but it's all that we live to see. This is your time. Take it. Don't hesitate. It's not so bad a thing. And try to avoid attacking journalists.

John: Ha! I suppose you're right, as usual.

Al: Goodbye, John Lennon.

[Al exits.]

John: Goodbye, Professor Al Moran. We four lads will be missing you, now.

SHORT INTERMISSION
(5 Minutes)

ACT 3 SCENE 1

Setting: Inside Al's study, night. Ginny is posing for Al and he is painting her picture. She is nude and drinking wine. Al is taking great care with the canvas as he sips wine. It is dark outside.

Ginny: Why are you some quiet, luv?

Al: I'm just fussing over that script inside of my head. I'm not sure if I'm cut out to do it.

Ginny: If Al Moran can't write it, who can? You're the resident expert.

Al: This Beatles thing is almost getting too big. I'm worrying about Johnny.

Ginny: No bigger than the bulge I see growing in your trousers. Johnny will be fine enough. Can't we leave off those bloody beat and jive boys long enough to enjoy ourselves?

Al: I'm enjoying myself….but I'm sticking to business.

Ginny: I mean business, bhoyo.

Al: I can't get a handle on the scouse accent thing.

Ginny: If anybody knows the lads it is you. They all know that, Al. John the most.

Al: Where shall it all end? What happens to Johnny in the end? Do they just use him up and destroy him, all for nothing?

Ginny: You're Catholic enough to know it all ends up with death.

Al: Why so gloomy?

Ginny: You're making me gloomy.

Al: I want you happy.

Ginny: Happy or horny?

Al: Painting you is more important than any script. The Beatles can wait. I am sure Brian Epstein has plenty of Hack writers, anyway.

Ginny: One day you should write a book about the Beatles, Liverpool, the Art College and me.

Al: Yeah, maybe, a book. That would be something. I really do worry about Johnny, though.

Ginny: Well, don't, you fool. I need your concern more than him.

Al: Ah, yes. Indeed.

Ginny: Ha, ha, mister.

Al: It's been quite a ride. Is that all that life is, just a ride, and then just for some?

Ginny: I suppose that's true. Those who miss it, oh well for them.

Al: And isn't that awfully harsh?

Ginny: It's life, luv. Accept it. Try and win at it.

Al: I guess you're right about that. Please move forty-five degrees to your right. Thanks.

Ginny: I have to pee.

Al: I could use a sandwich, anyway.

Ginny: You're such a pig. We are creating art, here, yes?

Steven G. Farrell

Al: I'm going to work on the script. I have to try to get it right, for John.

Ginny: Don't take so long. I am going to sleep...in your bedroom.

Al: Goodnight, my love. I won't be long.

Ginny: Goodnight. But I hope you're...long.

Al: How so?

Ginny: I meant all night long, my moon god.

[Ginny stands up and reveals her nakedness to Al. He is still impressed by her beauty. She approaches him and crumbles into his arms.]

Al: I thought you were off to bed....to sleep.

Ginny: Bed, Al, bed...both of us, together. No sleep...until dawn breaks.

[Al lifts her up and takes her into the bedroom where he gently puts her down on the bed. He begins to undress.]

Al: I have to work tomorrow.

Ginny: And you must work now.

Al: The manuscript can wait.

Ginny: I wasn't referring to any bloody manuscript. I meant you need to work...on...me.

Al: Your wish is my command, Ginny.

Ginny: I think your wish is for your Ginny...all night long.

[The two make love. The early traces of dawn reflect the pleasure on their faces. Ginny reaches a climax first. He follows shortly.]

Ginny: You, Al.

Al: You, Gin...ny.

[The early morning rays reveal the two exhausted and happy in one another's arms.]

Ginny: Nighty, night. Kissy, kiss. Al, luv.

[Al is looking into her face with tenderness as she falls asleep.]

182

ACT 3 SCENE 2

Setting: Outside college classroom, day. Al is typing at his desk when there's a gentle a rap at the door. He is stunned when Brian Epstein enters. The two men shake hands. Miss Hayes is taking up the rear.

Brian: I'm frightfully sorry for disturbing you, old man.

Miss Hayes: What? No cute lasses here to help you grade papers?

Al: Brian, this is a surprise.

Miss Hayes: So he does do some work after all.

Brian: We're all in Liverpool at the moment...a brief moment.

Al: Are the Beatles putting on a show at the Cavern Club?

Brian: We're here only for the movie screenplay and to visit our screenwriter. We're taking him out to a grand feast tonight. The Beatles and I want to treat you right, Al.

Al: That's very kind but I'd rather work on the script while I'm on fire. And I am on fire!

Brian: John rang me up about that but I must tell you that there are others working on script at this point in time. It's a bit of a contest, don't you see? Of course, Al, you're on our short list.

[Al doesn't like what he's hearing. Brian becomes visibly uncomfortable. Al then proceeds to herald the merits of his script.]

Al: How about this for a scene: the lads, John, Paul and George are in a rock n' roll band in dire straits for a drummer. The three of them are walking past a monastery when they happen to hear the sound of most beautiful drumming in the world. And guess what?

Brian: I can guess, Al, I'm afraid.

Al: The drummer turns out to be none other than the one and only Ringo!

Brian: And Ringo is a monk too?

Al: He is simply a novice Monk who tends to his prayers, garden and drum kit. What's wrong with that?

Brian: It sounds very Catholic.

Al: It stops being Catholic when Ringo tears off his robe to become a Beatle.

Brian: Sounds...well...er...promising.

Miss Hayes: It isn't *Hamlet.*

Al: John takes on a motor cycle gang, Paul dates a royal princess and George is chased by a lion.

Brian: Nothing fancy, professor. We're in a frightful hurry.

Miss Hayes; the Beatles are now an industry, professor.

Al: It'll be good.

Brian: Dash it off quickly, then.

Al: I'm getting there just now.

Brian: It should be roughly ninety minutes long, Dr. Moran.

Al: The working title is *I Should Have Known Better.*

Brian: Well, it is a pleasure, as always.

Al: The same here.

Brian: And, thank you, for the introductory letter and all. I just wanted to say that.

Al: You're welcome, it was just fate, and who can control that?

Brian: Many thanks, in any event.

Al: Good luck with my Beatles. Take care of them, mate.

Brian: I will. You can be sure of that. Goodbye.

Al: Brian, it has been a real pleasure meeting and knowing you. Best of luck to you, sir.

Brian: Thank you, Al. The same is true for you.

Al: Goodbye.

Brian: Goodbye.

Miss Hayes: We'll let you get on...with things...sir.

[Brian exits.]

ACT 3 SCENE 3

Setting: Al is making phone calls.

Voiceover: I should have known better. Ginny and I would be engaged. She told me the Beatles had started filming a movie based on the screenplay of Allan Owen, a Liverpool writer. Of course, I couldn't reach Brian Epstein at his office. None of the Beatles were answering their telephones; except for lonesome old George.

John: George, is that you?

George: Yes.

Al: It's me, Moran.

George: Our Albert!

Al: What's this about the Beatles filming before my script is finished?

George: What's this all about, then?

Al: Lennon and Epstein both engaged me to write a screenplay for your movie.

George: Take that up with John and Brian, Al, not me.

Al: What's the lowdown?

George: Search me, mate.

Al: I have great stuff down on paper, George. I filled the movie up with fine lines….and finer women…all for you, skin.

George: I keep telling you, Al, I don't know a blooming thing about it. I only play the guitar for the band. I play the lead guitar.

Al: Yes, I know that you play lead guitar for the Beatles! But I feel as if I have just been royally screwed over by the high and mighty Beatles, my very own mates. The Beatles! How is it even possible? It's mind-boggling.

George: It doesn't interest me, Moran.

Al: Don't feed me that line, Harrison!

George: Listen, professor, we're just here to make music. That's our lot in life, and we're pretty good at it, I might add, at least so far.

Al: What? I can't believe what I am hearing!

George: What's wrong with you, mate? You're lucky I even answered the phone. Look, Uncle Al, things change, so do the times, and people's lives.

You have to move on, and accept that. We're just not the same lads we once were in Liverpool, anymore.

Al: What could have possibly changed? Jesus!

George: Practically everything has changed, in fact.

Al: I think that is a pack of lies!

George: Calm yourself now, prof Al.

Al: Oh, my God!

George: Shout at those who you think made you promises, not me.

Al: The Beatles are now stepping on the little people who helped them up the ladder in the first place.

George: I'll see to it that you're paid for your time. Union scale, like. Send me the invoice directly and have done with your sulk.

Al: It's the principle of the thing. Damn it, George! Don't you understand?

George: You've gotten plenty out of the Beatles, lad. I'm not going to even start on all of the birds we helped you pull.

Al: You're all lousy sons of....

George: Ah, don't bother me.

Al: You are lucky that…

George: But wait, just a moment. Al?

Al: What now, for Christ sake, more torture? Why do you persecute me like this?

George: I just want to personally say thank you, before I say goodbye. And it was indeed a pleasure knowing you. So, thank you, sir, and goodbye.

Al: Yes. That's fine enough. It was great knowing you too, George. And thank you, too. Good luck is all that I can say at this point.

[The telephone line goes dead.]

ACT 3 SCENE 4

Setting: A montage of live action scenes and voice-overs.

Voiceover: The Beatles were introduced to my native country.

[Ed Sullivan is introducing the Beatles to his audience on CBS.]

Voiceover: I married Ginny Browne.

[Ginny and Al are standing side by side. John and Cynthia, best man and the maid of honor, stand next to them.]

Voiceover: The Beatles tried to make amends with me by giving me a small part in *A HARD DAY'S NIGHT.* Can you spot me in this scene?

[There is a brief clip from *A Hard Day's Night* where a platoon of London boobies are chasing the Beatles around the city street.

ACT 3 SCENE 5

Setting: 2012, on the Staten Island Ferry, day. Al Moran and Ginny Browne, now older, are in New York. There is a fifteen second clip of Gerry and the Pacemakers song *Ferry Across the Mersey.*

Al: I haven't heard that song in years.

Ginny: I haven't seen Gerry and his lads in years.

Al: John shot, George dead of cancer, and so many others scattered.

Ginny: But Al Moran stayed in Liverpool, England, for a spell, at least.

Al: And Ginny Browne came back to the Mersey to start her own woman's magazine....and made heaps of silver and gold doing it.

Ginny: That's Ginny Moran, mate. I have been a respectable married woman for years now. You might just treat me like one.

Al: Your husband has a beauty on his hands.

[Ginny squeezes Al's hands and looks gently into his eyes. There is a sad and gentle smile upon her lips. Her big brown eyes speak volumes. He begins to visibly grieve.]

Ginny: Al, I'm sick.

Al: Come back to me now, love. We'll see it out together.

Ginny: I have always loved you, darling. You know that, right?

Al: I shall never stop loving you, Ginny Browne Moran, no matter what, and ever since the very beginning. I've always loved you as much as we loved in the old days.

Ginny: Will your love be there for all eternity, luv?

187

Al: My love will last beyond all eternity, Ginny. Oh, God.

[Al and Ginny hold one another close.]

Voiceover: Jennifer Colleen Browne Moran passed away. The bright colors of life were forever washed away from my eyes.

[The ferryboat crashes through the dark wave.]

ACT 3 SCENE 6

Setting: Outside of a Catholic Church, day. Al Moran, crushed, refuses to step into the church. Gerry Marsden gently grabs a hold of Al's arm.

Gerry: You're Beatrice is awaiting her Dante…inside…Al.

Al: It can't be…over, Gerry. It just can't be.

Gerry: You're Catholic enough to know it's not over…and she's seeing you now…and smiling. That is the way it is with things. It cannot be changed, mate.

Al: You make death seem to trite.

Gerry: Trite? No, it's just permanent and ever-lasting.

Al: Oh, God. Right now, I don't require any reading from scripture!

Gerry: I was not trying to do that, Al. I was just giving you my opinion.

Al: Well, your opinion stinks!

Gerry: All that we have to do is walk through that door, and go beyond.

Al: Spoken like a true poet. I am not so sure I want to go through that door. And why have I been thrust into these strange places where I must reconcile strange realities?

Gerry: Professor Moran, please try and gather yourself.

Al: Okay, you're right. I will, now.

Gerry: It's really very easy. And after you face your fears, they melt away like butter. And that is just life.

Al: It's easy for some; but for those who have tasted of true beauty it is not so simple. Though perhaps, with some effort, I have more understanding.

Gerry: There you go, now. Follow me, then.

Al: Okay.

Gerry: Take my hand, then.

Al: Thank you.

Voiceover: God, how I still love Ginny. And I think often of John, Paul, long gone away George, Ringo and the rest. I dream of dirty Liverpool, the crumbling port city perched upon the Mersey River that will be the final resting place for my ancient Irish Yankee bones. I shall die a very lucky man.

ACT 3 SCENE 7

Setting: A graveyard, day. A large gathering is scattering after the final rites at a Catholic funeral. The characters voices are heard but they are not in the scene. The scene is shot from a distance.

Ringo: We all loved Professor Albert Moran.

Gerry: All of Liverpool loved our Albert.

Ringo: Ginny and John loved him the most.

Paul: He sent us sailing into the wide ocean. Will anyone say a few words?

Gerry: May God rest the beautiful soul of Professor Al Moran. I shall dearly miss him. I will always remember him for the rest of me life. Amen.

Ringo: Thank you, my dear Al Moran for our friendship and all that you did for us in our lives.

Paul: We are here…I want to say that…I…I love you, Uncle Al. I love you.

Gerry: I guess that's it, then.

Paul: Yes, it is.

Ringo: Come on, mates. Let's go drink away our sorrows.

Voiceover: On behalf of the Moran, Farrell, Powers, McNamara and Gleason families of Chicago, Illinois and Kenosha, Wisconsin I want bid you a happy voyage, Al Moran and Ginny Browne.

Steven G. Farrell

PAPER 8

BLACK AND GREEN SMASH MOUTH

It is a widely held belief of many boxing scholars that the sport of
professional boxing entered its modern phase when the 'Boston Strong'
flattened the 'Troy Giant' in the fifth round with his bare knuckles. John
L. Sullivan would become the pivotal figure in the transition of boxing from
London Rules (bare knuckles) to *the Marquis of Queensberry Rules* (gloves
over fist). However, Sullivan was still a primitive savage compared to his
successor, James J. Corbett, who was boxing's first truly modern
heavyweight champion. Both Sullivan and Corbett were Irish-Americans,
and they set the course for the dominance of their sport by their ethnic
group for the next several decades to follow. It wasn't until well into the
20th Century that African-American fighters began to emerge and,
eventually, to take over the sport. In this essay, I shall examine the on-going
struggle between Irish-American and African-American fighters that took
center stage in the boxing for almost 100 years before Yankee Micks
completely disappeared from the sport forever.

Sullivan held on to his diamond-studded championship belt for an
amazing ten years reign; mostly by ducking promising up and coming
fighters of both races. Perhaps at the head of the pack of denied challengers
were black men like George Godfrey and Peter Jackson. Sullivan was no
doubt one of the first athletes to figure-out it was more profitable to turn to
the footlights of the stage than to take a pounding beneath a hot sun while
risking the loss of the title. It was also physically less taxing and required no
roadwork. It had always been the 'Great' Sullivan's goal to score a quick
and hefty payday; and he could achieve his ends just as easily on the stage,
or by touring the country in well paid exhibitions sparing with rank
amateurs from the American hinterlands. However even somebody as
exalted as Sullivan found it necessary to put his crown on the line every few
years: if only to silence the baying of the sportswriters and the elite of the
boxing world. One must keep in mind that in the late 19th century there was
no formal boxing organization yet created to sanction or to promote fights.

Richard Kyle Fox, owner and editor-in-chief of the *Police Gazette*, did more to galvanize the champ to defend the crown with his printed hazing than anything else.

There had always been plenty of talented black fighters in the fight game in America since the introduction of the sport during colonial times, but they were usually regulated to fighting one another. As the wounds of the Civil War began to heal, blacks in the lower weight divisions began to make in-roads in comparison to the heavyweight class. George 'Little Chocolate' Nixon, a black Canadian, became the duly recognized bantamweight champion of the world in 1890. Joe Gans was another highly respected black man who eventually became the lightweight champion in 1902. Reflecting the blatantly racist tone of the day, reporters referred to black fighters as 'Ethiopians.' It is sickening for historians to note that there was no hesitation in bestowing such demeaning nicknames upon worthy black fighters like *"Kid Chocolate,' "Cool* Coffee Maker,*"* or the 'Black Prince.'

Towards the end of Sullivan's reign in the early 'Gay' Nineties, two of Sullivan's top three challengers were black: Godfrey, an African-American, and Peter Jackson, a West Caribbean transplant, who had built up his reputation primarily on the shores of Australia where there was much less rancor towards blacks than in the USA.

Sullivan dismissed both black men with such jeering remarks as "I will not fight a negro. I have and never shall," and "(Jackson) is a great sport, a high roller, and probably not in the best condition. Isenberg (*John L. Sullivan and his America*) writes: "It was Peter Jackson's misfortune that he was forced to confront the twin evils of institutional and personal racism." John L.'s drawing of the notorious 'color line' met with the approval of his manager, William Muldoon, and America in general. Sullivan went on to disqualify the vast majority of fighters by stating that he would not fight for anything less than a purse of $10,000, effectively putting his title out of reach with the lone exception of Corbett, who had the backing of the wealthy 'silver kings,' many whom were of Irish stock. As time went on Sullivan resolution cemented into hard stone that he would not step into a ring unless his opponent was an American white. Sullivan, who was reputed to be a mean son-of-a-bitch of the first water, didn't even have any kind words for Corbett, a fellow Yankee Mick, referring to him as a 'duffer' and 'the young dude.'

James J. Corbett, like Sullivan, was an urban Irish-Catholic and the son of immigrant parents who had settled in California. However, 'Gentleman Jim' had had the marked advantage over Sullivan by being born in an upwardly mobile middle-class family and within the city limits of a brawling gold rush boom town that was young enough to be free of the deeper rooted prejudices of Sullivan's puritanical Boston. It is also true that there was a vast educational difference between the two Irishmen. Corbett had no qualms whatsoever in fighting a Jewish boxer like Joe Choynski or a black man like Peter Jackson. He fought a grueling draw with the thirty pound heavier West Indian in 1891; and he had the class to praise Jackson by saying he was "credit to his profession." Labeled as the 'fight of the century,' the Sullivan-Corbett fight was fought over $45,000 in purse and side bets. The end result was the dethroning of the long-time champion. After being counted out in the twenty-first round, a battered Sullivan staggered to the ropes and addressed the audience: "Gentlemen, I have only one thing to say, once (and) for all, and that is this: 'this was to be, and is, my last fight. I have lost. I stayed once too often with a young man. And to James J. Corbett I pass the championship."

Corbett was white and American and, in time, he too referred to the belt as the "American championship," and he became steadfast in his refusal to fight any black men. Curiously enough Corbett felt that his 'own crowd,' the Irish-Americans, never forgave him for beating Sullivan. A young 'lace curtain' Irishman had defeated a 'shanty' Irishman in an America where social class prevailed as much as racial and regional credentials.

Corbett, who many consider the ring's first scientific boxer, held on to the crown for five years. His long reign was more about ducking troublesome opponents than it was about any skillful ring technique. In the 1941 movie, *Gentleman Jim,* Corbett is played by Errol Flynn while Ward Bond portrayed an over-the-top Sullivan, complete with a broad Irish brogue that the real John L. never spoke with. The baton was eventually passed on to 'Ruby' Robert Fitzsimmons, a naturalized American citizen and originally a Cornishman with an Northern Irish Protestant father (with pit stops in the fight worlds of New Zealand and Australia), in an 1897 upset with a 'solar plexus' punch in the fourteenth round. Fitz, who was to hold titles in three weight divisions during the course of his exceptional career, was a man of few prejudices who took on all comers. Unfortunately, once the crown was placed upon his head, Fitzsimmons received a great deal of outside pressures to limit those who would have access to a title shot. In other words: the title was not available to fighters of color. After Fitzsimmons lost the title to James J. Jefferies in 1899 the Irish didn't have a heavyweight champion of their own until Jack Dempsey took the crown back twenty years later.

Sullivan and Corbett, now elder statesmen for their sport, didn't have much to say about having an Anglo-Saxon Protestant following in their footsteps, but their ink became vile when James J. Jefferies was forced to come out of five year hiatus as the newly billed 'Great White Hope' to challenge Jack Johnson, the first officially recognized black heavyweight champion of the world, in Reno, Nevada on the 4th of July, 1910.

Sullivan loudly proclaimed: "A white man demeans himself by fighting a black," and "I do believe the negroes should fight in a class by themselves...of course we shall all like to see the white man win, but wishes can never fill a sack." By the way, chances are it was the novelist Jack London who coined the term the 'Great White Hope.' Corbett, who was always more politically correct than Sullivan and had once been a referee for Johnson in New York's Polo Grounds, had less to say but he was in Jefferies corner when the fight ended with a Johnson knockout in the 14th. Jefferies, like his predecessors, had also done his share of ducking, dodging and hiding before he officially retired the first time. "After one has achieved his ambition and reached the top, there is not the incentive to work as there was before. In other words, it's harder to work and, unconsciously, a fighter will neglect proper training."

James J. Jefferies, who was of Dutch and English lineage, was probably less prejudice than Sullivan or Corbett which could be due to the slowly changing attitudes about race in sports. Like Corbett, he had fought Jackson, but unlike Corbett he had won. Afterwards, Jeff stated: "I probably wouldn't have hurt Peter much when he was at his best." Jeff also had this to say personally to Jackson: "Don't worry, Pete, we all come to it in the end." There is an old photograph of Jefferies standing on a beach with two black youngsters; his arm is resting upon the shoulders of one of the lads. It is hardly the behavior of a bigot.

Carney (*Ultimate Tough Guy: the Life & times of James J. Jefferies*) contends that 'Jefferies initial response to Johnson's challenges may have been to draw the color line, which he appears to have done on at least one occasion. But he realized that this was ridiculous in view of the fact that he'd fought several black fighters.' Before moving away from Big Jeff, I'd like to share a quote attributed to him about Tom *'Sailor'* Sharkey, an Irish *heavyweight* boxer (who some scholars contend should be recognized as a brief holder of the crown) and a personal friend of his. "God never made a wayward child as lovable or hateful as an Irishman according to his mood."

Jack Johnson was never the gallant defender of the African-American community that many Americans still believe all of these years later, nor was he the sadist that many whites accused him of being during his prime. He was cocky but not arrogant. He wasn't a punishing fighter but he was a punishing counterpuncher. In boxing terms he was closer in style to Corbett than he was to Sullivan or Jefferies. The Irish champs, who had to fight many prejudices of the day, were never depicted as 'fiend incarnate' as the media proclaimed about Johnson. Ward (*Unforgiveable Blackness: The Rise & Fall of Jack Johnson*) describes Johnson as being 'independent, restless, with an ability to improvise, to attract attention, and to get around rules intended to tie him down.' Jack once had this to say about his handling of relationships with both blacks and whites: "I have found no better way of avoiding race prejudice than to act with people of other races as if prejudice did not exist."

Once he was the king of the boxing world, Jack refused to fight black fighters, giving his primary reason as being that there was no money in it. However, to his credit, Jack was never known to hesitate in fighting Irishmen from all over the globe like Sandy Ferguson, Jim Flynn and Victor McLaglen, who fared better as Hollywood actor in life. The hulking Victor also performed notably better in his fist fighting against John Wayne in *The Quiet Man.* than he did in his match with Johnson. When Jack Johnson toed the mark with Ferguson in Chelsea, Massachusetts, according to Ward: "Nearly everyone present was Irish and howling for Johnson's blood."

The colorful Johnson unhappily lost his crown in the 26th round beneath the blazing sun in Havana, Cuba. Sadder yet, many years later Jack showed up at Joe Louis' training camp before Joe's fight with Max Schmeling. Joe reputedly declared: "Get that black cat out here. I don't want him in my camp." The *'Brown Bomber'* was only too well aware of how unpopular Johnson had become with both blacks and whites as he went into decline. The part of Jack Johnson was skillfully played by James Earl Jones in the 1970 movie, *The Great White Hope*. There was a Hollywood prank played upon the audience when Jack Johnson became Jack Jefferson as I backhanded tribute to Johnson and Jefferies.

Jesse Willard, another Wasp from the sticks like Jefferies, was the white man who put the hurt on Johnson. He lost his one and only fight as champion when he had his teeth knocked out and block knocked off by Jack Dempsey in 1919. Jack Dempsey has the distinction of being the only Irish-Mormon to become a boxing champion of the world. Chances are the Irish crowd really never fully accepted Dempsey because of his religion, as well as the additional Scottish, Native American and Jewish genes he carried in his 190 pound frame. The native of Colorado actually had more in common with Jack Johnson than he had with either Sullivan or Corbett. Both Jacks had been boxing hobos, riding the railroad rods as they built up impressive records brawling in mining camps and in the back rooms of honkytonks. Both men were also virtually racist free and took on all worthy comers. Unfortunately Dempsey, who was a brave fellow who feared no man, allowed himself to be restricted by the rules of sanctioned racism due to Doc Kearns and Tex Rickard, the men who handled his career and promoted his fights. The big gates came in fighting white contenders like Tommy Gibbons, George Carpientier and Luis Firpo, while ignoring highly ranked black opponents like Harry Willis and Sam 'the Boston Tar Baby' Langford.

Dempsey, once again in a very similar fashion as Johnson, had very little credibility with the general public as his boxing career waxed and waned during *'the Roaring Twenties.'* He made poor public relation choices when he married a suspected prostitute and was accused of dodging the draft during World War One. Jack compounded his problems by appearing in a photograph of himself working in a shipyard sporting a new pair of fancy spates. The public felt duped. Even Jack Johnson taunted Dempsey by calling him "a slacker!" Later in his life, Jack Dempsey told Roger the sportswriter (*A Flame of Fire: Jack Dempsey and the roaring 20's):*"No matter how much I have I'm for the poor person. I'm for the white poor and the black poor who have it worse. As long as I live, I'll never forget I was poor."

Gene Tunney finally returned the crown to the urban Irish Catholics by defeating Jack Dempsey in 1926 and again in 1927 in two ten round decisions, including the infamous 'long count' Many Irish-Americans felt more comfortable with Tunney over Dempsey because he was truly one of their own. The fact was that the bookish and shy Tunney had only taken up the sport to defend himself against the Irish street gangs who had terrorized him and his brothers in their Greenwich Village neighborhood in Manhattan. In time the 'Fighting Leatherneck' lost the support of his own ethnic group because he turned out to be a 'no fight' champion. His lone fight was in 1928 against Irishman Tom Heeney before returning to begin a new life as a Connecticut Yankee country squire. More than a few in Irish America felt that Tunney had betrayed his roots by going 'high hat like a swell.'

It wasn't until June 13, 1935 when James J. Braddock defeated Max Baer, who was part Irish ancestry himself, in a fifteen round decision on Long Island that the Irish once again had a champion that they could truly identify with again. It can be argued that Braddock was the most loved of all Irish-American heavyweight champions since John L. Sullivan. 'The Cinderella Man's' stunning victory over the fun-loving Baer is still considered the greatest upset in boxing history. Braddock, who was really a very run-of-the-mill fighter, has become the epitome of the Irish-American fighter: a courageous underdog with more heart than talent. Russell Crowe intensified the myth in Ron Howard's film version of Braddock's amazing comeback.

Schaap (*Cinderella Man: James J. Braddock, Max Baer and the Greatest Upset in Boxing History*) contends that when news leaked out that Braddock and his family had been on public relief (welfare) earlier during the Depression it only increased his popularity, for the Irish-American had paid back every cent he had collected once he defeated 'Corn' Griffith in a preliminary bout before the Baer-Carnera championship match in 1934. Unlike most media generated publicity the news item meant to disgrace a man actually made him a hero to millions of American gallantly combating the doldrums of the Thirties. Schaap also replays the old story where Max Baer and Jack Dempsey are being interviewed in Dempsey's nightclub and the former champ was questioned by a reporter about the new champ's chances against the challenger from New Jersey.

"'He's (Baer) going to get hurt, that's what's going to happen.'"

"'Chasing women around is the best exercise I know," Baer said. "They're harder to catch than washed-up Irishmen.'"

Baer, who claimed Jewish ancestry based upon his father's heritage while he was reared in his mother's Roman Catholicism, stepped into the ring out of fighting condition and was shown up by Braddock, the pride of Bergen, New Jersey. By the way, Braddock's fight in 1929 with Tommy Loughran for the light heavyweight championship is the last time two Irish-Americans squared off for the a boxing title of any kind.

Braddock had enough savvy and street smarts to realize that he wasn't the stuff that true champions are made out of, so he held on to the crown by not fighting for two years. Schapp writes: "Even while the public was falling in love with Braddock, its new champion, it was drawn to the 'Brown Bomber' (Joe Louis). Braddock, in spite of his popularity, was regarded as a lucky Irishman who took the title from a lackadaisical Baer, but Louis at twenty-one was already hailed as the most complete heavyweight ever." The last of the Irish-American heavyweight champs had enough wisdom to negotiate a good contract for $32,000 before he stepped between the ropes that had been set-up in Comiskey Park, home of the Chicago White Sox, in 1937. Joe Louis, along with the sellout crowd, was stunned when the 'Cinderella Man' floored him with a solid sock to the jaw. The knockdown was Braddock's last shining moment inside on the canvas; for Joe proceeded to massacre him from that moment onward.

After the sixth round Bob Gould, James J's manager said, "I'm going to have the referee stop the fight." Braddock, in a mythic display of an Irishman's courage in a lost cause, retorted, "The hell you are. If you do, Bob, I'll never speak to you again."

Steven G. Farrell

Two rounds later the Irishman was floored for the count of ten and Joe Louis became the undisputed heavyweight champion of the world: a title he would hold for almost an entire decade. James J. was a decent enough practicing Catholic who refused to mention Joe's race at any time. Joe, in turn, referred to Jim as "the bravest man he had ever fought." As the Second World War loomed around the corner, most American seemed relieved to see an American wearing the crown over any European.

Joe Louis was a fighting champ compared to the previous heavyweight kings, but he was panned in the press for his lame opponents, who were collectively known as the 'bum of the month club.' The lone exception to the rule was Billy Conn, an Irish-American from Pittsburgh, who was the current light heavy champion of the world. The 'Pittsburgh kid' was handsome, white, charismatic and gifted in the ring. He was also young, cocky, quotable, Irish and strikingly handsome which made him a great draw at the box office.

Kennedy (*Billy Conn the Pittsburgh Kid*) wrote: "Many Irish-Americans identified with Conn's quest as an attempt to recapture that was rightfully theirs. At this point in the history of boxing the Irish had produced more champs than anyone else. Conn could restore the legacy of Sullivan, Corbett, Dempsey, Tunney and Braddock. The bout took place in Harlem, the capital of Black America, surrounded by a city with a large Irish population."

Conn, at 180 pounds, was knocked out by Louis, 199 pounds, in the 13th round in their 1941 match when Billy was way ahead on points on all of the scorecards. When chided by the media for trying to knock Louis out Conn replied, "What's the sense of being Irish if you can't be dumb?" An out-of-shape and aging Conn took on Louis in a rematch five years later, but he only lasted into the eighth round. Regis Welsh, a noted sportswriter, wrote later, "Conn, once a great fighter, just had too much Irish to control his fighting abilities once he gets burned up."

The end of Billy Conn's tenure in the ring as heralded the end of the Irish presence in the sport as well. It wasn't until the 1960's, with the emergence of Jerry Quarry, that the Irish-Americans had one of their own working their way up the ladder to eventually become the number one challenger in the heavyweight division. With his John Lennon haircut and his California cool surfer dude moves, Quarry had more in common with the Beach Boys than he did with his Irish counterparts like Sullivan, Corbett, Tunney or Braddock. He defeated former heavyweight champion Floyd Patterson and top contenders like Ron Lyle and Ernie Shavers. However, 'Irish Jerry' couldn't beat the big guns like Mohammed Ali, Joe Frazier or Ken Norton. Jerry Quarry was noted for three reasons: 1) he bled

198

easily; 2) he made numerous successful and unsuccessful comebacks; and 3) he was an Irish-American. Once when Jerry and his brother Mike, a light heavyweight, were put on the same bill against two black men, it was touted as "The Soul Brothers versus the Quarry Brothers" by promoter Bob Arum.

In 1982, 'Gentleman' Gerry Clooney of Long Island, New York, became the last serious Irish-American heavyweight fighter worth his weight in gold when he climbed through the ropes to tango with Larry Holmes for the title. Promoter Don King, in an effort to drum-up interest for the closed circuit audience, baptized Cooney as the 'Great White Hope' while Holmes snorted that Cooney was the "Great White Dope." In the 100 years since 1882 the race-baiting and name calling had jumped back from the Irish-American's side of the track to the part of town where the African-Americans resided. Ken Norton, a champ for a brief while, had started the bashing of Cooney before his own fight with the Irishman by boasting that he had a perfect record against Caucasians. Never mind Ken's record, for Cooney set a professional record by knocking Norton out in 54 seconds in the first round. Ali, who is partially Irish himself, never the one to praise white fighters, actually said before the Holmes-Cooney fight that Cooney could hit Holmes so hard "that his brothers in Africa would feel it." Cooney, like Conn and Quarry, was unsuccessful in his bid for the title belt.

Irish America has put out very few champions in any weight class since World War Two: Sean O'Grady and "Irish" Mickey Ward being the most famous. Eoin Cannon, a contemporary scholar of Irish America, heavily influenced this paper with his perceptive on the packaging of Irishmen in today's fight game. Cannon, in his groundbreaking essay, "The Heavyweight champion of Irishness: ethnic fighting identities today," makes the valid point that the Irish-American fighters still have a marketable image because their symbolic representation of being heroic. Cannon wrote: "The Irish fighter is the humble man of limited skills who wins by hard work, sheer courage…the Irish fighter is also has a cheeky, devil-may-care attitude." Cannon makes his strongest point when he claims that the Irish fighter has the 'inability to take the safe, smart route instead of the dangerous bruising one."

Halloran (*Irish Thunder: The Hard Life & Times of Micky Ward*) describes in colorful details Ward's three epic bouts with Arturo Giatti which took place after the events depicted in the movie *The Fighter*, featuring Mark Wahlberg as 'Irish' Micky. The odds are high that Micky Ward shall be the absolute last one in the long list of truly great Irish-American fighters.

In this paper I have attempted to trace the sometimes thorny but usually affable relationships between the leading Irish-American and

Steven G. Farrell

African-American heavyweight boxers, ranging from 1882- to 1982. The Irish day in boxing has long since departed and the African-American fighters, after a very long reign at the top, are now being tossed aside by talented Hispanic, Asian and African fighters, as well as a recent infusion of white Eastern European champion level talent (as predicted in Sylvester Stallone's *Rocky Four*). The playing of the race card, as well as the race-baiting, will probably forever remain a part of the most individualistic and psychological sport ever created by humankind.

PAPER 9

RETIRING FROM WRITING

One can retire from just about any job, hobby or pursuit without much criticism from the public at large; however, the lone exception being retiring from the practice of writing. Sometime, perhaps many centuries ago, there must have of been a dictum put in place by a great prophet or philosopher like Moses or Aristotle that decreed that a scribbler who puts down lines of words on a blank piece of paper must continue to do so until their very last moment on the face of this earth. It doesn't seem to matter whether or not that the author may have penned their last meaningful words years before their actual demise. It could be that there's this hidden gene inside of every writers biological make-up that convinces them that they have yet to produce their magus opus while the historical data clearly indicates that the vast majority of masterpieces are written long before most writers have finished with their literary tasks.

Rimbaud, the French poet, put the period to his last poem before he was 21 years of age. He had poured out what he needed to say before embarking on an action-filled life that included gun-running in Africa. William Shakespeare, the 'great Bard,' is yet another writer who knew when it was time to pack it in. He became a businessman in his home town and never was tempted to go back to his writing desk. These two great men are to be admired for knowing when to quit. However, most writers, especially American, British and European writers, seem to have felt that they were condemned to their chair and the midnight lamp to prove to the literary world that they still had the stuff of champions when they were just writing for the money, or to pass the time until they retired for good with death.

With the composition of *Retiring from Writing* this is my last-ditch attempt to set some sort of historical precedent here by knowing that this autobiographical piece will be the last 'creative' writing of my life. I have just turned sixty years of age (2014), and I have been taking my place at my writing table to hammer out writings of every known genre since I was twelve years old (1966). So I have had a very active writing career for the past 48 years. Of course, I grant to you, my reader, that I have not stockpiled any large sums of money in my bank account to encourage me to write any further, nor am I eagerly protecting a literary reputation. By occupation I am an educator; and I have been in the field, more or less, since 1979. Writing has been my spiritual vocation longer than my teaching career. Catholics would refer to it as being my true 'calling.'

I am resolved that *Farrell's Last Papers'* shall be the last literary manuscript I shall ever work on in this life. It will be my 11th and final published book. Chances are that it shall be a self-published work. As I have been putting together the work, it quickly became clear that my table of contents was made-up of 8 pieces, including one novella, one novelette one trilogy, three short stories, one essay and one stage play. The manuscript came to roughly 290 typed pages and it occurred to me that I might want to round it off to close to 300 pages, making it my longest work ever. A goofy notion came over me that since I am the 9th child in a family of 10 that 9 was a number has some sort of a symbolic significant to me. *Retiring from Writing* would give me additional pages to flesh-out my book and nine papers and the numerical importance of 9 meant something special to me. Finally, it quickly became crystal clear to me that this piece is the swan song of my writing life: this is the funeral march to the graveyard; each word produced being one more step to the final destination.

I, Steven Gerard Farrell, was born on July 31, 1954 in the city of Kenosha, Wisconsin, a factory town situated about halfway between Milwaukee and Chicago, Illinois. I was the 9th child of Grover and Edna (Kressin) Farrell. I was following in the footsteps of Joan, Colleen, John, Frank, James, Patricia, Barbara and Daniel. Robert, born in 1958, was the 10th and last child. Our ethnicity was Irish and German while our official religion was Roman Catholicism. Indeed, there was a member of the Farrell family in attendance at St. Thomas Aquinas School (65th street and 23rd avenue) from the early 40's until the early 70's. The old redbrick church and school have long since ceased to be. I believe the building is now serving as a charter school.

As I think about the many subjects I have written about during my writing life, it becomes very obvious to me that I have rarely attempted to put any memories of my childhood on paper. I'm aware that it could very well reveal severe psychological indicators about my reluctant to dwell upon my misty past in great details. I received a passing grade in *Psychology 101*. Since I'm breaking new ground by writing my farewell to my writing life, it strikes me as a cool idea to ignore the time-honored tradition of authors writing about the painful experience of growing up. I could slap on a pair of rose-colored glasses and produce some slop about golden ages of yore, baseball field triumphs, or first kisses beneath the harvest moon. I'll spare my reader all of that by merely stating that my childhood was white bread and normal for that of an American boy growing up in the Midwest during the Vietnam Era. Even now when I read biographies and autobiographies my interest doesn't kick in until the person has started their real human career at the age of 18.

My fondest memories revolve around seeing the Beatles play on the *Ed Sullivan Show* in 1964, going to my first Chicago Cubs' game at Wrigley Field in 1967 and graduating from Tremper High School in 1973. Among my worst recollections would be the Kennedy assassination in 1963, the race riots of 1968 and the breakup of the Beatles in 1970. The Wisconsin winters were long, cold and snowy. It was great to get the day off due to a winter storm; there also being money to be made shoveling sidewalks for elderly neighbors. I still think that freshly fallen snow looks enchanting after night fall. The long walks to school with my brother Robert in zero temperatures still makes my toes hurt from the remembered numbness. The days raced by with school obligations, where I was mainly a mediocre student. I only excelled in history. Sister Theodore, my 6th grade teacher, put the notion into my head that I was a historian and capable of telling a story well. My grades did improve significantly as I advanced upwards. By the time I was wrapping up high school I was on the honor roll six straight quarters. My athletic career was as average as my academic career. However, I did love to play softball, especially at Lincoln Park or on the playground of Columbus School. It seems all I did was play in one endless nine inning game during the summer of 66-69. By 1970, I was sadly aware I was never going to play right field for any major league team, so I focused on after school jobs like delivering newspapers, pumping gas and washing dishes. The Farrell family used to walk to Simmons Beach to swim and to picnic. When we had the extra coins, we actually took the bus out to the north side of town and the Washington Bowl swimming pool. If we were willing to walk home, we could buy a bag of popcorn at the Big Star. Attending the movies at the Roosevelt Theatre or the Lake Theater downtown was always a treat. I liked the action-packed adventure movies like *The 300 Spartans, El Cid* and *Taras Bulba* the best. *The Horror of Dracula* and *The Brides of Dracula* at the long-gone Kenosha Theater gave me nightmares for weeks. Of course, I saw the Beatles in *A Hard Day's Night* and *Help* when they were first shown in Kenosha. The teenage girls in the audience screamed though-out most of the screening; and I remember I couldn't make-out the Beatles' thick Scouse accent. I sure enjoyed the music.

Steven G. Farrell

Television was still a novelty back in the Sixties, and our family nightly schedule revolved around the programming of ABC, CBS, and NBC. *Andy Griffith* was on Monday, *The Beverly Hillbillies* were on Wednesdays, and *The Munsters (*and, later, *Batman)* and *My Three Sons* were on Thursday. The Farrell clan loaded up on the stagecoach for Dodge City, Marshal Dillon and *Gunsmoke* on Saturday nights and then we took the train to Virginia City, the Cartwrights and *Bonanza* on Sunday nights. Our father enjoyed puffing his Dutch Master cigars as he proved allegiance to his Irish heritage by watching the *Jackie Gleason Show* and the *Ed Sullivan Show.* I wonder how many of my readers remember when Richard Kimball finally caught up to the one-armed man on *The Furgitive.* My sister Barb and I were the only ones to dig the British export of *The Avengers,* starring Patrick Macnee as John Steed and Diane Riggs as Mrs. Peel. The television shows were as fresh and colorful as the music on the airwaves out of Chicago (WLS and WCFL): the Beatles, Sonny and Cher, the Rolling Stones, Tom Jones, Gerry and the Pacemakers, the Buckinghams, Chad and Jeremy, the Who, the Beach Boys, Aretha Franklin, the Temptations, the Monkees, Herman's Hermits, Ray Charles, Bob Dylan and so many others. By the early 70's my taste went to harder rock like Led Zeppelin, Mountain, Deep Purple, the Doors and Black Sabbath.

In the early days of June, 1973, my childhood formally ended when I graduated from high school along with over 700 seniors. My parents, my brothers and I took a week-long trip to San Francisco to see the Golden Gate Bridge, Chinatown and two Giants' games at Candlestick Park. The Zodiac Killer was still on the loose, but he didn't bother us hicks from Wisconsin. The trip was the first time I had ever left the Milwaukee-Chicago area. I read James T. Farrell's *Studs Lonigan* and Charles Dickens' *David Copperfield* around this time. I also began to consider the possibilities of becoming a novelist myself. I consider the symbolical end of my childhood as actually occurring on August 15, 1974 when my best friend Danny Hautzinger and I caught a greyhound bus to Milwaukee to begin our military service. I can't claim I was anything other than a raw recruit when I showed up to boot camp at Fort Leonard Wood, Missouri. Drill and ceremony, long marches in the hot summer sun, and the rifle range were the least of my concerns when compared to the intense loneliness I experienced. I also didn't care much for sharing an open barrack room with seven other young homesick men. I was in, and won, my only fistfight during boot camp. I scored a technical knockout over a redneck from northern Wisconsin. The longest eight weeks of my life ended with graduation and the presence of my proud parents in the audience. My advanced training took place in Virginia at Fort Lee. The highlights included another visit from my parents, along with my brother Dan (we connected in D.C) and seeing a Virginia Squires ABA game in Norfolk. I won the second fight of my career by decking a black dude from Houston who refused to return my iron after I had lent it to him. He tried to even the score by chasing me with a board with nails in it. After a month's leave, I was shipped over to West Germany. My permanent duty station was an Army base not far from Stuttgart. I was a supply clerk for the 903rd Maintenance Battalion. I was screamed at by a general for not saluting him as he rolled by in his jeep. I was a Specialist Four by the time I received my honorable discharge. Mostly the soldiers partied and terrorized the surrounding villages. Munich is still the most enchanting city I have ever visited in my travels. How charming it was to see the sun set as I sat on a hillside in the English Gardens. I walked by a convent full of young nuns in formation on the front lawn, who cheerfully waved at me as a walked by. Heidelberg was a quaint medieval university town where I could easily imagine that Einstein, Faust and young Frankenstein may have studied among the test tubes and chalkboards. I joined a tour group to Paris, France, where I shamed my nation by asking what was so important about the Mona Lisa: it did seem so small and lame next to many of the more impressive paintings of the French and Dutch Masters. I visited the notorious red light district of *Pigalle* but the whores were on strike. I did my penance for having bad intent by checking out the Cathedral of Notre Dame. The Hunchback wasn't available for autographs. I was eating cheese and bread on the shore of the Seine when a group of young girls in berets and striped shirts began to wave to me from a bridge. I toasted them with the bottle of wine I was swigging from, but I couldn't entice them to join me. I purchased a stereo from the PX and listened to my music from back home. My brother would occasionally send me tapes of old favorites like Pink Floyd or Alice Cooper. Speaking of Alice, I saw him in concert right around the time I saw the Who play. I regret not visiting the Berlin area, where my maternal grandfather's ancestor tilled the land and served in the Kaiser's army; his grandfather having served in the Franco-Prussian war before settling in Minnesota. The favorite part of my military career was receiving my discharge papers and walking into a lounge in Kennedy Airport for my first drink as a civilian. I celebrated by buying a round for everybody in the place. Later on a bearded Jewish rabbi said to me, "Welcome home, soldier."

I moved back to the family house on 65th street and 18th avenue, but our days were numbered on that block. Our old neighbors had all relocated to Pleasant Prairie or Bristol and our surroundings were becoming dumpier and more dangerous with each passing day. Muggings and home invasions were the order of the day. I adjusted to civilian life by hammering out my first novel, *Dreamingabout a Word,* which grew eventually into an unpublishable 300 page. Gerry Mackrell, who was amazingly like Steve Farrell (the name Mackrell is the Scottish variation of Farrell), was the hero of my first book. I hooked up with Dale Andresen, an old school buddy of mine, and we spent most of the summer playing golf, swimming and playing basketball. When he left to go to school in Madison, I mostly hung around with my brothers until the autumn term began at the University of Wisconsin-Parkside. I sure felt that fall was an especially grey and lonely one as I collected Thin Lizzy albums and thought vaguely about re-upping in the Army. My alienation ended in the spring term when I took a course in Irish theatre and met Terry Sexton, a fellow Irish-American and a local folksinger. He introduced me to his Bohemian crowd in the Student Union at the university and I soon grew a beard and began to listen to jazz, blues and Irish music; only the Irish music really took. In a freshman literature course I pushed aside Hemingway and Fitzgerald when the professor assigned to the class *On the Road* by Jack Kerouac, a novel that probably influenced my life more than any other I had ever read before or since. The Beat generation was long gone but Terry and I did our utmost to revive it as we listened to Tom Waits and read the rest of Kerouac. I appreciated the poetry of Allen Ginsberg but much of the output of that American literary movement didn't move me very much. New York City was the place to go for many of the students from UW-Parkside for spring break. There was Broadway, Barnes & Noble Bookstore, McSorley's Ale House and Hell's Kitchen to explore. We walked past the Chelsea Hotel where Brendan Behan, Norman Mailer and James T. Farrell had all lived in the past. It was my mission to connect with r Kerouac's ghost at the Kettle of Fish in Greenwich Village. The Empire State Building put me in mind of King Kong's climb. City Island had excellent seafood restaurants. I graduated from UW-Parkside in the spring of 1979 with a B.A degree in Communication and a B average. I was the fourth one of the ten children in my family to receive any sort of college degree: the number would eventually be six. I left campus to take on a series of dead on jobs in Kenosha. I was hammering away at my novels and drinking more than anything.

Terry had moved to Boston for work, so I followed him with my college sweetheart in tow. I was never as bored in my life as when I worked with an adding machine inside of a general ledgers office for a company on Soldier Field Road. My office overlooked the Charles River where the Harvard team would go rowing back and forth several times a day. I imagined myself to be like Franz Kalka, the Czech-Jewish novelist, who found himself trapped at a clerical job during the day to earn his keep for his night writings. Going to Fenway Park to see the Red Sox play was fun, especially when 'Yaz' was on the field: on his way to over 3,000 career hits and 400 or so home run. The Celtics at the Garden were better to watch because Larry Bird and Kevin McHale led them to a NBA championship when I was living in the Allston-Brighton neighborhood of Boston. The endless invasions of cockroaches, the decline of my romantic interest in my female roommate and the lure back home to Kenosha finally ended my stint in Massachusetts but not before I did some traveling in Maine, New Hampshire, Rhode Island and Connecticut. The only state in New England that I missed was Vermont and, to this day, it is the only state I have never stepped foot in. Terry and I actually went to Lowell, home town of Jack Kerouac. It was Massachusetts' version of Kenosha: a Catholic blue collar town of rain swept streets, battered taverns and old ghosts like Dr. Sax.

There was nothing for me in Kenosha but a battered couch in my younger brother's place on 7th Avenue. An empty bank book inspired me to catch a bus for Rockford, Illinois where my brother Jim had an attic where I could sleep and write. My stint in northern Illinois is notable for only 3 things: first, I moved to Chicago for a few weeks and holed up at the Mark Twain Hotel on Division Street; second, I encountered anti-Catholic sentiments for the first time in my life from a nurse I worked with who was from some KKK inspired Midwestern town; third, I worked for a few months with a very beautiful woman from nearby Freeport who later served as the model for Ginny Browne, the main character in my Beatles novel *Mersey Boys*. Her name was Jeannie and I located her on the internet after almost thirty years of silence between us. She's happily married with children and entitled to her privacy. I will say I was thunderstruck by her like I had never been before in my life. Another female friend by the name of Debbie advised me to apply for graduate school at Northern Illinois University in DeKalb as I was heading up a blind alley. My G.I Bill of Rights was due to lapse so it seemed logical that I go back to being a student rather than working the third shift at a low-paying hospital as a psychiatric technician.

Earning my Master of Arts degree was one of the most difficult things I had to undergo in my life. I had a B plus average but I really had to tackle the books and rewrite my papers numerous times to barely make it through the program in about 17 months. It was fun being on a campus again; one having a football team in the Huskies of the Mid-America Conference. The girls were still beautiful like when I was an undergraduate but the students were more Republican than they were at UWP. Ronald Reagan was proving to be the most popular president since Franklin D. Roosevelt. I lived in a converted chicken coop on the edge of town, walking the two miles to school as I had no car. I grew a beard and gained a reputation as being a Walt Whitman type of eccentric campus character. I washed dishes in a dormitory for extra cash and I did my drinking at the

Shamrock with students about eight years younger than myself. My final paper submitted to my committee revolved around the handling of terrorism by the mass media. I had to rewrite the thing a few times to eradicate my pro- Irish Republican Army leaning passages. My best friend was a young man by the name of Steve Fassler, who eventually set-up his own training film company in California.

I graduated with yet another degree and I returned to the unemployment line. My brother Jim hurt my feelings by saying he could wipe his ass on my worthless degree. It was a cruel thing to throw in my face when I was struggling to keep from drowning Steve had taken a job in Connecticut and invited me to try my luck on the east coast a second time. To give Jim credi,t I have to state here and now that he staked me the airfare. I found an office job within a few days of arriving in Stamford. One day, as I waited in the autumn rain for my bus to work, it crossed my mind that I was sick of living and that death appealed to me like it had never done before. Then it occurred to me that I only had one true desire left, and that I was to visit Ireland. My Irish dream sustained me through those feral days of 1986. A telephone call from Dr. Kurt Ritter, the Department Chair of the Speech Communication Department at Texas A&M U University, changed my life forever. The offer of a lecturer position pumped new hope into my heart. Many northerners have some sort of knee jerk reaction whenever you mention the state of Texas to them. However, I love the Lone Star State because it put me back on the right track for the first time since I graduated from Parkside in the late Seventies. Moving to College Station was, next to going into the Army, the second biggest move of my life. Sometimes I wonder if I really took the position because I had never been south of Virginia before. One night as I was taking a stroll on a warmish winter night, it dawned upon me that every step taken took me one step further southward than I had ever been in my life.

I had a blast among the Aggies! I taught *Public Speaking* and the *Fundamentals of Speech Communication*. I carefully nurtured my reputation as being a lovable Irish Yankee scamp from Chicagoland. I honed my teaching skills and learned how to argue with students over grades. I was deep in the heart of the Bush family's Texas: wild cats, cattlemen and cowboys. I made it to Houston for Astros and Oilers' games. I caught a bus to Dallas for a Rangers game as I still didn't know how to drive a car at the age of 32. I boarded a never ending bus ride to New Orleans where I rambled up and down Burgundy and Canal Streets. Louie Armstrong ghost personally steered me to his old haunts in Story Ville. I almost got in a fight in an Irish pub with a tourist from England when I called out for Irish rebel songs like *Rifles of the IRA.* I ate red beans and rice and red hot Cajun and Creole foods.

In March of 1988 I finally flew over to Ireland. I mostly hung-out in Dublin, Cork and Limerick. I chased to ghost of Phil Lynott, singer of Thin Lizzy, across the O'Connell Street where I lost him in the foggy dew. I drank in pubs once patronized by Brendan Behan and Patrick Kavanagh. I stumbled across the neighborhood where Sean O'Casey, the playwright, lived years before during the time of the Troubles. Pilgrimages to the Abbey Theatre and the Gaiety were obligatory. I saw O'Cas*ey's Shadow of a Gun Man.* and Behan's *Borstal Boy.* Murphy's Stout in Cork was even more delicious than Guinness. I met a Paddy who started giving me grief about being a Yank until he discovered that we shared the same last name of Farrell. I left Shamrock Airport knowing that I would return. The following year I took various train trips that took me from London, England to Cardiff, Wales to Liverpool, England to, finally, Edinburgh, Scotland. In spite of my life long anti-British sentiments I found the United Kingdom to be a fascinating place with many hospitable folks. I saw the great Jeremy Brett in a play about Sherlock Holmes in the West End. I stayed with a friend from Texas A&M at his flat in Notting Hill Gate. The Welsh were a dark, quiet and sweet people with a mythic Merlin past. The Scots were a hail and hearty people, who drank with gusto and who constantly reminded me that the notorious grave robbers, Burke and Hare, were Irishmen who gave their city a ghoulish reputation. I rode the Tube with Londoners wearing bowlers and spiked punk rock hairdos.

I made a spiritual connection with the port city of Liverpool and its mighty Mersey River that Gerry Marsden had sung about in the song *Ferry across the Mersey.* I stayed in a bed and breakfast right across the street from the registry where John Lennon married Cynthia Powell. I drank in the corner pub where they held their wedding reception. I took a Beatles' bus tour that took us to the childhood homes of John, Paul, George and Ringo, including the poverty stricken Dingle. I almost cried when I saw the street sign of Penny Lane and the tour guide pointed out the roundabout. Strawberry Hills made me think of the murdered John and the video the Beatles made for their song. I took that ferry boat ride to the other side to Speke and nobody charged me because I was a tourist. I made a special point to find the Liverpool Art College where John Lennon had been a student. There was a fish and chip shop that I ate in where John used to hang out whenever he was cutting his classes. I was tickled to find a harbor side street called O'Ferrall. I didn't like the bitter so I switched to Guinness when I was sitting in the Ye Old Crackle, another local of Lennon's. The inkling of an idea began to take place in my brain: what about a story where an American college professor taught at the Liverpool Art College, circa 1960, and he befriended a young John Lennon, a poet and a rock and roll rebel? The professor would be named Al Moran in honor of two Chicago gangsters: Al Capone and Bugs Moran. I start to create the greatest female character of my writing career: Ginny Browne. She would beautiful, talented and strong-willed. She was to be the Muse who would serve to draw John Lennon and Al Moran together; and the same Muse to tear them asunder.

At the same time the Beatles' novel was brewing inside of my mind, another germ of an idea began to grow alongside of it: I had become possessed by the bug to write my first flown-blown play. The subject of my entry into the world of theatre was to be John L. Sullivan, the heavyweight champion of the world from 1882-1892. Sullivan was one of the first Irish-Americans to become a popular culture hero to the entire nation at large. John L. was also an interesting rogue would be a fascinating man to research and to write about. My two works would take me about eight years to complete; most of the writing being done when I was living over in Utsunomiya, Japan. After a few years in Texas, it felt like it was time to move on to other things, so I applied to an advertisement in a Peace Corp newsletter for an English Teaching position at the Utsunomiya English Center in the Kanto region. It was time to say goodbye to my best friend Chris Wisenbaker and to fly across the Atlantic to make new friends. Once again I was determined to seek adventure and to make my fortune in the world. My intention was to put in one year in Asia before entering the doctorate program at the University of Oregon in Eugene. I stayed in Japan for five years and I never started work on my final degree.

Being jet leg and smelling the raw sewage that waffled up through the slits in the sidewalks gave me a bad first impression of my new home. I immediately lost twenty pounds because of all of the rice and noodles I was eating, as well as having trouble manipulating the use of chopsticks to navigate food to my mouth. It took a while to get used to sleeping on a futon, riding buses and living in a closet-sized apartment. The Japanese are hard-working people with many outstanding qualities to admire, but as students of the English language I found them rather boring and unimaginative. I quickly lost my interest in teaching and I focused more upon traveling and reading the works of Hearne, the Irish writer who had written many books about Japanese folklore in the last century. I fell in love with a Japanese woman and we lived together as man and wife until it was time for me to re-enter my own culture. We explored Hong Kong, Singapore and Seoul together along with her daughter. She inspired me to start work on a third writing project: *Zen Babe*. I would recreate Babe Ruth's barnstorming venture in Japan just before the outbreak of the next big war. I would include Moe Berg, the catcher who had turned spy. We were also able to purchased tickets to the *Big Egg Dome* in Tokyo to see George Harrison and Eric Clapton in concert. Later on we saw the Tyson-

Douglas heavyweight championship fight in the same place. My best friend was Tim Tagg, a Welshman. My only major disappointment in Japan was that nobody seemed to be overly interested in Buddhism, a religion that I had long admired. The Japanese seemed to practice a hodgepodge of religions: Shintoism, Buddhism, Catholicism and Agnosticism. Visiting temples was just a national hobby in my book.

As my love for the Japanese woman started to fade, I began to hear the siren call to return home. I was forty years old and I needed to get serious about my human career again. I rejoined my brother Jim, who was now living in Delevan, Wisconsin, located somewhere between Kenosha and Rockford. I spent three years there working on *The Scousers, Boston Knuckles* and *Zen Babe*. Other than my writing, it was a chronic waste of time that ended when I became a homeless drifter out west. I bounced from city to city and hotel to hotel, living on my credit cards until I went broke. I spent time in Seattle, Portland, Anchorage, San Francisco, San Diego, Los Angles, Salt Lake City, Cody, Jackson Hole and Omaha. I took in Mariners Giants, A's, Padres and Dodgers' baseball games. With my tail between my legs I returned to Kenosha to park inside of my sister Pat's guest room as I caught my breath. I was still recovering when I took on an adjunct lecturer position at UW-Parkside, my old college. It was only part time, but it was instrumental in helping me regain my footing. By June of 1998 I was flying back overseas to teach English: this time I was trading the Pacific for the Atlantic, and Japan for the Kingdom of Saudi Arabia. I spent the next year thinking of Lawrence of Arabia and losing my sanity in the great and endless desert. Days with temperature highs over 120 were not uncommon. I never really warmed up to the Arab culture the way I did with that of the Japanese, but the Arabs were fairly friendly and I kept myself from receiving a whipping at the infamous Chop Chop Square. I worked for Aramco Oil Company at their industrial school in the Dhahran area. I did very little traveling within the Kingdom as the restrictions were very strict, but I did cross the causeway over to Bahrain to drink whiskey. I took a jaunt over to Bombay where I spent my time with an Indian woman who showed me a good time... and other things... as I spent my oil money on her. For the first time in my life I actually felt rich and my bank account grew. Indian food was hot, the women's clothing was bright and the weather was blazing hot. I thought of Kipling as I took in the sights.

Twice I was able to visit Ireland and Northern Ireland: Dublin, Longford (ancient homeland of my clan), Sligo, Wexford (Vinegar Hill), Waterford, Belfast (I dashed past the Orange Lodge before they could sniff-out my Fenian leanings), Derry (walked around the water fountain in the city center mentioned in the song *The Town I Loved So Well*), Galway Bay, and the Aran Islands. What beauties I saw in untamed Connemara. I explored the insides of the very last of the eight medieval O'Farrell castles (called Mornin Castle) near Granard. I made it to Ballymahon, birth place of Oliver Goldsmith. I probably spent about a month in Ireland spread out over two trips. I actually marched in an Easter Parade with Gerry Adams in honor of Patrick Pearse, Michael Collins and the other heroes of the great uprising. On a more peaceful note: I visited the grave sites of W.B. Yeats and the legendary Queen Maeve. An old lady pointed out to me the apartment where James Joyce lived with his wife Nora; and I saw the pistol of the Big Fellow (Collins) in a museum. Another highlight was when I watched the Irish defeat the Australian in a high scoring rugby match at the stadium where the British Black and Tan massacred numerous spectators out of spite. I stood on top of an old Celtic fortress and looked out across the Atlantic Ocean. I felt some sort of raw and ancient power surge through my aging body. I felt a thrill when I stepped in the 'Free Derry' area in Belfast with the painting of the IRA gun man on a wall overlooking the street below. There was also a jaunt to the Netherlands and Belgium where I mostly drank and hung out in the notorious red light districts after many sexless months in Felix Arabia. My short time in Saudi Arabia enabled me to round-out my international traveling credentials. I didn't really bond with any of my fellow teachers, many of whom were actively gay and not interested in a fat and middle-aged American from the hinterlands of the Midwest. The order of the day was to live and let live; and I was fine with that laissez faire attitude. After repairing my economic situation, it was time to give my country another chance at providing a life for me.

After several months of hanging around my old haunts, I was once again on the verge of hiring on as an English teacher. I was in the process of locating a position in either Poland or Kuwait when I friend directed me to a local Catholic school that was searching for a warm body to teach Social Studies for middle school children (ages 12-14). The contract offered a salary of only $26,000. It was a big comedown after teaching at universities and oil companies. The thought of putting down roots at the age of 45 really appealing to me; and I did settle down in the southeastern corner of Wisconsin for the next six years and four months: a long commitment for a Celtic wanderer such as myself. It did give me a chance to re-establish my credit, as well as to learn how to use a computer for the first time. I purchased my first new car and rented houses in the Forest Park section of the city. I enjoyed teaching history and geography to the noisy brats on 22nd Avenue. When we became bored with Caesar or Napoleon, we would turn off the lights and tell ghost stories and urban legends. I became very adapted at creating stories at the top of my head about mummies in Cairo, Susan the Vampire in London and other fibs. My best tale dealt with my encounters with a Yeti snowman in the mountains of Tibet.

To keep some goals in front of me I decided to visit the last ten states I had never been to (Tennessee, North Carolina, South Carolina, Arkansas, South Dakota, Kansas, Oklahoma, West Virginia, New Mexico and Delaware) and the last MLB baseball teams I had never visited at their home stadium (Pittsburgh Pirates, Detroit Tigers, Baltimore Orioles, Cleveland Indians, Philadelphia Phillies, Kansas City Royals, St. Louis Cardinals, New York Mets, Florida Marlins and the Washington Nationals). I had these two fun distractions to keep me busy and to take myself away from writing. I took some night work at colleges in the Milwaukee area; and I even taught a class or two at trusty ole Parkside, where I taught a section of Media and Society. With certain sense of delighted shame I must confess that I landed inside of a major mid-life crisis that made me addicted to having relationships with much young women; one who stole my automobile one night after she had satisfied me.

Over the Christmas break of 2005 a job offer materialized out of the blue. I was offered $10,000 more in salary as a full time instructor in the Speech-Communication Department at Greenville, South Carolina.

"It's time to move on again," I said to myself as I started to breakdown a life that I had had for the past seven years. It was not an easy task to perform; for I had adjusted to being back in Kenosha, as well as to being a crusty old history teacher. However, the rumors circulating through the hallways of the school indicated that the place was on the verge of closing its doors. I didn't want to find myself being laid-off in my fifties, so I jumped at the chance to once again re-invent myself. Loading up my bags inside of my G6 Pontiac was one of the hardest things I ever had to do. It was snowing by the time I entered the flat state of Indiana. The snow had turned into rain by the time I reached Kentucky. I pulled over to a motel off the side of the highway to rest and to watch the Chicago Bears defeat the Green Bay Packers in a Monday night matchup. Noise in the parking lot around midnight compelled me to look outside of my room's window. Silence streams of late night zombies were walking in the fog for the entrance of the place. I shriveled in my bed until the dawn's early rays began to fill my room. I felt better when I reached the Smokey Mountains that connected Tennessee with North Carolina. Somewhere up there in Davy Crockett territory I kicked out the ghostly memories of the past seven year block to focus upon what was in front of me.

Here it is already September of 2014, and another nine years of my life have slipped on by. In a few minutes I shall close up my office in UT 224 and cross the hallway over to 219, where I have to deliver a lecture in my Interpersonal Communication class. After the madness of seven years in a middle school, it's rather mundane to be teaching adults. I teach courses in

Steven G. Farrell

Speech-Communication.. I have risen from the rank of Instructor to that of Associate Professor, the highest position I have ever had in my long teaching career. I have presented scholarly papers at two national conventions for the American Conference for Irish Studies (Savannah, Georgia and Madison, Wisconsin) which is the only time I have ever done so in my life. I have taken part in seven symposiums on subjects ranging from the St. Valentine's Massacre to Cicero. I have been the coach of the college's intercollegiate speech & theatre team. Recently I have organized a Monster Movies night for every Monday in October, featuring such classics as *Dracula, Frankenstein, The Wolfman and Abbott and Costello Meet Frankenstein.* I have published essays, articles, reviews, plays, criticism and stories in about two dozen magazines (online and hard copy). I have even been interviewed four separate times on the radio. I don't travel as much I did when I was in Wisconsin, limiting myself to one trip a year where I hook up with my friend Chris Wisenbaker for a NFL or MLB game; this year we're meeting in New Orleans to see the Saints host the Bengals.

My time spent in the Upstate has been the most successful in my entire life, but I know I have declined in a very real physical sense. At the age of 60 I am considerably different from the man I was at 50. Starting a new life was much harder this time around than it had been in the past. Homesickness didn't catch up to me this time until I had been in South Carolina for about a half year. I then I began to miss everything about Kenosha: from the pizza to Lake Michigan. My blues were compounded by the death of my brother Dan at the end of my first year in the south. We buried him on a beautiful autumn day in early November as the Irish bagpipes wailed and the colorful leaves rushed across the grounds of the cemetery. An Irish singer from Chicago sang *Danny Boy.* He was buried next to my father. In 2009, they were joined by my brother Jack and my mother. By 2010, my brother Frank had joined them in the after-life. We had lost our sister Colleen in 2002. I still grieve for them all, and my life has become a lonelier planet without them.

In 2008, I finally broke into Internet by having an essay, *Mickey Machine Gun is Back!: The Return of the Irish-American Gangster to the Silver Screen,* accepted by Talking Pictures, a British publication. The article has been republished by Crime, Audience and the Irish-American Cultural Institute. I received a big charge telling people about my entry on to the computers of the world. Later that year I self-published two of my books: *Boston Knuckles*, my play about John L. Sullivan, and *Zen Babe*, my Babe Ruth in Japan novella. I was happy to get them up and made available to the outside world. By 2009, I had a third book published: *Liverpool Roared*, a full-length novel. I had taken my Beatles novel, *The Scousers,* and made it more fictional. John, Paul, George and Ringo became Darcy,

214

Conn, Keith and Roddy. Ginny Browne and Al Moran survived the original novel, and actually went to Chicago to get married. I expanded the part of Ginny Browne; the final scene on the ferryboat between Al and Ginny being the best I had ever penned. Self-published is better than not being published at all. I was fortunate to find Jeanne Putnam in Greenville to serve as my typist and proofreader. She had been a student of mine that I had taught as adjunct at USC-Upstate. Jeanne and her husband, Ronnie Putnam, have been my best friends in Greenville for several years now.

In 2010, I sent a copy of my play to Audience magazine and it was accepted by M. Stefan Strozier, publisher, thus beginning a four year relationship with Mike that would eventually end in tragedy for me. Mike eventually published five essays, three stories, two pieces of criticism and my John L. Sullivan in four editions of his magazine. He also encouraged me to put together my essays and stories, that I entitled *Farrell's Irish Papers,* into a book that was published by his book company World Audience Publishers. It was still only a print on demand situation but it gave me a New York publisher. I wrote a very short novella, *Bowery Ripper on the Loose,* that Mike found an Australian artist to do the nifty cover design. The story revived Jack the Ripper in 1938 and had him matching wits with a street gang called the Irish Clowns. I actually got a few positive reviews for the book with online magazines. So my experience with Mike was off to a good running start, and we actually met in New York when I ventured there for a convention for the Irish American Writers & Artists. The two of us went to the Meadowlands to see the Giants play the Bills. It was on the train ride back to Grand Central Station that I mentioned my Beatles novel to Mike; his eyes lighting up and signaling the start of one of the worse episodes of my life. The book was eventually released on kindle and in a limited edition of 50 copies in November of 2012 by World Audience Publishers. However, by April of the following year, I had fallen out with Strozier and I republished the Beatles novel, *Mersey Boys,* with Create Space and under my own publishing imprint of Celtic-Badger. I had had to go through Amazon.com to have Mike's copy of my novel taken down and mine set up. There was also a clash over who owned the copyrights. It really didn't matter in the end, because Mike Strozier left (or fled) New York City for Jamaica.

To complicate matters, Mike and I had decided to film *Mersey Boys* as a very low budget film, featuring Off-Broadway actors in all of the roles. Mike decided that New York City could stand in for Liverpool and that the Staten ferryboat could pull duty as the Mersey ferryboat. Auditions were conducted and a cast was found. From the photographs he sent me I selected Joanna Pickering, a very experienced film actress from England, to play the female lead of Ginny Browne. The two of us became fast friends

215

and we're still in contact two years later. As I hurriedly wrote a screenplay based on my novel; at the same time I wrote a stage version as well. I thank Mike for lighting a fire beneath my butt to get me started: it was the last good thing the man did for me. Suddenly he turned into Orson Welles and his ego swamped the production and destroyed it in the end. He wanted to star in the role of Al Moran while also producing and directing the film. He even began to rewrite my script and he had no handle on the Scouse accent whatsoever. It became a nightmare, including angry exchanges of e-mails. Just enough of *Mersey Boys* was filmed to provide a short trailer that was online for a few months to generate interest in the project. Overall, the clip wasn't so bad but Mike was no Al Moran. Whatever was filmed is gone with Mike's disappearance. The man is gone forever out of my life. I prefer not to carry any malice inside of my heart for a guy who did me a few good turns. I was appalled as I had spent a considerable amount of time sending out press releases which was picked as a news item by many magazines. I even was interviewed by the *Kenosha News* and *The Irish-American Post*. The experience left me red-faced and ashamed. To salvage a bad situation I went ahead and published the screenplay and stage play under my Celtic-Badger flagship. Joanna Pickering gave me permission to use her likeness on both books. She will forever be Ginny Browne in my eyes. I must also be honest and admit that I sunk money into the affair.

Joanna Pickering has been a breath of fresh air in the life of this dusty old scholar. Even with the best of friendships there seems to be a fair share of overwrought emotions, edgy e-mails and angry explosions between the two of us. I, a 60 year old American, am never going to see eye to eye with a European woman half my age. I still have her picture hanging on my bulletin board just outside of my office door. Somebody asked me if she was Bridget Bardot, the French actress from the Sixties. We discussed raising the money and producing *Mersey Boys* ourselves. It is the stuff of pipe dreams. When I do eventually pass away the rights of all of my books shall pass into the joint hands of Jeanne Putnam and Joanna Pickering.

I purchased an Irish walking stick online for what I claim is a conversation piece instead of admitting that my rheumatism has given me a pronounced limp. During the 18th century the shillelagh was used as a weapon in the notorious faction fights that took place in Ireland between rival clans and political parties up in Ulster. It was a lethal tool of destruction, but I use as it something to get my bulk up and down steps and across the campus. Old age has laid her hands upon me. The siblings I have lost in recent years all died between the ages of 55 and 71, so I am convinced I have now entered the final one/seventh of my life, or the last 14%. The world is as violent and as desperate as it was when I first entered it 60 years ago, but I still acknowledge that it is full of magic and miracles.

My life has been an adventure. It's nearly over now; now I'm easy. I haven't written it all down because I can't remember it now after all of these years. I also have no wish to bore anybody with ancient grudges, old flames and worn-out dreams. I suppose I flatter myself that I did very well for a Midwestern Catholic from a blue collar family. I certainly was never a candidate for 'white privilege' and anything I have I earned in my life has been done all by my lonesome.

So now I round back to the theme and title of this last line in the final nine papers for my last book: *Retiring from Writing*.

Steven G. Farrell

POSTSCRIPT

As the year 2014 was rapidly approaching its' demise, Dr. Dan Robbins, department head of the Theatre Department at Greenville Technical College, asked me to do a favor for him. Dr. Dan requested that I play a small supporting role in the school's presentation of Charles Dickens' *A Christmas Carol*. For the first time the college was going to use faculty members, along with young children, to act alongside of students. The cast and crew reached thirty in number: quite a huge production for our college. I immediately accepted before seriously considering the long rehearsals, as well as my complete lack of experience upon the stage. Although I have written two plays (*Boston Knuckles* and *Mersey Boys*), I have never been in greasepaint before in front of a live audience. My boss, Dr. David Burke, played the part of stingy old Ebenezer Scrooge while I played merry old Fezziwig, who is featured in one of the scenes with the Ghost of Christmas Past. Not only did I have to wear a white fuzzy wig and a too tight 19th century suit and vest, but I also had to dance a hornpipe with Mrs. Fezziwig (Dianne Chidester of the Social Sciences Department) and four young couples who played our daughters and their suitors. I acquitted myself well in a four show run that drew well over 600 spectators. What great fun it was to be strutting and dancing as such a bigger-than-life and jocular fellow as merry Mr. Fezziwig. I even signed a few autographs after the shows and the little children in the lobby all were delighted to see me and they knew the dear soul's name. What a fine finish to my short autobiography!

Steven G. Farrell

ABOUT THE AUTHOR

Steven G. Farrell is originally from Kenosha, Wisconsin, but he currently resides in Greenville, South Carolina. He is an Associate Professor of Speech-Communication at Greenville Technical College. His *Mersey Boys* trilogy (novel, play and screenplay) were published in 2013 by Celtic-Badger Publishers. The *Mersey Boys* film script was published by Off the Wall Plays of London, United Kingdom and Johannesburg, South Africa in August of 2013. Farrell has published numerous books, articles, essays, stories, reviews, plays and screenplays over his long writing career. Two of his essays (*Mickey Machine is Back! The Return of the Irish-American Gangster to the Silver Screen* and *Galloping Gallagher Deserves the Gallows: The Irish Rogue in Film*) were inducted into the Irish Film Archives in Dublin, Ireland in March of 2009. World Audience Publishers of New York published his collection of essays and stories, *Farrell's Irish Papers, in 2010* and his novella, *Bowery Ripper on the Loose,* in 2011.

CPSIA information can be obtained
at www.ICGtesting.com
Printed in the USA
LVOW10s0137131117

556063LV00013B/183/P